Happy &
Joe & Pat Nowern
Charles & Ann Riddle
4-18-24 — 90 yrs. old.

Notorious in Nashville

The Jordan Mayfair Mysteries
by Phyllis Gobbell

Pursuit in Provence

Secrets and Shamrocks

Treachery in Tuscany

Notorious in Nashville

Notorious in Nashville

A Jordan Mayfair Mystery

Phyllis Gobbell

Encircle Publications
Farmington, Maine, U.S.A.

NOTORIOUS IN NASHVILLE Copyright © 2023 Phyllis Gobbell

Paperback ISBN 13: 978-1-64599-488-6
Hardcover ISBN 13: 978-1-64599-489-3
E-book ISBN 13: 978-1-64599-490-9

Library of Congress Control Number: 2023945647

ALL RIGHTS RESERVED. In accordance with the U.S. Copyright Act of 1976, no part of this publication may be reproduced, distributed, or transmitted in any form or by any means, or stored in a database or retrieval system, without prior written permission of the publisher, Encircle Publications, Farmington, ME.

This book is a work of fiction. All names, characters, places and events are either products of the author's imagination or are used fictitiously.

Editor: Cynthia Brackett-Vincent

Cover design by Deirdre Wait
Cover images © Getty Images

Published by:

Encircle Publications
P.O. Box 187
Farmington, ME 04938

info@encirclepub.com
http://encirclepub.com

Chapter 1

A hush hovered over the room.

Her voice. What was it about that voice? The way it came from something deep inside. Longing. Regret. Old pain for what was lost. Etched in a fresh face. How could a twenty-five-year-old possibly know all of it? But you believed she did when you heard her sing.

I've never been a fan of country music. Never followed country music, except for summer visits with my grandparents in south Georgia, when the radio was always tuned to the big clear channel, WSM, out of Nashville. Hearing a classic like Dolly Parton's "I Will Always Love You" can still take me back to that simpler, sweeter time.

After those long ago summers, I didn't pay much attention to country music.

But Willow Goodheart's voice grabbed me, pulled me into what she was feeling, made me hold my breath.

> *The first chill of fall in the air*
> *The smell of wood smoke in your hair…*

The lyrics, unpretentious but elegant, and the hymn-like melody with a hint of blues. Her quiet, rhythmic picking on the acoustic guitar. All of it. And the voice.

Not like any country song I'd ever heard.

Your heart's first small crack
The part that you never get back...

The haunting verse climbed into the chorus that rang with raw honesty, with the resonance of an old soul.

There are things that will vanish,
But they don't fade away.

Then, as Willow held the audience under her spell, another voice boomed from behind us. "That's *my* song, Missy!"

A disheveled man, weathered face, wiry beard, staggered from the bar at the opposite end of the room from the stage. "*Mine!* You stole my song!" He lurched forward, heading toward the stage, stumbling into a table of four women. Their drinks spilled. The women shrieked.

"It's *mine!*" he kept yelling.

Willow went silent in the middle of a line. The stillness in the room turned into a roar of disgruntled chatter. Several men, including Kyle, my daughter's significant other, jumped up, but before they could rush to rescue the women, a linebacker-type from the bar swung a huge arm around the man's skinny neck. And then, grasping his scrawny arm and gray scraggly ponytail, swept him out the door.

"Stupid drunk," Kyle said, under his breath. He sat down and reached for his beer.

"Who *is* that?" Holly whispered.

"He's Notorious." Kyle took a long pull from the bottle.

"Notorious for what?" I asked.

"For drinking like a camel, it would seem," Alex said.

"Delbert Haskins. Singer, songwriter. He was almost somebody once." Kyle shook his head. "His stage name was Notorious."

It's much smaller than you'd think, that stage where so many huge careers have been launched. The stage where one song, performed at the right moment, with the right person in the crowd, could be a ticket to stardom.

"Lotsa dreams shattered here, too," Kyle had said, earlier that chilly, damp April night as we'd waited in line to get into The Bluebird Cafe. As we shivered, Kyle, who worked at the Country Music Hall of Fame, entertained us with stories about The Bluebird. Not to be outdone by Alex, my history-loving uncle who was in town to promote his new book about Nashville.

There was a certain mystique about this place, to be sure.

You'd never imagine what this small café has meant to country music if you just passed on Hillsboro Road and saw it tucked in a commercial strip. Along with the likes of a hair salon, a dry cleaners, and a bridal shop. Construction going on all around. You might wonder at the long line waiting to get in. Kyle said there was always a long line, these days.

After we'd waited forty-five minutes, the doors finally opened, and we entered a warm, welcoming room. At one of the four-tops, so snug with the other tables that I could smell the aftershave of the man next to us, we ordered drinks and bar food and waited for the show to start. Waited to see Willow Goodheart.

"It's not easy to get on the schedule now," Kyle said. With sandy hair, cropped short, hazel eyes, and a narrow, clean-shaven face, Kyle was your standard good-looking thirty-year-old. Something distinctive, though, in the slight smile that turned up at the corners. He never seemed to take himself too seriously. "Used to be, a kid could come to Nashville straight off the farm, spend his last cents hitchhiking across the country with his daddy's Gibson," he said. "Not even hoping for the Opry, just hoping to play The Bluebird. And if he had some talent, he could get on stage, Writers' Night. Like tonight. Sometimes that was enough."

"Wonder how Willow got a spot," Holly said. She was nearly as tall as Kyle, a match for him in the *attractive* quotient, though I was more than a little biased. "She left a message, saying she was playing here tonight. I tried to reach her but no answer, and she didn't call back."

Willow was the niece of my old friend, Aurora DeMille. Sorority sisters at UGA, we met up again in Athens at a homecoming game the year Willow and Holly were both new to Nashville. Because of our connection, and because Aurora is the ultimate networker, her niece and my daughter became friends and shared an apartment for a time. Until Holly took a new roommate: Kyle. That was, how long ago? Could it possibly be four years? Hard to keep up. I wondered if Holly and Kyle were ever going to get married, but they seemed happy enough. Joyful, in the way young couples often are before time begins to wear away at the edge of bliss and love has to begin the really hard work.

"And then *Nashville* came to town," Alex put in, sounding like the professor he used to be. He taught me and all of my sorority girlfriends at UGA. "Producers built an exact replica of The Bluebird for the TV series, and it was a staple of the show, every episode. Sometimes the music was…" He winced. "Not entirely bad. Nothing exceptional, but entertaining."

Our orders arrived. Beer in long neck bottles, tacos, BLT, pizza, and fried chicken tenders. Each of us had ordered but we wound up sharing. All of it tasty, if not exactly healthy.

Kyle said, "Since *Nashville* was such a hit, it's hard for locals to get in anymore. Tickets sell out the minute they go online. Tourists fill the place now."

"Like us," I said. Georgians, both of us. Me from Savannah, Alex from Atlanta.

Alex frowned, pushed his glasses up on his large nose. "Like *you*, Jordan. I don't feel like a tourist anymore. Actually, I feel quite at home here." My uncle had spent extended periods of time in Nashville the previous year, gathering material for his book. A follow-up to the three travel guides he'd written before COVID, when traveling to exotic countries was something we took for granted.

We might have talked about the evenings he'd passed the time here at The Bluebird, listening to country music. Not what I would've expected of my uncle, from old Georgia stock. He started to tell something about Taylor Swift, when she was fourteen.

But the show began. The room quieted.

"Howdy!" said a kid with a thin mustache that I could almost believe was painted on. His face seemed much too young for whiskers, but he knew how to connect with the crowd. Some of them yelled back, "Howdy!" He was a musician with some skill, but there was nothing notable about another drinking song, reminding me why I hadn't followed country music. An hour or so of forgettable songs passed before Willow took the stage.

I hardly recognized her. I hadn't seen her since she and Holly lived together. No more than five-foot-two, with long, straight, hair so blonde it was nearly white, Willow looked vulnerable, as she settled on a high stool with her guitar. She used to be curvy, a shape a man would let his gaze linger on. A healthier-looking Willow, one with an easy way about her. But now she seemed hungry, in a way. Starved, really. Starved for what, it was hard to say. It would be natural for her to be nervous, her first performance at The Bluebird. Even if she were a seasoned artist, she might tremble, playing her first show in this hallowed place. But Willow seemed so shy, so fragile, almost as if she were only fifteen.

I couldn't help wondering what she'd been doing to herself. Maybe someone who was advising her convinced her she needed this persona. I hoped it was that, and nothing else.

Her voice was whisper-soft as she thanked everyone for coming. "I've been writing songs, oh, I don't know, all my life it seems," she said. "And I'm gonna sing one that I 'specially like. One that means something to me. And I hope it means something to y'all, too."

Then those first notes. And Willow Goodheart was immediately unforgettable.

And then there was the drunk's outburst.

It took a while for the noise to die down, but eventually, the room turned silent again. Willow settled on the high stool, cradling her guitar. "Well, that was weird," she said. "Guess somebody got overserved." A soft ripple of laughter followed as she began to strum her guitar.

This time, she seemed a little shaken, and why wouldn't she be? But she found her voice and finished to wild applause that left no doubt. The crowd loved her.

Loved her even more, I thought, because of the drunk, Notorious.

Chapter 2

Aurora and I went way back. Way back before we were sorority sisters.

Aurora Gray grew up on a farm in south Georgia, just down the road from my grandparents' farm where I visited most summers till I was fourteen. Over the years, I got to know the Gray family. Sweet Aurora, with her silvery voice, who knew every Top 40 hit, who let her older sister Hilda boss her around. Their kind-faced mother who never cared how many cookies we ate before supper, and her soft-spoken daddy, who seemed to always be reading the Bible when he wasn't out working on the farm.

Imagine what a surprise—what a joy—it was, my first day at the University of Georgia, when I caught sight of Aurora. I didn't recognize the stunning young woman at first. I was at the head of a long line where I'd waited to check in at freshmen orientation. Aurora came running from across the room in her short, tight skirt, calling, "Jordan! Jordan Carlyle! Is that really you?"

This was a few years before I became Jordan Mayfair.

Already I was five-ten. Aurora was not much taller than when we'd played together on that Georgia farm. Probably five-four. Embracing her, I felt like she was still the same Aurora, just made up like a movie star.

A moment later, I knew she wasn't that girl.

When we finished hugging, she addressed the students in line behind me. Big smile. Straight, white teeth. She'd had braces. "You don't mind if I cut, do you?"

If they minded, they didn't say so. Aurora, the reserved, complicit farm girl, had reinvented herself. Safe to say she would not let anything stop her from getting to the head of the line from that time on.

The doorbell at Aurora DeMille's spacious Belle Meade home chimed the first bars of a familiar tune. If you didn't go to the University of Georgia, you might recognize the notes as "Glory, Glory, Hallelujah" from "The Battle Hymn of the Republic." Alex and I knew better. We exchanged a look. Alex shook his head.

I couldn't help laughing. "Only Aurora would put the UGA fight song on her doorbell."

The door clicked. Aurora had told us she'd have the remote. Just ring the bell.

Inside, I called to her, and she answered, "Come on in. You know where to find me."

With an injured back, Aurora spent most of the time in her elaborate media room, in an overstuffed recliner, surrounded by remotes. Dressed in black sweatpants and matching T-shirt with sequins, she wore lipstick and mascara, and her short blonde hair was perfectly styled. If I didn't know better, I'd think she was dressed to go out or had just come in from a casual dinner.

She clicked off the giant flat-screen TV. Seventy inches, she'd told us. "How was it? How'd Willow do? Oh, wait, get yourselves something to drink first." Aurora reached for a delicate bone china cup, taking it from a saucer. "I'm so sick of tea. Can't wait to get finished with these painkillers. Y'all help yourselves to the good stuff."

"Tea's fine for me," I said.

"Alex, I'll bet you could go for something stronger. I always keep good brandy on hand. That's one of my rules." She gave a nod toward the liquor cabinet in the corner of the dark-paneled room.

"I could be tempted," he said.

"Let me make my tea, and I'll tell you all about the evening. Willow was awesome, by the way," I said. "Can I get you anything?"

Aurora handed me her teacup. "Refill, please, and then, if you'll do the honors, Alex, I really don't see how a splash of brandy could hurt me."

Settling on the sofa, across from Aurora, I pulled my feet up under me. A magnificent grandfather clock ticked quietly toward ten-thirty. The night felt much later, reminiscent of nights in our sorority house, staying up till first light streaked the sky.

Alex obliged Aurora with brandy in her tea. Raising his eyebrows, he held out the decanter to me, and I said, "I could be tempted."

"I'll leave it to you ladies," he said, starting toward the door. Then turning, he held up his brandy snifter. "To you, Aurora, and your hospitality. The Extended Stay Suites are nice enough, but the amenities you offer are beyond compare," he said with exaggerated formality.

"Oh, go on, Alex," she said. "Why should you stay in one of those places when I have five bedrooms? If I'd known you were in Nashville last year, you could've stayed here then."

"You're too kind, Aurora," he said, with a deference that was *so* Alex. Aurora was a single woman who was once his student. My uncle would never have considered moving into her house for the weeks he'd spent in Nashville.

He bid us goodnight and took his brandy upstairs.

"Tell me about Willow." Aurora twisted a little. Feeling her back twinge, I could tell.

"She was amazing. Everyone loved her." It was hard to find the words to describe Willow's performance. I tried, then finally said, "I couldn't help thinking about you, Aurora."

"Me?" She gave a little laugh. "Why me?"

"Don't be coy," I said. "Your voice. I can still hear you singing "Dancing Queen." You must have been twelve, maybe younger, but your voice was not a child's voice. I don't know enough about music to explain technique. I just know you had an incredible talent."

Her smile showed she was pleased, but she gave a wave of dismissal, then sipped her tea and set the cup back in its saucer. "Good times," she said.

"And in college, singing in that band. You could sound like Cindi Lauper or Linda Ronstadt. Or Whitney Houston. You could really do Whitney."

She sang a few lines from "I Wanna Dance With Somebody (Who Loves You)," moving her torso a bit, then making a face, showing she hurt. "Yeah, those were some good days, but they're long gone. Now when I sing in the shower, I sound like a crow."

"I don't believe that for a minute. My point was, when Willow sang, I thought of you."

"Willow's way more talented than I ever was. If the stars align, I think she can make something of her gift. But it's hard." Aurora drank more tea, and when she spoke again, there was something more serious in her voice. "I worry about her. Worry, like she's my own child."

The door she'd opened provided an opportunity for me to say, "Willow's lost so much weight since I saw her. I know that was a few years ago, but I hope she hasn't bought into the myth about perfect body image that makes young women starve themselves."

Aurora nodded. "Yeah, I wondered the same thing when she stayed with me last year. Did I tell you she had COVID? I hadn't seen her in ages. We'd text is all. Young people aren't much for conversation on the phone. But she called me when she got sick, and I said, 'You're coming to my house so I can take care of you!' Maybe I should've been more forceful all along. She didn't put up a fuss. Except she wanted to ask one of her friends to bring her here. And I put my foot down then. 'No, absolutely not! I'm coming to get you,' I said. 'What's your address?'"

Aurora reached for her teacup, drained the last drop. Her hand was shaking a little. The cup rattled against the saucer when she put it back.

The worry showed in her made-up face. "It was such a shabby place, on some dark side street in East Nashville. That's why she didn't want me to see it. I brought her to my house. She was awfully sick. Kept testing positive for ten days. Then, she stayed on for the next month. Seemed happy to be here. I told her she could live with me, like she did when she first came up from Georgia, but she said no. She was writing songs and anxious to get a singing career going. But she always was a little vague about… well, everything."

There was something in Aurora's eyes that I couldn't read. "I was… *relieved*… proud but relieved, too, that she'd made the cut at The Bluebird for Writers' Night. And then I had to go and slip a disc! Willow understood why I couldn't be there. I know she did. But what a tragic twist of fate!"

I said, "She came over to us after the show, and we talked, just for a minute, as everything was clearing out. She asked about you."

Aurora's face seemed to relax. "She's a sweet girl. Not at all like her mother. Best thing Hilda ever did was send Willow to me. I wanted her to go to college, but that didn't work out." She reached around to touch her back and gave a deep sigh. "Guess it's about time for my oxy."

Punching a remote, she made her recliner lift up so she could stand. She used a four-pronged metal cane. Her quad, she called it. I walked with her to her expansive master suite.

I almost didn't mention the drunk who'd said Willow's song was his. But I did. "Even with all of that commotion," I said, "she handled it like a pro. She went on to wow the audience."

Aurora leaned on the quad, lines in her brow that could be pain. Or something else.

"What a terrible accusation!" she said. "Who did he think he was!"

"Kyle told us he was some washed-out singer that used to go by the stage name Notorious," I said. And saw a flash of recognition in her eyes. "Have you heard of him?"

Aurora let a moment pass, then straightened herself, nodding. "Probably. There was a time, after Henry died and I was still young, that I went out a lot. Got to know the music scene. Yes, I remember that name. I might have heard him play. Nashville used to be a small town."

She patted my arm, signaling we were finished, and we said goodnight.

In college, Aurora was able to keep up an appearance. She didn't want anyone to know she was a scholarship student, straight off the farm. That was not the image she wanted for herself. She was a sorority girl. A singer with a band that played covers around campus. Her transformation was complete after she graduated and moved to Nashville, when she married an investment banker and settled in Nashville's wealthiest, most exclusive locale.

With me, Aurora had always been more transparent. But maybe not so transparent now. I only knew there was something she wasn't saying. Something about that man, Notorious.

Chapter 3

A crisp, bright morning dawned on our second day in Nashville. I dressed in sweats and T-shirt and joined other runners, bikers, and dog walkers on the streets of Belle Meade at 7:00 a.m. Past the Belle Meade Country Club, I got a glimpse of tennis players on the outdoor courts and envied them. Aurora had promised we'd play tennis, as we'd done in college. Sadly, by the time I arrived in Nashville, she'd injured her back.

With wide, tree-lined Belle Meade Boulevard cutting through the three square miles, the small city, incorporated within the larger city of Nashville, is mostly white and overwhelmingly wealthy.

Aurora hit the jackpot when she married investment banker Henry DeMille.

And when his heart suddenly stopped on the ninth hole of the Belle Meade Country Club golf course, just six years into their marriage, Aurora became an enormously rich widow.

I kept to the side streets, like Aurora's street, tucked away from traffic. Fine, impeccably landscaped homes were closer together than those on The Boulevard, but still impressive.

After an invigorating run, I headed toward Aurora's house. I thought about her and me, how both our husbands had died when we were much too young to be widows. I thought about my hundred-year-old house in Savannah, and the repairs and renovations that it had required as I raised my five children. About the motley assortment of students from SCAD, the Savannah College of Art and Design, who play touch football and throw frisbees in Forsyth Park. About the little art galleries, antique stores, and cafés in the Historic District, where I know the owners.

Aurora lived in a fairytale world. Lovely place to run. Lovely place to visit.

But I had not missed out.

"You must be feeling better!" I called to her.

Aurora sat at a wrought iron table on her patio that overlooked a garden, profuse with spring-green and new blooms in an array of colors. All made up, she wore a flowing caftan.

Breakfast foods were laid out on a bright blue and yellow tablecloth, the Provencal print I'd given her on another visit.

"Feeling *much* better. Can't bend without pain, but I'm sitting up straighter. Come, join me," she said. "I saw Alex drive away. Where'd he go?"

I took the chair across from her. "He was meeting a reporter at The Loveless Cafe. Holly set up an interview with someone she and Kyle know. Small paper, not *The Tennessean*, but Alex was glad to get the local publicity for his book."

"You know what they say. All publicity's good as long as they spell your name right!" Aurora reached for the silver coffeepot and poured a cup for me. "I love Alex's travel guides."

"This one's different, not just a 'must see and do.' He writes about how the city has changed." And is not shy in painting a picture of the New Nashville, I could've added.

"I'm sure it's delightful!" She took an olive from a white bowl. "Yazda's big on olives."

In the kitchen I had stopped to chat with Yazda, a pretty Kurdish woman in jeans and an embroidered blouse. Skin the color of weak tea, and dark, shining eyes rimmed in thick black lashes. Outstanding culinary skills, I now learned. The small, individual bowls held boiled eggs, cheeses, pastries—not too sweet. Something Aurora called *tahini*. A paste with a nutty, earthy taste. "It's vegan and gluten-free," she said. "Yazda turned me on to it. You have to try it!"

"Does she cook for you full-time?" I asked.

"Oh, heavens no! She's done dinner parties for me for years, but coming every day, no, just since my back went out." She raised her forefinger, making a point. "And you notice she's not wearing one of those aprons like the cooks in the big houses used to wear. In case you're thinking Old South."

"No, I'm thinking of Alex's book, *Rise of the New Nashville*," I said. "He doesn't just criticize what's new and out of control, as he calls it. He writes about all that Nashville has to offer. Points out how the city has been enriched by so many nationalities that have settled here. So many cultures."

"Me, I'm fine with immigrants," Aurora said. "Yazda's fabulous. I have a Vietnamese manicurist and a landscaper from somewhere south of the border. They're great, too. But some of my friends, some of the nicest people, otherwise, say the most *terrible* things about… you know, other races, other ethnic groups. Sometimes I could just *scream*. They get this stuff from talk radio." She raised her palms and looked helpless. "It's too bad politics and religion get in the way of friendship so much these days. I try not to let that happen. One thing I learned from sorority life, and that's loyalty. Above all, loyalty among sisters. Don't you agree, Jordan?"

I had a sudden flash of the sorority sister who tried to kill me. Aurora wouldn't know about that, and I had no intention of bringing it up.

Her cell rang. The timing couldn't have been better.

She checked her phone on the table next to her and said, "Gotta take this."

It was business, I could tell from her tone, so I left the table to give her privacy. Coffee in hand, I went into the yard, past the flower garden, to a gazebo at the edge of her property, bordered by a privet hedge. I looked at the back elevation of her house, examining it with my "architect's eye." It wasn't one of those mansions on the Historic Register, but it was an expansive mid-century Greek revival, well-kept and so white, it must have been freshly-painted.

Aurora had married thirty years ago and had lived here ever since.

Thirty years and many things about my friend's life that I did not know.

The call went on until I'd finished my coffee. Fine with me. I was enjoying the warm April breeze. In Savannah, it would still be pleasant, just starting to edge toward summer heat.

Too far from the patio, I couldn't hear what Aurora was saying, but I could see her gestures. Aurora talked with her hands when she was excited. After a while, when I saw her put down the phone and pour more coffee, I went back to the table.

"Sorry about that, Jordan." Before I could say I hadn't minded at all she said, "That was my friend, Odelle. I want you to meet her. She's an architect. We're part of an advocacy group, trying to save a building that ought to be a historic landmark. She's coming over to bring some photographs and plans. Maybe you can advise us, being from Historic Savannah."

Odelle Wright must have been six feet tall. I don't often find women taller than my five-ten, but I had to look up a bit to meet her eye to eye. Her white hair made me think of Albert Einstein, but otherwise, nothing was out of place. She wore a tailored black pantsuit showing the collar of a pale blue blouse. A shade that complemented her smiling blue eyes.

Aurora had told me that Odelle Wright was eighty years old. It was hard to believe.

Gathered in Aurora's office, the only room in her house that I'd describe as cluttered, we drank sparkling water and sampled the cookies Yazda had set out. Something like gingersnaps.

"Your back's still giving you problems, Aurora? It's been a while, hasn't it?" Odelle said.

Aurora sighed. "It's better. The orthopedist says these things just take time."

"You never said what happened. Did you fall?" Odelle asked.

"No, I was trying to lift something that was too heavy. Thought I could take it to the basement. Silly of me!" Shifting in her chair, she said, "I *hate* talking about it!" and began to tell about my architectural work in Savannah, my experience with renovations of historic properties.

Earlier, she'd said to me, "Don't say, 'real estate development.' Right now the word *developer* is *anathema!*" To Odelle, she didn't mention my business affiliation with my brother, Drew, who is *that word*. "I am *sure* Jordan has come up against a few crooked developers," she said, before taking up Odelle's credentials.

I wanted to make the point that I'm a fierce advocate for historic preservation, and when my little brother gets out of line, I can handle him, but I let it slide.

"You can't walk on any street in downtown Nashville without passing a building that has Odelle's fingerprints on it," Aurora said. "How long have you had your own firm? Forty years?"

"Forty-one," Odelle said. Impressive. I would have been twelve years old.

"She built a foundation for women in architecture," Aurora said, proudly.

Odelle raised her palm, showing manicured pearl-colored nails. "Please! Let's stop all this back-patting." She laid a large manila envelope and a roll of plans on Aurora's desk.

Back and forth, they related a story that, as Aurora had surmised, was not new to me. A developer comes to town, buys an old building, wants to tear it down and build a high-rise. In Savannah's Historic District, where I live and work, developers have a bunch of hoops to jump through. As Odelle explained, Nashville's standards were more complicated. The building in question was near, but not part of, Music Row, where historic overlays had been put in place.

"The Nashville Coalition for Historic Preservation is an advocacy group," Aurora said. "It has no real rights, but we've worked with developers. Successfully, I might add. If they're reasonable, we can often get a compromise. Sometimes even a win. But this guy is slimy."

"He's a New York transplant. A notorious con man," Odelle said.

Notorious. The word made me glance at Aurora, try to catch her eye, but I had the feeling she deliberately looked away. She kept talking and gesturing, telling about the developer who started as a hedge fund manager. "Corporate raider, buying distressed companies, breaking them up and selling the parts. Leaving whole towns without jobs. Insider trading was what finally got him. He gave up one of his partners, and the SEC offered him a settlement. Fined him and banned him from the Securities Industry. So he comes to Nashville and starts buying up real estate. Makes promises to sellers about what he'll do with their properties, but before you can say 'liar, liar, pants on fire,' he levels them. That's what he wants to do with this building."

I was stunned that Aurora was so knowledgeable about all of this, but maybe I should not have been. She was always bright, graduated *magna cum laude,* and she was married to a financier for six years. Seemed she had a keen business sense but could project whatever image she wanted.

"What's the building you're trying to save?" I asked.

Odelle pulled some photos from the manila envelope and explained. The property was a two-story house, built in the 1920s. It was not architecturally significant but for years had housed Eagles

Nest Music Publishing that had a reputation for promoting young songwriters. "Providing a 'nest' before they could fly, I guess," Odelle said. "Legend has it Hank Williams wrote his first song at Eagles Nest. The publishing house was a vital part of the music industry until the eighties. All those years. Several renovations, with a studio on the back end. The studio's fascinating, too, the acoustics. The way they got a particular sound, the reverb."

She spread out the photos. "But ownership changed hands over and over. The last owner had a massage parlor in the house and just boarded up the studio. Then, we'd heard rumors. Tommy Kahn had his eye on the building. But when the sale was final, it seemed rather sudden…It was announced last week."

I sat up straighter. "Tommy Kahn is the notorious con man?"

Aurora's eyes widened. "You sound like you know him, Jordan."

"I don't know him," I said. "But I've heard the name."

I didn't say I'd heard the name from Holly. She worked for Tommy Kahn.

Chapter 4

My children were all grown up, but still, sometimes, I couldn't help worrying.

The youngest of the five—twins, Michael and Catherine—lived in Atlanta, where they stumbled on the usual bumps that are part of college life. Failed romances, professors that were unreasonable (their word), too much work, too little money, not enough time for their social life (they claimed). Or too much social life (my thought). The middle child was Julie, the brainiest of all, with a Cornell degree, who'd had the hardest time finding a job. Now she had a promising position in business, at a nice hotel in Chicago, if only she could live with the sharp winds and deep snows and contain her longing to come back to Savannah where it was warm. Next to the oldest was Claire, a jewelry designer in Santa Fe. Fiercely independent, she told me next to nothing about the particulars of her life. COVID had made Claire and Santa Fe feel even more distant.

The oldest, my firstborn, was Holly.

People who know me and know my family say that of all my children, Holly is the most like me. We are the same height, five-ten, and we've often been mistaken for each other at a distance because of how we carry ourselves. Apparently we both have what people call a *purposeful* stride. Her hair is similar to mine but more ginger-colored than my auburn. Our blue eyes are shaped more like cat-eyes than round. And for better or worse, Holly has my sense of what is fair, or more accurately, a sense of what is unfair.

That's not always a good thing. Because I know myself, know the way I dive into other people's messes, which is often too much like diving into a dumpster full of toxic materials. And I know, though it sounds inconsistent, that I often guard against feeling too much, too deeply.

Thoughts about Holly kept edging into my mind as Odelle unrolled worn-looking plans on Aurora's desk. Holly had worked for Tommy Kahn ever since she came to Nashville. If he was a slimy, notorious con man, how much did Holly know?

From the photographs and faded blueprints with tattered edges, the Eagles Nest came to life for me. I asked, "Where did you get these?"

"The contractor who built the last addition is a friend. He's retired but he dug them up for me." Odelle reached for one of the 8 x 11 photos. "Some of these, we took recently. Skye did."

"Skye, from the Coalition," Aurora clarified. "We were trying to get the building declared a historic landmark. We started the process months ago but I'm afraid we dragged our feet."

Odelle said, "Maybe we did, but it's not easy to hurry it through. I don't know how it is in Savannah, Jordan, but here we have to work with the Metro Council. One of the councilmen is on our board, and he's great. So many of them, though, are obsessed with the city's growth and blind to everything else! That's all they care about! All the out-of-control growth."

"The Historic Zoning Commission has the final vote," Aurora said, "but we aren't there yet. None of our efforts to work something out with Tommy Kahn have paid off. He won't even return our calls. If he follows his playbook, he could have the wrecking ball there tomorrow."

I had the urge to tell them that Tommy Kahn was Holly's employer, but something held me back. Some protective instinct.

Eventually they'd know, but I had to wait to say it until I found out more from Holly. Tonight, Alex and I were supposed to have dinner with her and Kyle at their house. I doubted I could do anything to help save a historic building, but maybe I could save Holly from—from what, I wasn't sure. Maybe Tommy Kahn was slimy, but was he doing anything illegal, here in Nashville? And what did it all mean for Holly?

Alex was in fine spirits when he returned to Aurora's house in the early afternoon.

I remarked that it must've been a long interview.

"Yes, it was. But after it was over, I drove downtown and delivered chocolates and wine to some of the fine people in Nashville who helped me with my book." He ticked off names on his fingers and ran out of fingers. Staff in the mayor's office, the Metro Police Department, the courthouse. A couple of attorneys. Librarians. "The ladies at the main library could not have been more gracious when I was stumbling through the Archives last year."

Librarians love Alex. Love his intelligent inquiries. And he is so appreciative. Especially librarians of a certain age, who practically fall over themselves to provide what he needs for his research. I always find it amusing that Alex is oblivious to what I see so clearly.

Aurora took us to her bright sunroom. Today, since she was a little more mobile, she had avoided her recliner in the media room, where she'd spent so much time. The sunroom, like her entire house, was tastefully decorated, the latest trends in interior design. Casual furniture with comfortable cushions, suitable for a sun porch, but the room was enclosed in glass, with Roman shades. White tile floor, an area rug in muted shades of gray, beige and brown. Alex settled in a modern-style club chair. We did not have to ask him if the interview was a success.

"Such a nice young man," he said. "Accomplished. And witty. Caleb Hunter. He said his parents named him after one of the spies that Moses sent to check out Canaan, the Promised Land. Twelve spies, and ten came back saying it was too dangerous to go in. But Caleb and another said it was a land of milk and honey. 'Trust in God, and possess the land,' they said."

"Oh, we were big on Bible stories at my house," Aurora said, clasping her hands. "I remember that one."

"Caleb and Joshua," I put in. My Catholic family was not like Aurora's Baptist family, but I had some memory of Bible stories.

Alex said, "Caleb told me, with a kind of reverence, 'I have always felt the burden to tell the truth and be fearless.'"

A quiet moment passed, as the words took hold. I thought I would like this young man.

"I believe it," Aurora said. "I always pick up the *Nashville Voice* at the grocery store and Caleb Hunter usually has a piece about crime or affordable housing or Nashville traffic. And shady politicians. He doesn't shy away from writing what people might not like to hear. Last week, he wrote about how the city we've known is being torn down all around us." Her eyes narrowed as she remembered one of his lines. "He said, 'You are only a true Nashvillian when what was here before is more real than what is here now.' Isn't that so perceptive!"

"I thought he did book reviews," I said. "Sounds more like investigative journalism."

"He's a staff writer for the *Nashville Voice*." Alex's expression was pensive. "I've been reading his articles since last year, when I stared my research. Oh, I know he interviewed me because of Holly and Kyle, but I'm sure, from the questions he asked, that he read my book. We talked at length about how Nashville is exploding with no clear vision of what it wants to be."

"Will his review come out this week, in time for the Parnassus event?" Aurora asked.

Alex rubbed the bridge of his nose. A nervous gesture, I've noticed. "I'm not sure he'll actually write a review. He didn't promise. But he didn't seem like the kind of young man who would tell me how much he admired my book if he didn't mean it." Alex took off his glasses and wiped the lens on the cuff of his white shirt that peeked from his tweed jacket. Always the professor. "He mentioned he's working on a series. He didn't say what, but it must have something to do with the issues I covered in the book because he spent so much time with me."

Maybe no book review, *per se*, but I said, "If a daring young reporter writes an investigative piece and quotes you and mentions your book, that's a good thing, Alex."

"I can't wait to read it," Aurora said. "I called Parnassus, but they've sold out till Saturday. Oh, I'm sure your event will be a big splash! Stacks of copies, people rushing to grab one. But I wish I had it right now. I'd read it straight through."

"Then we'll have to do something about that, Aurora. I already have a signed copy for you in my room." Alex stood up, looking quite chivalrous, a look he carries off very well.

"Remember we're having dinner with Holly and Kyle tonight," I said.

"Yes, and I have copies for them, also," he said. "And a nice Bordeaux."

"I think I'll rest in the recliner," Aurora said. She stood, moving tentatively. She winced, must have felt a stitch in her back. Her phone rang as she took hold of her quad.

She answered, made sounds of approval, and then, "*We* didn't put them up to it." Finally, "I don't know if it'll make any difference to Tommy Kahn, but the publicity can't hurt our cause." She didn't sound entirely convinced or convincing.

Ending the call, she made her way to the media room. Slowly.

Telling me about the protest that was taking place at that moment in front of the Eagles Nest building. Students seemed to have gathered initially, and a crowd from Music Row had joined in. "That was Skye from the Coalition," she said. "She was there. It didn't seem to her that the protest was very organized. Just a lot of yelling and chanting. She mentioned a permit. If they're students from Vanderbilt and Belmont, they should know they needed one, but if it's spontaneous…"

Aurora reached the chair and let it ease her to a reclining position. I asked if I could get her anything. She shook her head and closed her eyes.

I knew she needed to rest, so I didn't ask the question, but Aurora answered it, anyway.

"Skye estimated fifty or sixty so far. The TV stations are arriving. And the police."

Alex laid his book on the parson's table at the foot of the elegant stairs.

"I looked in on Aurora. She's sleeping in her recliner. I'll give her this later," he said.

I had been on the patio, checking my phone for a report about the protest at the Eagles Nest. Looking for "breaking news," and there it was. Even a video, a few minutes old.

"Want to take a ride?" I asked Alex.

"No thanks. My editor left a message about a TV interview. Something she just set up. I need to call her back. Where're you going?" He reached in his pocket and handed the car keys to me. "You have that look you get when you're about to head straight into the arms of trouble."

Chapter 5

The protest had gained momentum.

Cars lined the streets near the Eagles Nest. I drove around the area a couple of times and found a place to park three blocks away from where the crowd had clogged the street. The fifty or sixty that Aurora had mentioned looked more like a hundred now. They may have come from the universities in the area, Vanderbilt and Belmont, and from Music Row, but it was impossible to identify a particular subset of the crowd. And not everyone was on the same side. One young Black man with his fist in the air was wearing blue hospital scrubs. A young woman, head covered in a hijab, wore skinny jeans and cowboy boots. Some may have worked in nearby offices, judging from their business attire. High-tops, loafers, and construction boots. Spiky pink hair, cowboy hats, and dreadlocks. Tattoos, piercings, and beards.

"Save our Nashville!" voices rang out.

Near me, a gray-haired professor-type man yelled, "Troublemakers! Rabblerousers!"

I stood at the edge of the crowd, taking photos to show Aurora, amid lots of others snapping pictures with phones. TV photographers documented the scene that we'd probably see on the evening news. Uniformed police threaded through the crowd, looking unsure of what to do. No one was causing trouble, but there was a restless energy, an underlying current of anger. More people arriving by the minute.

In the midst of the noise and the surge of hostility, I thought I heard my name. Looking around, I saw wild white hair and someone waving. Odelle Wright called, "Jordan! Over here!"

I waved back and we headed toward each other, through a sea of bodies and chants.

"Are you here alone?" she said, not quite shouting, but almost.

"Yes!" I had to raise my voice, too. "I didn't expect to see you."

"I couldn't stay away," she said. Leaning closer to me, so I caught her Estée Lauder scent, she still had to speak up. "My father played at the Opry. He was a fiddler. A studio musician, too. Right here, at the Eagles Nest. No one remembers my father now, but he was friends with all the legends. If you asked any of them, they'd tell you his name should still be ringing on Music Row."

She smiled, and I could see the flood of all those memories in her eyes.

"I can see why this isn't just any old building to you," I said, "but I'm amazed at this turnout, this kind of energy, to save a building. Even in Savannah's Historic District, where most citizens believe historic preservation is not just the right thing to do, but also profitable, I've never seen anything like this."

Odelle nodded, sadly. "You're right. Have you seen all the steel and glass on Music Row? It's been happening for years now. Block after block of old buildings obliterated with hardly a peep from anybody except the Historic Commission and our Coalition. We've managed to get some historic overlays on Music Row, and that makes it more difficult for developers, but the billionaires from New York and California are hard to fight."

"Looks like a lot of people are passionate about saving the Eagles Nest," I said.

"I think it's something more than this building, Jordan. Much more," Odelle said. "Nashvillians are finally waking up to what's happening to our city. The Tommy Kahns don't just demo old buildings without respect for Nashville's history. They don't blink at paying millions of dollars for houses, making the housing market terrible for most buyers. They buy apartments and condos and raise the rents, pricing middle-class renters out of the market. They seduce our elected officials and candidates with their big money. Oh I could go on—"

But suddenly our attention turned to a large SUV, edging toward the protestors, who stood their ground. A black Navigator. Painted across the side was *Nashville Property Solutions, LLC,* and under the company name, *Progress and Prosperity.* The Navigator stopped and its doors opened, letting out three young men and two young women, all of them lithe and clean-cut, outfitted in white shirts and khaki skirts and pants.

"Tommy Kahn. That bastard," Odelle said, lowering her voice this time.

Something caught in my throat for an instant. But thank God, Holly was *not* one of the petite, blonde, young women, with blinding white teeth that couldn't have been out of braces very long. The young men's uniformity was just as striking. Medium-build, rolled-up shirt sleeves, hair that looked more like a stylist's work than a barber's. Like automatons, they all hurried to the back end of the Navigator and unloaded signs. All of it, perfectly choreographed.

The activists for saving the building had no signs, a consequence of their spontaneity. Tommy Kahn's troupe moved into the crowd, spread out, and began to distribute their signs as hands reached for them. I was surprised how many hands. The signage was professionally done: *"Property owners have rights"* and *"Protect property owners' rights"* and *"Progress and prosperity go hand in hand."*

A counter-protest organized by Kahn's people in a couple of hours.

A police officer with a bullhorn climbed to the steps of the house, ordering, "Go home, everybody! Break it up now or face the music! Go home!" But the noise level continued to rise.

Not far from us, a red-bearded man in a muscle shirt that showed bulging biceps took a sign from one of the girls. Promptly, he threw it on the ground and stomped on it. The girl, half his size, began to pound his back with the other signs she carried.

The rest of it happened so fast, the way people always describe it when they try to recall a traumatic event. It was like someone turned a knob and the level of violence went up to *Riot,* or someone lit a fuse and there was a pause, then an explosion of fists, knees, and curses. Pushing, punching and flailing. Shouting, shrieking. The signs became weapons. Someone threw a brick, and then another. More screams and cries. I felt panicky, wondering if somebody in this mob would bring out a gun. I remembered from Alex's book that in Tennessee, adults don't need a permit to carry.

I took a couple of photos, then reached for Odelle's arm. "Let's get out of here!" I said, pulling at her. She seemed dazed for a moment, but nodded then, grabbed my hand and followed me toward the street. The crowd surged around us as we threaded through, everyone jostling for space. Police blew shrill whistles, and again the order came through the bullhorn: "Break it up! Go home NOW!"

Behind me, I heard Odelle cry out and her hand dropped from mine.

I whirled around. "Odelle? Oh no! Odelle!"

She was pressing her temple. Blood running through her fingers, streaking her pale face. And then, in a kind of slow motion, her knees buckled and she sank to the ground.

A crowd tightened around us. "Get back! Give her some air!" I shouted. My voice cracked as I yelled, "Somebody call 9-1-1!" and I heard someone on his phone, saying, "An old woman's hurt bad. Her head's bleeding. Send an ambulance…"

Kneeling beside Odelle, I fought my fear and tried to comfort her. "It's all right. Help's on the way. You're gonna be fine." I could smell the blood that gushed from her head and I could see the terror in her eyes, like she wanted to believe me but couldn't quite. From my shoulder bag, I pulled out all the tissues I had and pressed against the wound. Someone handed me more tissues, but immediately the white wad turned red, drenched with blood.

The feeling of absolute helplessness washed over me, but I squeezed Odelle's hand and whispered, "Stay with me, girl. You're doing great."

She closed her eyes. Her other hand was fumbling with a brick that lay beside her. It must've been the brick that hit her. Her fingers curled around it. I could tell from her grimace that she was trying to lift it but didn't have the strength.

"Jordan… take it," she said.

Why would she want it? But I took the brick, my fingers stained with blood.

"Hang on. The ambulance is on its way," I said, as I dropped the brick in my purse.

The wail of a siren sounded. I thought Odelle might've lapsed into unconsciousness, but a moment later she opened her eyes and tried to speak.

I leaned closer. "I'm here, Odelle. What is it? What are you trying to say?"

"Help them," she whispered, "save…"

And then her voice faded away.

Chapter 6

I was useless in the E.R.

Someone finally got around to calling me up to her desk. I was embarrassed that I didn't know anything about Odelle except her name. Nothing about her insurance. Not even her address or telephone number or the name of the firm she'd founded forty-one years ago.

"Who *are* you, honey?" the woman with tight gray curls and owlish glasses asked.

I couldn't even claim to be Odelle's friend. I'd just met her this morning.

"My name's Jordan Mayfair," I said. "I was there when she was injured. I asked one of the paramedics which hospital and came here because I thought somebody should be with her."

I'd made sure Odelle's purse went along in the ambulance. Now I wished I'd kept it. "You can get her information from her wallet. Probably an emergency number," I said.

She gave me a dubious look. "You can wait over there."

Before I could move away from the desk, a short, stout Black woman in pink glittery tennis shoes appeared, breathing hard. "Are you Jordan Mayfair?" she asked, and without losing a beat, she took the chair I'd relinquished and turned her attention to the owlish glasses. "I'm Skye Donelson. I work with Odelle. What do you need to know?"

Fifteen minutes later, Skye sat down beside me in one of the plastic molded chairs.

"I was at the Eagles Nest!" she said. "But when the bricks started flying, I high-tailed it outta there. I heard the siren and knew somebody was hurt but didn't have a clue it was Odelle!"

I had called Aurora as I made my way to the hospital. Skye said she was already back at the Coalition's headquarters when Aurora reached her.

"Aurora said you'd be at the E.R. Look for the tallest woman in the room, she said. Nearly six feet tall with dark red hair." Skye touched my arm and I noticed her long, hot pink nails. "Lucky you. The tall part. I like my hair better." She patted her brown braids.

I wasn't sure how to respond. I smiled and hoped that was enough. "Lucky that you showed up," I said. "I couldn't provide any information about Odelle. We just met today."

"How serious is it? A concussion?" Skye asked.

"A concussion, I would think, or worse. The brick struck her temple. There was so much blood. She knew who I was, but she seemed to go in and out of consciousness." I remembered the last time she'd closed her eyes and the deathly pallor of her face.

We were quiet for a moment, and Skye said, "Aurora told me your name's Jordan Mayfair, that you're visiting your daughter. I know a Holly Mayfair from yoga at the Y. She looks a lot like you, just younger."

"That's my daughter." I expected the kind of comment I always hear about Holly. How smart she is. And kind, which is the best compliment, in my book.

Skye narrowed her eyes. "She works for the prince of frickin' darkness, you know."

I stammered, "Tommy Kahn," and felt my stomach begin to knot.

Another silence fell. After a moment, she stood up. "I'll be outside if they tell you anything, which I'm sure they won't. I'll be making some calls and saying a prayer."

"*These old buildings are not just bricks and mortar,*" Alex read out loud from the *Nashville Voice*. "*They house our past, reminding us of the graceful Southern city Nashville once was, reminding us of who we were and who we might still be. Old buildings like the Eagles Nest are a sacred trust, a treasure, unique and irreplaceable.*"

Alex shook the newspaper and folded it. "A talented journalist, that young man."

Caleb Hunter's article in last week's *Voice* sounded more like a literary eulogy for a once-great city than an ordinary newspaper article or even an op-ed. The *Nashville Voice* was what Holly called an alternative weekly, aimed at a younger audience, edgier than anything in *The Tennessean*, the Nashville newspaper that was struggling to keep its head above water, to fend off the merciless competition of digital information outlets.

Holly put out a chips-and-dip plate with apologies. "I had to work late," she said. "And I hope you like spaghetti. I meant to do better."

I said, "What's better than spaghetti?" I could see the strain around her eyes and felt an ache, a mother's worry. I wanted to ask about her work, but now was not the time.

Kyle poured the wine Alex had brought. "Is Tommy Kahn gearing up for the protestors tomorrow? They'll be back, you know, and they'll be organized next time."

Apparently Holly's significant other hadn't felt the same vibe her mother had felt.

"I don't know! I didn't have anything to do with that!" No mistaking Holly's tone now.

The charge in the air left us all silent for a minute. All of us reaching for chips and dip.

Holly and Kyle lived in East Nashville where the old working class neighborhood was being pushed, block by block, into oblivion—800-square-foot houses with sagging porches stood next to four skinny houses shoehorned into a quarter-acre lot, next to stunning renovations, in keeping with their historic character. Holly and Kyle rented this 1929 bungalow. Kyle worked at the Country Music Hall of Fame with the owner, who had bought and transformed the sweet little arts and crafts house before moving on up, to affluent Green Hills.

High stools and a bar separated kitchen appliances from a small dining table and chairs. Holly and I sat on the kitchen side, facing the men. Mouths full as we let the tension subside.

After a moment, Holly said, "I'm sorry," and reached over to touch Kyle's wrist. He took her hand and squeezed it. She spoke, directly to him. "You know what I've been working on. It's... tedious." Then turning to me, "Nothing to do with the Eagles Nest. Not really. You know, I was only the fourth employee that Tommy hired, nearly five years ago. Now there are seventeen of us. All kinds of business ventures, and we're not all involved in every one of them."

If Tommy Kahn was crooked, it would make sense not to let any employee know about *all* of his businesses. To trust only those who were easily manipulated with details about the ventures that were less than honest, ethical, or legal. That would leave out my daughter.

"Holly works too hard," Kyle said. Poor Kyle was trying, but I expected Holly to bristle.

I was wrong. She sighed, "Yes, I do, but that's all going to change." Then quickly she added, "Can we please talk about something else?"

Alex picked up the earlier thread of conversation. Caleb Hunter's piece in the *Voice*. Seemed we couldn't get completely away from old buildings, but I tried. "Tell them about your interview today, Alex." Like most old roosters, he was more than willing to crow.

And then he said, "Caleb had the highest praise for both of you."

"I met Caleb when he was on a story about the Hall of Fame," Kyle said, "and we started hanging out. He was playing hoops at a community center with some kids he knew. Now I play with them, too."

"The kids that sing," Holly put in.

Kyle nodded. "Caleb thought it was amazing for a community center to have a singing group like that. Boys and girls and the old guy that directs them, they practice every Sunday night, not for money or credit, just because they love music. So he started interviewing them, writing about where they come from and what they want to do with their lives."

"Last time one of his pieces ran," Holly said, "before Caleb got... well... *distracted*, someone started a scholarship fund for these kids, through Belmont's music program."

I had the feeling I'd had when Alex came back from meeting Caleb at The Loveless Cafe, that he was a young man who would go places.

"None of us can afford to go out much, so most weekends we hang out here," Kyle said. "Sometimes he brings a girl but most of the time, no."

"I like to cook for him," Holly said. "He'd eat shoe leather if I put cheese on it."

"Speaking of food, you want me to start the pasta? I'm starved," Kyle said.

I would've offered to help in the kitchen, but this was better, seeing them work together, side by side, making spaghetti, salad, and garlic bread. For a few minutes, their own little world.

Though I knew something was bothering Holly, she put on a face, the rest of the evening. She could always put on a face.

In the living room, as she was pouring coffee, Kyle's phone rang. "It's Caleb," he said, answering, "Hey, man, what's up?" He stepped away to another room, and we kept talking about the TV interview Alex had learned about today. It was already scheduled for Wednesday.

"Presleigh Deere is the young woman," he said. "My editor spelled it. P-r-e-s-l-e-i-g-h D-e-e-r-e. She said it's bad form to misspell her name. Is that a stage name?"

"I think it's for real," Holly said. "She can show her claws, Uncle Alex. Be careful."

Before she could elaborate, Kyle returned. "Caleb had some news about the protest," he said. "The police made a few arrests and finally broke it all up around dark." Then his voice rose in disbelief, his smile turning up at the corners of his mouth, giving him that appealing boyish look. "And my man Caleb came home with a black eye!"

Holly's breath caught. "Who? I mean, was it…" Like me, she must've been thinking about Tommy Kahn's crew at the protest.

"It wasn't about the protest," Kyle said. "It was Notorious."

Kyle told us that Notorious hung around the Country Music Hall of Fame. "Out front, playing his songs, the closest he'll ever get to any hall of fame. Not many people listen 'cause he comes off as just another homeless guy. He's not homeless, though. Has a room somewhere. Isn't even panhandling, but he'll take it when I slip him a few bucks. I talk to him when I'm leaving work. If he gets my attention, he won't shut up. Always wants me to hear this great song he just wrote. Sometimes if he's not too wasted, the old buzzard can make that guitar ring."

At the protest, Kyle said, Notorious had spotted one of the TV photographers who was talking to Caleb. "He started yammering about Willow Goodheart and how she stole his song. About up-and-comers that steal from *real* songwriters. The photographer tried to get rid of him, telling him, 'Talk to this guy. He's a reporter for the *Voice*.' Caleb had heard about what happened at The Bluebird, but he didn't have time for Notorious, didn't believe anyone had stolen a song from him. Finally, Caleb told him to get lost. Told him nobody would ever believe a used-up drunk's story."

"That's pretty harsh," I said, "even if it's true."

"I guess Caleb could've chosen his words better, but he was there to cover the protest and this drunk wouldn't get out of his face. Notorious took a swing… and connected." Kyle shook his head and laughed a little. "Caleb said nobody was more shocked than Notorious. First hit in twenty years."

Chapter 7

Noise and restlessness, signs and banners provided a backdrop for the TV reporter's video from the Eagles Nest. "No violence this morning," he said.

Leaning back in her recliner, Aurora was watching her gargantuan television when I came downstairs, still sluggish from a fitful night's sleep.

I couldn't remember when I'd ever slept past nine. Yesterday had left me with an exhaustion that was not just physical, yet my brain wouldn't rest. I saw first light streak the sky before I finally drifted off, into a deep, drug-like sleep. No telling how long I would've slept if Holly hadn't called. She was taking the day off and wanted to meet me at Radnor Lake.

Aurora's day must have started early. "I talked to Skye. She helped with getting a permit after she left the hospital yesterday." Aurora clicked on *mute*. "Will you look at those signs? *Property Owners rights. Second Amendment rights.* What about women's rights? God help us!"

Lots of *Save Our Nashville* signs, too. Looked like everyone was waving something. Though no signs were as professional as the ones Tommy Kahn's mercenaries brought yesterday.

"Skye went to the hospital this morning. She was with Odelle when the doctor came in," Aurora said. Odelle had seemed confused and agitated. "Didn't recognize Skye. The doc said they'll be running all kinds of tests today. The memory loss may be temporary, or could be permanent. Probably some memories will come back. Her age is a factor, not in her favor. It's so tragic!"

"Heartbreaking," I said. One blow to the head, and her entire world may have disappeared. I wondered about the brick that was now in my bag. Why had Odelle wanted it?

"Did you drink all the coffee?" I said.

"Are you trying to say I'm wired? Well, I prob'ly am! But I didn't forget you. I had Yazda make a full pot before she left."

She called to me as I filled my cup in the kitchen. "Help yourself to whatever you find. I had breakfast *hours* ago. Alex came down and nibbled and then went back upstairs to work."

When I returned to the media room with a small breakfast plate and coffee, the clip of the demonstration was over. Aurora had turned the sound back on. A heavily made-up blonde whose bright lips screamed *Botox* sat across from a bald, well-dressed man, coat and tie, well-trimmed mustache and stylish eyeglasses. An intelligent look.

"That's Presleigh Deere. *Mornings with Presleigh*," Aurora said. "Alex told me about his interview tomorrow. Oh, it's good for book sales, I guess, but she's always itching for a fight. All about ratings. She's sort of a... well, she's a witch. And I'm being kind."

Presleigh Deere's voice was low, way too seductive for a morning show.

"Once again this year, student test scores dropped in Tennessee," she said. "Why shouldn't we hold teachers accountable for the poor performance of their students?"

"He's with the teachers' union. A sacrificial lamb, I'm afraid," Aurora whispered before the man answered.

He leaned in, earnestly. "We all know that many factors affect student performance. The setbacks we suffered during the pandemic were huge, and we're still recovering. Teachers were on the front lines, tirelessly putting students above their own well-being—"

"I see," Presleigh said curtly. "Isn't it true the teachers union opposed guidelines that the legislature tried to put in place? Surely you don't think teachers should be just be free to teach anything they please in the classroom?" She gave a flouncy little wave. "Without oversight?"

He forced a smile. "It's unfortunate that the state legislators don't trust their own professional educators. Teachers are the ones who spend their days with students. I notice legislators are not particularly happy with oversight in their lawmaking, either." He spoke with conviction, with *heart*, I suppose. "Teachers are some of the most dedicated professionals you'll find. Many go above and beyond, every day, with their own time and their own money."

"Oh yes," Presleigh moaned. "Where have we heard it before? Overworked and underpaid. Even with every summer off. Tell that to cops and firemen."

"Oh, she's a piranha!" Aurora cried out.

The rep for the teachers union was surely not a novice when it came to tough interviews, but a close-up showed beads of sweat on his forehead. "It's no small thing to be educating the next generation," he said, unable to conceal the edge of frustration. "These guidelines you mention come down from people with their own agendas, not people who are trained to teach."

Presleigh raised her voice. "You believe teachers should tell our kids what to think?"

The man straightened, and the trace of a smile made me think this was a question he'd wanted Presleigh Deere to ask. "No, we believe in teaching kids *how* to think, not *what* to think. Would you go to a politician for a root canal? Would you want a politician to perform an appendectomy on your child?"

Point for the teachers' rep! But Presleigh Deere hurried past the questions and called for a commercial break.

Aurora switched off the TV. "Always stirring the pot, that woman. I guess that's television for you, but I sure hope Alex can handle her."

I felt a rise of protectiveness for my uncle. "This is not his first rodeo," I said, but at seventy-five, he was not as fast on his feet as he used to be. I was worried that Presleigh Deere could make a good man with a fine mind into a rating spectacle.

Radnor Lake State Park was a natural area in South Nashville with marshes, trails, and woods. Alex, in his book, had called it "the best-kept secret in Nashville."

Only minutes from the parking area and Visitors Center, Holly said, "I'm quitting my job, Mom."

We'd started out on the trail. Holly had chosen a short loop, she said, because she didn't have much time. She didn't say what else was on her schedule, and I didn't ask. I just let her talk. And she began to spill it all.

"I didn't know how corrupt Tommy was. Not for a long time. I didn't like what he was doing, but it was legal, as far as I could see. So I thought, well, it's business. That's all." Holly was setting a brisk pace, leaning forward. She might have been heading into a strong wind.

"First time something really got to me, it was this woman who came in with a notice she'd received about a rent hike. These apartments the company owns, an older complex off Wedgewood. She'd been paying $1,100, and the new rent would be $1,750. The woman worked two jobs, Dollar Store and a convenience market." Holly took a sip from her water bottle without slowing. "Like I told you, we all work on different projects, and I didn't know anything about those units, but I asked Sharla, the girl who did. She shrugged and said, 'Talk to Tommy.' Well, that didn't go anywhere. He laughed at me and called me a bleeding heart."

Holly looked at me for the first time, her eyes full of sadness as she remembered. "I had to tell her. She had a child with spina bifida, Mom. The little girl was at Harris-Hillman, the school for children with disabilities, and the woman had it worked out with a neighbor who kept the little girl before and after the bus came. She said, 'I'm barely making it, where we live, but my friend helps. Do you know how hard it is to get somebody to take care of a child with spina bifida? I can't move. But I can't afford that much rent! What can I do? What would *you* do?'"

Holly didn't say how that story ended. I could only surmise that she wasn't able to do anything to help. I saw in her expression the battered conscience she carried.

She told another story of a man in one of the other apartment complexes that had mold. Not long after he moved in, he began to have joint pain, nosebleeds, and shortness of breath. When his ears started to bleed, his doctor told him it was exposure to black mold. He asked the property manager for repairs to the unit, for help with medical bills, then, finally, for moving expenses because he knew he had to move out. Holly was not involved, but she got the story when she was in the elevator with Tommy Kahn one day, and the man, coughing blood into a handkerchief, confronted him. Not only had his requests been denied, but now Tommy said, "You know you can't break your lease." The man said, "I'll sue you! You've ruined my health!" And Tommy said, "You do that. Sue me."

I hadn't said anything until now. "Aurora and Odelle told me how Tommy Kahn handles historic properties. Staying just within the law. It's the same with raising rents and refusing to let someone out of a lease. All legal. But that doesn't make it right. Your good conscience is whispering to you, Holly, and I'm glad you're listening." I was breathing hard, trying to keep up. Though my legs were as long as Holly's, her fury was driving her.

Finally she slowed down, then stopped when we came to the part of the trail that edged Radnor Lake. A beautiful lake. Still. Peaceful. Holly moved to the side, as others had come up behind us. And then we began to walk slowly. She kept her voice low.

"There's so much more, Mom. I can't even talk about all of it."

I wished I could comfort her. But I couldn't. I couldn't make everything all right. Just wait for her to say it in her own time, I told myself. I waited.

We met four women pushing strollers. Laughing, talking, all at the same time.

Our pace was slow and deliberate.

Up ahead, there was a commotion. As we came closer, we saw that a large tortoise was taking its own sweet time crossing the road. Hikers stopped to get pictures. But not Holly.

We passed on. And when all of that was behind us, Holly said, almost whispering now, "He's guilty of PPP fraud. You know, the Paycheck Protection Program, supposed to help small businesses during the worst of COVID. I've known what Tommy was doing for a while. More than a year."

My throat tightened. Just wait for the rest of it, I told myself.

Holly seemed confused by my silence. She frowned. "You're not thinking *I* was part of it, are you? I kept my mouth shut, and maybe that was wrong, but I wasn't involved in the scheme."

For an instant, I'd been fearful of what she might tell me next. But that moment was a glitch. She didn't have to tell me everything. I knew what was true about my daughter.

"I believe you, Holly," I said. "My worry is whether you're in danger. Because of what you know. Is that why you're quitting now?"

"I... I don't think I'm in any danger," she said. Not very convincingly.

We had reached Otter Creek Road, a point where we could continue the hike on a longer trail or return to the parking lot. Holly didn't pause. She headed toward the parking lot. She sounded weary when she said, "I'm so sick of going to work every day, thinking about it."

All I could say to her now was, "You should give notice immediately. Please, Holly."

"I don't think I'm in danger," she said again. And almost whispering, "Not yet."

Chapter 8

"Will you take me to the hospital?"

Aurora met me at her front door. I didn't even get a chance to hear the UGA fight song.

"To see *Odelle* is what I mean!" She laughed, moving back to let me in. "The look on your face, Jordan!"

"I couldn't imagine why you needed to go the hospital. You seem fine," I told her.

She was all made up. Tight shiny pants and loose silky top. Ferragamo ballerina pumps.

"I think I can manage with my quad. I'll be slow, but if I can't do it, well, I'm sure they have wheelchairs, don't they? Oh, I know it's a lot to ask, Jordan, but I'm *dying* to see Odelle."

I was worn out from the hike with Holly, after a restless night, worn out and now worried, but Aurora was putting me up for a week so I didn't see how I could refuse her request.

"Just give me a few minutes to make myself presentable," I said.

She called as I headed upstairs. "Nashville's new rush hour starts about three o'clock now. If we hurry, we can beat it."

It was a shock, seeing her there in an ICU bed. Odelle looked every day of her eighty years. Hooked up to an IV line. Hospital gown hanging on her thin shoulders. Thick bandage covering her temple, taped to her cheek and scalp, where they'd shaved off her hair. The chilly room smelled of disinfectant.

Odelle's eyes were closed.

A nurse, one of those young nurses with a fresh, hopeful face, was checking the IV tubing. She glanced at us and back at the empty bag hanging on the metal pole.

"Will she wake up if we speak to her?" I asked, just above a whisper.

"Prob'ly. She sleeps a lot but has a few lucid moments. Might be a little confused." The nurse's high-pitched voice made her sound even younger than she looked.

"What's she getting in the IV?" I asked.

"Just saline. We're just keeping her hydrated." She headed to the door. "I'll be back with a new bag."

Aurora had already moved to the side of the hospital bed, reaching for the bare, wrinkled arm. I stepped up behind her as she spoke.

"Odelle, it's me. Aurora." Her voice broke as she leaned closer. "Oh, honey, I'm so sorry about this. What's the world coming to? Something like this happening to somebody like you."

Each inhalation and exhalation was painfully slow, followed by a long pause. I dreaded each pause, thinking she might not breathe again. Aurora kept whispering her name, and finally Odelle opened her eyes, a hazy blue now. She looked at Aurora, but not a trace of recognition. Maybe her response was just reflex, a reaction to hearing her name.

As Aurora kept talking to her, rubbing her arm, the door opened.

A man came into sight and spoke, his voice impatient. "I just need to ask her a few questions. I won't be long." Salt-and-pepper hair. Coat and tie. Questions? Was he a detective?

The young nurse moved in front of him, too small for her body to block him, but she spoke with surprising authority. "Like I already told you, she's not able to talk to you. I can't let you see her right now."

He glanced at Aurora and me. "She's able to talk to them. I'll wait."

My uncle is always accusing me of inserting myself into the middle of things that aren't my business. It seemed like the right time to do just that. I walked over to the door and told the man, "She's not talking to us. She hasn't said a word. Doesn't even recognize her friend."

"Who *are* you?" he said.

The nurse stepped around me and took hold of the door handle, pushing. Not pushing me out, exactly, but the effect was the same. I moved into the hall as the door closed.

"Are you family?" he asked. Now that we'd been shut out, he stepped back but still sounded like someone used to getting his way.

"A friend. Are you a detective?"

He answered with a gruff "Detective Slater." He pulled back his jacket and flashed a badge so quickly, it could have come from a cereal box. "I need to ask what she knows about the attack."

"She doesn't know anything," I said. "I was there. People were throwing bricks. I'm sure she couldn't tell you who threw the brick that hit her."

"So you were with her." It was not a question. He didn't sound so cross now that he thought he might get information from me.

"Yes, I was with her, and I'd tell you if I knew anything more, but I don't."

"You saw people throwing bricks. Sometimes you don't know what you know."

"I saw bricks flying. And then Odelle and I started pushing through the crowd, trying to get away." A thought came to me. I reached for my phone and began scrolling through my photos. "I took some pictures. Here. On these last ones you can see some bricks in the air, but I don't have anything to show what happened to Odelle." I held up my phone for him to see.

Nothing in his expression indicated whether my photos were

useful, but he asked if I'd send them to him. "Any others from that day? Everything you got, I'd like to have," he said, taking out his phone. "Can you air drop?" I shared all ten that I had from the protest.

"Have you checked with the news photographers that were there?" I asked.

He gave me a skeptical look. "We've checked with the TV stations," he said, with an inflection that was supposed to make me feel stupid. And I did, a little.

I shrugged. "Just trying to help."

"What's your name?" he asked. I told him. I even gave him my phone number, though he didn't ask for it. He typed my information in his phone.

"I doubt the brick was aimed at Odelle, but she's eighty years old and it looks like some real damage was done," I said. "Somebody ought to be held accountable."

"We have footage from the TV stations—just like you suggested, Ms. Mayfair," he said, with the first trace of amusement he'd shown, "and we arrested some of the agitators. But we can't hold anybody for what happened to her until we have something more than we've got."

He tucked his phone back in his pocket and left. I put my phone back in my purse, thinking about the brick that I still carried around. Would there be anything on it to identify who threw it? I could've mentioned it to the detective, but I wanted to give Odelle a chance to tell me why she'd given it to me.

If she ever could.

The new bag of saline hung on the metal pole. The young nurse was still there, washing her hands at the sink. She glanced at me. Maybe she expected me to say something about the pushy detective, but I didn't.

"Don't tire her, OK?" she said, finished drying her hands, and left.

I stepped up to Odelle's bed, beside Aurora. Again, Odelle's eyes were closed. "Anything?" I whispered to Aurora. She shook her head.

I lifted the brick from my bag, overcome by a feeling of something like dread. Still whispering, I told Aurora, "I think it's the brick that struck her. She wanted me to take it."

"Why?" Aurora said.

"I don't know."

It was an odd thing to do, but I thought maybe… just maybe… so I held it in front of her and said, "Odelle? See this? Do you remember this brick?" I saw the dark blotch on it that was dried blood and remembered trying to stop the blood pouring from the wound.

She opened her eyes. Same cloudy look as before, but I could see this time she was trying to focus. Then she lifted her hand, just barely. I knew what she wanted. Still holding the brick, I put her hand on it.

"Can you remember giving this brick to me?" I asked.

Slowly, she nodded. Her dry lips parted. A few seconds crawled by.

"What are you trying to say, Odelle?"

Raspy voice, almost a croak. "Take it… save…"

The same words she'd spoken at the Eagles Nest.

That was all.

Chapter 9

"I'm not a destroyer of Nashville's history," declared the man who could have modeled for *GQ*. Impeccably dressed. Classic handsome face, dark curls tamed by a stylist.

"That's Tommy Kahn. Damn him!" Aurora said, leaning forward in her recliner, eyes fixed on the TV, her remote in her hand.

Not the crooked, slimy, con man I'd imagined, but when did they ever have horns and cloven hooves?

Tommy Kahn spoke into a reporter's microphone. "I've made it my business to *rescue* properties before they turn into slums."

At first I thought he must be in front of the Eagles Nest, but the camera pulled back, and I saw Greek columns in the background. The Parthenon.

When Holly first moved to Nashville, we'd toured the celebrated urban park. Like her great-uncle Alex, Holly loved playing tour guide. She'd explained that the spacious site was named Centennial Park because it was the location of the Tennessee's Centennial Exposition in 1897. For the occasion, Nashville constructed an authentic replica of the Parthenon in Athens, Greece. An amazing architectural achievement, in the heart of Nashville, Tennessee, with a huge statue of Athena completed more than a hundred years after the Parthenon was built. A must-see for tourists, as Alex would say.

Tommy Kahn made an expansive gesture toward the Parthenon. "*This* is history. The classical architecture and all it signifies. Not some old run-down building, infested with rats. Yes, I've been inside the Eagles Nest. The cost to make that building habitable, to bring it up to Codes, would be staggering, and then, what would you have? Still just an old building that a few people are sentimental about. Nothing that brings progress and prosperity to Nashville."

The low, sultry voice that interrupted was familiar. "What would you do with the Eagles Nest property, Mr. Kahn?" The camera switched to Presleigh Deere, then back to Tommy Kahn.

"What *will* I do with the property *I own*? The property I paid a fair price for?" He let that sink in. "I'm not at liberty to say what partners we're negotiating with, but I'll tell you this much. What we build on the old Eagles Nest site will be another monument to Nashville's character." A few cheers and a smattering of applause followed. Probably no protestors from the other side knew about the press conference. Just his own small crowd that he'd brought with him.

Presleigh Deere faced the camera, winding up the segment. Aurora muted the TV. "Can you believe it? A monument to Nashville's character? Like the strip mall that's going up on Nolensville Road in the middle of a Kurdish neighborhood. Tommy Kahn bought a row of pretty little rental houses from several different owners. The renters were all Kurdish families. They're all very family and community oriented. Three or four generations living together, Yazda said. Not the haven for drugs that Tommy Kahn claimed. They kept up their homes. Planted flowers. The owners all sang the same tune. Skyrocketing taxes had forced them to sell, and they were as shocked as anybody when Kahn's bulldozers showed up. Whether that's the truth or not..." She punched her remote, groaning as the chair reclined.

All of it had taken a toll on Aurora. The arduous trip to the hospital, slow-going, especially on the way back. Odelle's critical condition, and the name the nurse finally gave to what I suspected— TBI, traumatic brain injury. The hour Aurora had sat on a hard plastic chair by the bed, waiting, hoping her friend would say her name. It never happened.

The skin of Aurora's face and neck sagged as she lay back in her recliner. Her Botox treatments probably smoothed the wrinkles on a good day but today had not been a good day.

"Why don't we wait about going out for dinner?" I said. Alex and I had promised to take her to her favorite restaurant, which happened to be a Belle Meade landmark, Sperry's.

"Oh no! I *need* it!" she said, a note in her voice that I hadn't heard since we saw Odelle. "I've been locked up in this tomb ever since my damned back went out."

I said, "I get it. Maybe after you rest a while, you'll get a second wind."

"A little nap does *wonders* for me," she said.

A nap sounded marvelous. A nice cup of tea and a little nap.

In the kitchen I put on a teapot and found some teabags with exotic-sounding names.

Everything Aurora had said touched a chord of sympathy in me. Sympathy for ordinary low-and-middle-income families caught up in Nashville's rapid, unrestricted growth. Savannah was not immune to "progress and prosperity," though not so out-of-control. Some of what Tommy Kahn said could've come from my brother's mouth. Making money by developing property was legal and not always unethical, but it did seem that the rich got richer and the poor got poorer.

My mind turned back to PPP fraud. Thinking about Holly, knowing there was more she had *not* told me, touched another chord, a chord of fear, as I turned off the whistling teapot.

Sperry's, an upscale steakhouse in the heart of Belle Meade, was a Nashville tradition. "Nearly fifty years old, and not much has changed," Alex said, as we sat at a small table in the dimly-lit bar, waiting to be seated in the dining room.

"A favorite hangout of the bluebloods, all these years. I remember the first time Henry brought me here," Aurora said with a note of nostalgia. "He knew *everybody*, shook hands, introduced me all around and he made a point of saying where everybody lived. 'On the Boulevard, near the club. On Tyne, across from the golf course. On Jackson,' and so on," she said, in a kind of sing-song. "Not that *Henry* was a blueblood, oh no, he wasn't one the old Nashville families, he'd only lived in Belle Meade for fifteen years! But, you know," and she rubbed her thumb and forefinger together. The rich never spoke of money.

"And I remember that night, Al Gore was in the bar, and Amy Grant was in a party seated at a table next to us." Aurora laughed. "Oh, were my eyes ever wide!"

The server, her ponytail bouncing, came to take our drink orders. "Where have you been, Ms. DeMille? We've missed you!" she said, eyeing the quad she'd set against the wall. Aurora explained at length. More and more, I was finding that the world was run by my children's peers. The Gen Z kids, barely in their 20s, had taken over the jobs of servers and cashiers from the millennials, who had become the professionals. Here, in this Old English-type room with its highly-polished dark wood and red accents, a cheery old bartender with white tufts of hair would have completed the picture, but, instead, we had a preppy young barman who barely looked old enough to serve alcohol to the baby boomers that made up so much of Sperry's clientele.

The men at the bar laughed with each other, an air of familiarity among them. Even the man at the end of the bar, next to the wall. When he turned to get the bartender's attention, I recognized him from his speech in front of the Parthenon. Tommy Kahn ordered another drink, then said something to the guy next to him that must've been off-color, from the way they hooted.

Alex and Aurora had turned their attention to someone else who was entering the bar. "That's Caleb, the reporter," Alex said, scooting back his chair. Caleb raised his hand at Alex and headed to our table but stopped when Tommy Kahn shouted from the bar.

"Caleb Hunter! Let me buy you a drink!" Kahn turned on his barstool, stood up, swayed a little, and took hold of the edge of the bar. "The publicity you gave me in that rag of yours would've cost me a fortune!" he said, with a derisive laugh.

The chatter in the room died down. The men at the bar looked around at Caleb. All of us seemed to be waiting for a snappy comeback from this master of words. But there was none.

"Come on over!" Kahn taunted. "What's the matter? You can slander me in the press but you don't have the guts to say something to me face to face?"

No doubt in my mind now. Everything I'd been hearing about Tommy Kahn came together. A notorious con man, a crook, and a bully. Facing TV cameras in front of the Parthenon, he played his part well, but I was convinced that *this* was the real Tommy Kahn. The loudmouth bully. The only surprise was that he'd quit playing the more appealing role once he arrived at the popular watering hole.

A long, tense moment passed, and it seemed Caleb was frozen in place. Yet, there was nothing on his boyish face that showed the bully intimidated him. If anything, his calm expression reminded me that he was a reporter, accustomed to observing trouble of all kinds.

And then, finally, Caleb walked over to him. "I think you mean libel, not slander. And it's not libel when it's true," he said.

The bartender delivered Kahn's drink, looking unsure about what else he should do. Kahn picked up the squat glass, two fingers of amber liquid, and swirled it around. Threw back a swallow. Held the drink in both hands. "You don't know what you're up against, you snot-nose kid. That rag lets you spew your bullshit, but you don't know what real power is!"

Caleb fixed his gaze on the glass, Kahn's fingers tight around it. With a hard look into Tommy Kahn's face then, he said, "For Chrissake. Go home, Tommy. Go home and sleep it off."

"You sanctimonious little bastard," Kahn said. Apparently noticing Caleb's black eye for the first time, he said, "Who gave you that shiner? Somebody else you trashed in the paper?"

Caleb turned away, ignoring him, but Kahn took a couple of wobbly steps and grabbed his arm. Caleb glanced back, as a splash of whiskey hit him in the face.

A moment of absolute quiet followed.

Caleb's flinch was his only reaction. Tommy Kahn was the one who looked shocked.

"Keep watching the front page, Tommy," Caleb said, without bothering to wipe his face. "I'm not through."

And he walked away.

Chapter 10

Sometime in the middle of the night, I awoke to a pitch black room. That old fear of the dark had once more taken me hold of me.

My night light had burned out. My every-night light, the one I needed after the trip to Ireland, after being confined in a dark, claustrophobic priest hole.

This night, when I bolted straight up in bed, I hadn't been dreaming about the priest hole. This dream was more like a vision. My grandmother, a dipper in her hand, was whispering the story that she told me time and time again when I was a child, spending summers at her farm.

The well in her back yard had not been in use since my granny was a little girl, herself, but the horror came alive each time she warned me about the deep, black hole. Told me he was her firstborn, the laughing six-year-old boy who climbed trees and swung into the creek from a grapevine and made all kinds of mischief while my grandmother took care of three younger ones, my mother just an infant. One morning, the little boy, Artie, disappeared. At the end of a heart-wrenching day, they found him in that long-dry black hole, his skull crushed.

And now the story came to me again, rising out of deep-rooted fear. Was it possible that my unreasonable dread of darkness reached back that far? Even before the priest hole?

My room had its own bath. I left that bathroom light burning, the door ajar. Eventually, I slept.

In the morning, I woke feeling gloomy, even before I drew back the curtains and saw the gray clouds billowing in the sky. As if a shadow had drifted over me. A sense of foreboding.

Now I was thinking about Holly, something lurking in a dark corner of my mind. About Odelle Wright and what fragile creatures we were, that a single random act of violence might erase all of our memories. And a kind of dread about Alex's interview on the morning show, that unexpected, unfamiliar stab I'd felt when my self-reliant uncle said last night, "You *will* go with me, won't you, Jordan?"

Aurora was watching the local news, none of it good. A shooting in North Nashville. A fire in an apartment complex in Antioch, leaving several families displaced. Police had dragged a body from the Cumberland River, near one of the city's homeless camps.

Rain on the way. Aurora offered her umbrella when we left for the studio.

Her final word: "Don't let her bait you, Alex!"

That, I learned, was Presleigh Deere's strategy.

Kaz, the tattooed and pierced producer of the show, took Alex into the studio and let me stay while others showed him where to sit, attached a microphone to the lapel of his tweed jacket, and dabbed powder on his nose, which Alex didn't much like. Then Kaz said, "You can watch him on the monitor in the green room," and he led me through a maze of corridors.

A country singer from Milwaukee named Jenna was waiting in the green room for her turn on camera. Visibly nervous, clomping around in cowboy boots. Eager for company, or so it seemed to me, she settled in a chair across from me, and we chatted while I waited for Alex's interview to begin.

"Wonder why they call this a green room," she asked.

"It's just a term from show business," I said. "The room where people wait to go on."

"But it's not green," she said.

I pointed to the TV monitor where the interview was starting. "That's my uncle." I didn't intend to be rude, but Jenna must've understood. She started pacing again, and texting.

"You don't seem to like our city that much, Professor Carlyle." Presleigh Deere wasted no time, starting out on the offensive.

"You can call me Alex," he said. "May I call you Presleigh?"

The professional interviewer lost a beat before she replied with a cross "Of course." Not prepared for my uncle's Southern chivalry, which I knew was genuine.

"Actually, Nashville is a charming city, one of my favorite places," Alex said.

"*Really?* I don't get that impression from your book." Presleigh affected a little frown.

"You may have missed my point," he said. "The things that spell Nashville are disappearing so fast. Too fast. *That's* the point."

Alex seemed to be holding his own so far, barely. But as I watched from the green room now, I remembered Aurora's warning. *Don't let her bait you!* Presleigh picked up a copy of Alex's *Rise of the New Nashville* and turned to a bookmarked page. "Some of your criticism, I have to say, is pretty harsh." And she read, "'*Nashville is becoming a reminder of New York City's Times Square in the 70s. A tawdry parody of itself.*' Now that really stings, Alex."

He pushed his glasses up on his nose and cleared his throat. If he were in the classroom, he'd clasp his hands behind him and take a few steps. All to give him time to choose the right words. Presleigh's wry smile seemed to indicate she thought she had him.

"You are much too young to remember any of this," he began, with a smile, "but Times Square was at one point the crossroads of the world. And then in the 70s it became the back alley of the greatest city in the world. That's the comparison I was making. Here in the shadow of the Ryman—the original Ryman, the mother church of country music—Lower Broadway has become a commercial strip with neon lights flashing and music blasting, a theme park devoted to the sale of booze. Not much left to remind us of the time when Kris Kristofferson and Willie Nelson wrote songs at Tootsie's and left through the back door that led to the Grand Old Opry."

Gaining momentum, he spoke earnestly. "You can find singers and musicians with remarkable talent performing in the bars, but they complain that no one listens, the crowd is boisterous, the noise overpowering. And the music that pours from the bars out onto the streets has nothing to do with the roots of country music. You know, don't you, that country music began as the common man's poetry. Much of that has been lost."

"I think you're a little old-fashioned," Presleigh said, with a cynical laugh.

Alex took a deep breath. "I'm sure I am, Presleigh," he said, "and this will sound old-fashioned to you, too, but I'm going to say it. I believe that new or old, the truth still matters. Many Nashvillians that I came to know when I was researching my book expressed the same hope for their city. The hope that what was *true* about Nashville might someday rise again."

It was a great line that made me want to cheer. Inwardly, I *was* cheering. But Presleigh breezed right over it and announced a commercial break. Already? In a way, I was relieved. The interview so far had kept me on the edge of my seat. I was sure, to an audience that didn't know him, Alex sounded like one more old fuddy-duddy, out of touch with New Nashville.

"I don't guess your uncle would like my music," Jenna said. "But, you know, I'd *like* to sing about things that matter. Real love. Real heartache. I know what he means about things that are *true*. But people want to hear about, well, about knocking boots." She sat down again, in the chair across from me, and leaned forward. "Jenna isn't my real name, you know," she whispered. A confidence. A secret. "It's Mary Jo Pierce. I had to change it. But it feels so… phony."

I reached across and squeezed her clammy hand. All I could say was what I would tell a daughter of mine. "If you sing from your heart, Mary Jo, I think the audience will feel what's true in you."

But many talented artists who followed their hearts were never commercially successful. I knew it, and so did she. Jenna knew what she'd had to do even to get here, to sing on Presleigh Deere's morning television show.

The next segment began with Presleigh's re-introduction of Alex, to which she added, "I must say, his book is not very complimentary of our city." She turned to him. "One of your complaints is the party buses, the pedal taverns, all the transportainment vehicles. Are they *really* so much worse than partying in the bars? What's the harm in having a good time?" With a sideways glance, she said, "I'll bet you did a little partying when you were young, Alex."

Again, he pushed his glasses up on his nose. "I suppose I did. Actually, I still enjoy having a good time, Presleigh, even at my advanced age. But 'a good time' on Lower Broadway has taken on a new meaning. Public spectacles. Brides-to-be celebrating by vomiting up their evening over the side of a party bus. Degrading the young women and denigrating the city."

"So you don't like the bachelorette parties," Presleigh put in quickly. "Surely you know that these parties have been a great blessing to our economy."

"Blessing?" I said under my breath.

Alex didn't quibble over her word. He looked thoughtful, then said, "I'm all for love and marriage. But this kind of entertainment is mostly about tequila and the so-called woo girls that can't hold their liquor, which ends up on the sidewalks of Lower Broadway."

Presleigh shifted in her seat. She seemed a little uneasy but still in control. "Let's talk about the economy. We all know that Nashville has its growing pains, but tell me, Alex, don't you think growth is the key to progress in any great American city?"

"Growth *can* be good, but all you have to do is walk through a cancer ward to see that all growth is not beneficial to an organism," Alex said. "A city is a living thing, and the kind of growth that Nashville has experienced is not healthy. What matters most is the character of a city. And I fear that Nashville's character is slowly being strangled by out-of-control growth."

"That's the negative view. Tourism brings millions of dollars to our city." Presleigh was having trouble maintaining that low, subdued voice. Now her words had a sharp edge. "Not just tourists. People are moving here in droves because they love Nashville!"

"As a result, housing prices have skyrocketed," Alex said. "Property taxes have taken an exorbitant hike. Ordinary Nashville residents are priced out of their own city. Firemen, teachers, and policemen can't afford to buy homes here. And let's not forget that the commercial development is generated mostly by out-of-state developers who care nothing about Nashville's character. The local politicians bow down to them and give them outrageous incentives, turning a blind eye as they destroy what has made Nashville unique."

"All of the dollars poured into our economy, you don't see as a good thing?" she said.

Alex continued to sound like a professor, trying to urge a deluded student back onto a path of reason. Gently, he said, "What you see as a cure, Presleigh, I see as a disease. There has never been a junkie that didn't think *more* was better. My book is simply a plea to a small Southern city that barely recognizes itself anymore. A warning that it's not too late to save this city from the wrecking ball of loss, disguised as progress."

I wanted it to end there. Alex had not just stood up to her, but he'd made some powerful comments that would no doubt resonate with some of the audience. Make them want to buy his book, surely. But Presleigh would not be outdone.

"My next question was going to be about your family in Savannah, Georgia—developers, aren't they?—in that beautiful historic city. We could talk about what's happening in the Historic District that's changing the character of *that* lovely city. But, sadly, our time is up!"

Aurora was right. Piranha. Witch. And worse.

A minute later, Kaz stuck his head in the door of the green room. "Jenna? You ready, girl?" To me, he said, "I'll bring Mr. Alex back here in a few." Then winked. "Your uncle's a cool dude."

Something in his manner said, *But don't expect him to ever be asked back on this show.*

Alex might have made a stop at the men's room. Or maybe Presleigh Deere was keeping him, raising her contrived voice, telling him that *she* was supposed to get all the good lines. As I waited, a news break came on the TV monitor.

"The body that was dragged from the Cumberland River this morning has been identified. Police say the victim is Caleb Hunter, a staff writer for the *Nashville Voice*."

My breath caught. I heard more words, but the only ones my brain could process were *dragged from the Cumberland River.* I cried out to the empty room. *No! No!* Impossible! Just yesterday, Alex had breakfast with Caleb at The Loveless Cafe. Just last night, we saw him at Sperry's! It had to be a terrible mistake, I told myself, as we do when the truth is too awful.

My phone rang. I grabbed at it, absently, then saw it was Holly.

She was wailing. "Caleb's dead! They pulled him out of the *river!*" As I tried to murmur some small comfort, her voice rose to a shriek. "It's my fault! It's all my fault!"

Chapter 11

The ominous weather forecast were the last words I heard before I exited the green room.

"*Possible rain today and throughout the week. Storms moving in over the weekend.*"

The pewter-colored sky carried the threat that the weatherwoman promised, as Alex and I left the TV station. I offered to drive to Holly's house, and Alex tossed me the keys. It was his Audi, but I thought he was too distracted to drive. He was unusually quiet, deep in thought. Ordinarily we would have rehashed the interview, but now it didn't seem to matter all that much. Not in comparison with a young man's untimely, gruesome death.

My mind couldn't shake what Holly had said: *It's my fault!*

Her call had been short. A few words, mostly weeping. I asked where she was and she said, "At work, but I'm going home."

"I'm coming to your house," I said, "as soon as Alex and I can leave the TV station."

And so we wound our way through the streets toward East Nashville, through the infuriating downtown traffic, across the Woodland Street Bridge above the Cumberland River. The river I would never think of again in the same way.

"Maybe you need a stiff drink," Alex said, pouring whiskey for himself.

Holly dabbed her eyes with a tissue and shook her head. "I can't. I have to think."

I brought in a tray with hot tea, which I've always believe cures most ills, or at least dulls the pain of the most common heartbreak. I poured from the teapot, and Holly, sitting beside me on the small sofa, helped herself to cream and sugar. I prepared my tea the same way.

"I have to think," she said again. "I don't know how I can ever make this right. Caleb is dead." Her eyes grew even more glassy. She let the tears spill, as if she wasn't aware of them.

Making things right could get you in trouble. I did not understand all about the burden she was carrying, but I knew just enough to make me fear for her.

Alex, in a leather armchair across from us, sipped his whiskey, looking thoughtful. "Such a shock," he lamented. "I barely knew Caleb, yet I feel a tremendous loss. You and Kyle were very close to him. My heart aches for you."

"Thank you, Uncle Alex," Holly whispered. "Kyle is devastated. It's just horrible, the way Caleb was murdered"—she blinked back more tears—"and found in *the river…*"

I hadn't heard *murdered*, but what else could it be? I waited for Holly to elaborate. She stared into her teacup. And then, after a minute, she said, "I went to work this morning and typed up my resignation letter. I wanted to give it to Tommy personally, but he wasn't in the office. I had a call from Kyle at about a quarter of ten. He was a wreck." Another silence. A long moment. "A sergeant from Police Headquarters who knew Kyle and Caleb were buddies had called to tell him," she said. "He was shot twice. The sergeant said it might've been somebody from the homeless camp, down there by the river."

"Any idea what Caleb would've been doing there?" Alex said.

Was he shot, and then fell in? Or pushed? Or shot somewhere

else, then his body brought to the river? It always takes a while for answers, and the truth seems to follow at a distance.

"It doesn't make sense," Holly said, shaking her head, helplessly. "His wallet was gone. No I.D. on him, but the police that dragged him from the river knew him. He wrote about crime and hung out with cops. I guess he hadn't been in the water that long. He was snagged on a tree or roots or something. He was… not the way bodies get when they're in water a long time."

A tiny hope rose, that someone got it wrong, and then sank. His name wouldn't have been released to the media if it wasn't official.

"They contacted his editor from the *Voice,* and he went down to the morgue," Holly went on. The *morgue* seemed to bring on a new flood of emotion. Holly wept a little more, softly. I leaned toward her and put my arm around her trembling shoulders. A quiet moment passed, as she got her bearings. "I'm cold," she said then, and left the room.

Alex and I were talking about Sperry's when she returned with a sweater. "Caleb was coming over to our table," Alex recalled. "I wish we could've had a word. Not that it would've changed anything, but I suppose we always try to imagine a different chain of events."

"Caleb was there when you were at Sperry's last night?" Holly asked.

Between us, Alex and I supplied the details, Tommy's taunting, Caleb's restraint, and then the drink that Tommy splashed in Caleb's face.

I said, "Caleb told Tommy, 'Keep watching the front page. I'm not through yet.'" Words that might take on a new meaning now. "Do you know what he meant?"

Holly's expression suddenly turned dark. She closed her eyes for a moment, then said, "It's my fault. Caleb is dead because of me."

Her tears had dried up for now, it seemed.

"Remember what I told you about Tommy and the PPPs?" she began.

"I know nothing about that," Alex said.

"You didn't tell me much," I said.

One day more than a year ago, she explained, she'd filled in for Sharla, who was sick. Sharla was working on something for Tommy Kahn that had a deadline, and Holly realized the company was applying for a PPP forgiveness loan. "I didn't think anything was wrong with that," she said. "You probably applied for a loan, you and Uncle Drew, didn't you, Mom?"

"No. We could have, but we didn't." Trying not to sound pious. "We were fortunate. We still had work with some good clients like SCAD. It was just Drew and me. It was a little harder for a while, with some small projects on hold, but we weren't hurting like so many others."

"The whole point of those loans was to keep small struggling businesses from going under," Alex said, adding with a scowl, "not to enrich companies like Jared Kushner's."

"I heard that Tom Brady's company got a million dollars in PPP loans, after he'd just signed with the Bucs for $50 million," Holly said. "Tommy Kahn was just another guy like that who'd take advantage of a deal, I knew, but I didn't think it was a crime. Except… some of what I saw that day on the documents was not accurate. The number of employees, monthly payroll, the company's gross income and expenses, all if it was inflated. And there were names of subsidiary companies that I'd never heard of. I jotted down addresses. That was all the time I had that day. But I couldn't leave it alone."

"Like your mother," Alex said, though clearly he wasn't making light of Holly's story. Over the next weeks and months, she had run down the addresses of the companies. The addresses turned out to belong to vacant lots, empty buildings or new buildings that were going up. She recognized some of the names listed as corporate officers of those fake companies. One was a man from a public relations firm that Holly knew from working on another project for Tommy. He was not the CEO of a construction company.

"I told Kyle what I'd found, and he said I must not be looking in the right place for the right answers. I'd been misled. 'A little knowledge is a dangerous thing,' he said, quoting some old proverb. Kyle always wants to believe the best about people. So I dug deeper. Any chance I got, staying late or coming in early. I made copies, a few at a time." She grew even more pale.

"Weren't you afraid, Holly?" I asked, feeling my blood run cold, just the thought of her covert activities, imagining what a man like Tommy Kahn would do if he found out.

"Yes! Curious at first, then, I've never been so frightened! Kyle finally said I had a tiger by the tail. He said we should ask Caleb what to do." A pause, letting it all sink in. "Caleb started investigating. I fed him documents, and it started spiraling into a huge story. Not just about Tommy. The private lender had to approve the loan first. The bank should've caught the false information. The banker Tommy used is somebody who knows a lot about our company, somebody I thought was a stand-up guy. I knew him from some other work we'd done."

A click at the door made us all jump. Kyle came into the room, and Holly went to him. He wrapped her in his arms, and they held on like each was the other's lifeline. The sorrow etched in their faces more telling than tears. "I didn't know you were coming home," she said.

"Ethan told me to leave."

I remembered that Ethan was not just Kyle's boss. He also owned this house.

Alex held the Glenlivet bottle up to Kyle, raising his bushy eyebrows.

"Exactly what I need," Kyle said. He headed to the kitchen and brought back a short glass, talking at a fast clip. "Been a helluva day. I was on the phone with Caleb's brother, heading to my car, and Notorious was outside the building, playing his songs, like he does. Next thing, cops are swarming around him, telling him he had to go with them. That they have questions about Caleb's death. And he's yelling, 'I didn't do it! I swear!' And then he looks at me and cries out, 'Man, do something! Help me!'"

Kyle took hold of the Glenlivet bottle, but he didn't pour a drink. He set the bottle down with a thud. "Notorious is a drunk, but he's not a killer," he said. "Dammit, what am I supposed to do?"

Chapter 12

"What if Notorious *did* kill Caleb, and you're defending him?" Holly followed Kyle to the front door. "My God, I can't believe you want to help somebody that might be your friend's killer. Why do you have to get involved?"

"Because nobody else is gonna lift a finger for an old drunk," Kyle said. "I can't really *defend* him. I'm not a lawyer, but maybe I can find him one that'll do it *pro bono*."

It was uncomfortable, to put it mildly, hearing the exchange that had gone on since Kyle came home. Food is my default when I'm otherwise helpless. I'd found deli ham in the fridge and made sandwiches that we ate at the kitchen bar. To be accurate, Alex and I ate, while Kyle and Holly simply picked at their food and debated the innocence or guilt of Notorious.

Holly said, "The police wouldn't have come after him if they didn't know something."

"Probably it's what happened at the Eagles Nest. You know, Notorious gave Caleb a shiner. So they followed up. Police like to tell the public they have a 'person of interest.'"

"He's a drunk, Kyle, and people *do* things when they're drunk," Holly argued.

"Notorious talks big, but he's all bark, no bite. And why would he be at that homeless camp, or anywhere near the river? He has a room somewhere around Shelby, I think."

More back and forth, and then Kyle stood up. "I'm going down to the station."

"*Why?*" Holly stood up, too, and went after him.

"To see what I can find out. What they have on Notorious."

The argument went on until he opened the front door. He turned and gave her a quick kiss. "I gotta do this," he said.

Holly had said Kyle liked to believe the best about people. There it was.

"Caleb would understand. He'd want the truth," Kyle said, closing the door behind him.

Alex and I had remained silent during the heated discussion. Now I tried to smooth things over. "It can't hurt to get more information. Assuming the police will tell Kyle what they know."

"I guess. He knows some of the cops, and you wouldn't believe how gossipy cops are." Holly joined us back at the kitchen bar and took a bite of the sandwich. Looking thoughtful. She swallowed, then said, "If Notorious is guilty, well, I know where Kyle's loyalty lies. I know where his heart is."

She pushed back her half-eaten sandwich. "I gotta do something, too. Would you go with me, Mom?"

And that was how Holly and I wound up at a retail strip on Edmondson Pike, at the offices of the *Nashville Voice*.

It was not the kind of newspaper office I'd ever been inside. Not like any in movies or on TV. No rows of desks occupied by harried, hunched-over reporters and writers on computers. Against a backdrop of file cabinets of various sizes and tables with coffee-making supplies wedged in among stacks of folders, a kid with glasses and bushy black hair peered over more clutter. "Hi," he squeaked, grabbing up a mask, hooking it around his ears, covering his mouth and nose. I got a glimpse of the computer screen, a video game he'd muted.

Holly stepped up. "I'm Holly Mayfair, a friend of Caleb Hunter. Can I see the editor?"

"Caleb, aw, man." He called out, "Dad? Somebody wants to see you! Caleb's friends."

A cell phone jingled and he picked it up. "*Nashville Voice*," he said, sounding not so squeaky. "Umm, can I take a message? …Yeah, it sucks… Nope, Meredith went home. She was really upset… OK." He clicked off. "People keep calling about Caleb. He was a great guy. Everybody liked him."

Not everybody, but I nodded.

The kid went back to his video games. There was only one well-worn chair in the room, but we didn't wait more than a minute. A door, opposite the front door, flew open, and the man whose bulk filled the doorway said, "I'm Walt Meyer. Come on back. We can talk in my office."

He was something shy of 300 pounds, I judged, at six-four, maybe taller. Though his khakis sagged a little below his belly, something about his physique made you think he was once muscular, a jock. Bushy black hair like the boy's but a bald spot shining in his crown. His white shirt had sweat stains under the arms. I hadn't realized it till now, but the temperature in the claustrophobic space must have been close to eighty.

The hall was no more than ten feet long. Probably a bathroom at the end, an office to the left. Was that one Caleb's? Walt took a right. His office was barely large enough to contain a wide desk, swivel chair, and two other chairs, with stacks that might not have been moved in weeks. It appeared the *Nashville Voice* wasn't used to having company.

"Don't be put off by Tuck and his mask," he said. "He thinks everybody's got COVID."

"It's OK to be cautious," I said. Most of the nation, including myself, had made their peace with the pandemic. If you'd had your vaccines and tried to be careful about crowds, you hoped you wouldn't be infected, or if you were, you'd have a mild case.

"My wife's mother died. Went on a ventilator and that was that. Tuck was real close to his grandma. She wasn't even that old. Just fifty-nine." He finished cleaning off the chairs and made a gesture for us to sit. "I pulled him in to help out today cause we're so shorthanded."

"How old is he?" I asked. Holly shifted from one foot to the other. I could tell she wanted to get down to business, but it seemed that a little small talk couldn't hurt.

"Sixteen. You're wondering why he's not in school." Walt's swivel chair groaned as he sat in it. "He's already earned all his high school credits. He'll graduate next month and go to Yale in the fall. On a full scholarship," he added, with a proud smile.

"Impressive," I said. "Congratulations on having a brilliant son."

"He's sort of a genius. Also sort of a goofball. A good kid. He really is." Walt glanced at Holly and must've sensed her impatience. "Sorry about all the yammering. Police called me this morning to go downtown and identify Caleb's body. I can't seem to get my mind straight."

"I feel the same way," Holly said.

"Tell me your name again."

Holly did the introductions. I could see she expected her name to resonate with him, but he showed no sign that it did. "What can I do for you?" he said.

"Caleb was working on a story. A big one. He said you knew all about it."

Walt's congeniality turned quickly to business. "Holly Mayfair?" he repeated, as if he might remember. "I don't believe Caleb ever mentioned you to me."

"I suppose he'd want to protect me. That would be like him. I put him onto the PPP fraud story. I work for Tommy Kahn." Sadness crept into her eyes, but somehow I knew she would not cry. Tears might come again, but not now. She was on a mission. "I saw Caleb for the last time yesterday afternoon. We met at Starbucks and I gave him some more documents."

Holly had said she had to hurry home from Radnor Lake, she had something to do, but I didn't know she'd met Caleb, the day before he was murdered.

"When we left," Holly said, "Caleb told me, 'I want you to know, my editor is in the loop and he's one hundred percent trustworthy.' He was so *grim*. I didn't take him seriously enough."

The big man lowered his head, and after a long, heavy breath, said, "Looks like you and I are gonna have to trust each other."

I asked about the restroom, to give them a chance to talk. Then I joined Tuck and would've struck up a conversation with him, but he seemed too occupied, with calls coming in and his video games. There was one chair, so I made myself at home and picked up last week's *Voice*. I read the article Caleb wrote when the sale of the Eagles Nest became public. Alex was right about Caleb's eloquent voice. "*Old buildings like the Eagles Nest are a sacred trust, a treasure, unique and irreplaceable.*"

Another story caught my eye, an attempted abduction on Lower Broad, the previous weekend. A man approached a twenty-one-year-old woman just outside one of the bars after closing, flashed a gun, and told her to come with him to a waiting SUV. She resisted and attracted the attention of some men who were leaving another bar. As they came to her rescue, creating a scene, the would-be kidnapper fled, escaping in the SUV. He was middle-aged with an accent. "*Maybe a Russian*," the woman told police.

The article, also written by Caleb, ended with, "*Sex trafficking has been operating in Nashville shadows for the past decade. This attempted abduction under the glaring lights of Lower Broad is reason to worry that the emboldened traffickers have come out of the shadows without fear.*"

Another piece with Caleb Hunter's by-line told of two recent deaths of tourists from drugs laced with Fentanyl. The third tourist, who was revived by medics, said he and his friends thought they were getting cocaine. The drug deal took place in broad daylight, one o'clock in the afternoon. Caleb wrote, "*Lower Broad is where tourists come for a never-ending party. Music City has become Party City, where anything goes.*"

Caleb's articles, sharply critical of what Nashville was becoming, or had become, wouldn't please everyone. I wondered how many enemies he might have. Not just Tommy Kahn.

Holly and Walt came out after twenty minutes or so. It seemed clear they'd achieved a comfort level with each other.

As we departed, Walt called out, "Be careful, Holly." She gave a solemn nod.

That little exchange didn't do anything for my comfort level.

Holly turned on the ignition but didn't back her Honda out of the parking space.

She explained what her next move had to be. Walt needed the rest of the documents she'd found and saved on her computer. "Everything's password protected. I can't access them once I've left the company, so I need to do it now," she said. "I suppose I could wait about giving notice, but something tells me I should get out now."

"The sooner, the better," I said.

"I wonder if Tommy knew Caleb was about to expose him. The thing you heard Caleb say at Sperry's, to watch the front page… Tommy had to know. And he might be close to figuring out I was his source."

When your children are grown, you're helpless in the face of their decisions. Hostage to mistakes you fear are coming. All I could do was go along with Holly, help her if I could.

"I don't necessarily *need* someone with me, but I'm so jittery," she said.

I could feel, beneath the jitters, the steel of her. She could do whatever she set her mind to, but I'd be more worried if I *didn't* go with her to get those documents. The last ones.

"Everybody heads at out five sharp," she said. "We'll wait till five-thirty. I have a key card."

"Tommy Kahn must trust you."

She shrugged, then backed out of the parking space. "We all have key cards. Easy to track who goes in and out, and when."

It wasn't as if I'd never taken a few risks, myself, but I was terrified for my daughter. My heart kept drumming, *Get out now! Get out now!*

Chapter 13

The word, KAHN, lettered in gold, three-feet high on glass, greeted us as we stepped off the elevator on the tenth floor. Holly tried to insert her key card. It didn't work.

"Shit!" she said. "Sorry, Mom. This happens sometimes."

She tried again, with no luck. Then she began jamming it, one time after another.

"No, don't do that! Take your time." It occurred to me that she might've been locked out already, but I said, "Let me try."

She handed me the key card, and I inserted it. It worked.

"I guess you have the touch," she said.

"Not really. I just tried to be… calm." I didn't really feel calm, though.

Another paradox in New Nashville. The Kahn suite, in the steel and glass downtown high-rise, somehow felt less substantial than the *Nashville Voice* office, located between a clothing consignment store and a small appliances repair shop in a tired commercial strip.

Work was accomplished at the *Voice*. Important work. This suite looked like a stage set.

The main lights had been dimmed but not shut off. In the spacious lobby, cold as a tomb, here in April, the high-end, ultra-modern furniture was impressive. The artwork made the room feel like a museum. Each painting probably cost more than my annual salary.

Most striking was the wall of glass. The panoramic view of East

Nashville, past the river, *that* river, was spectacular.

I thought of that word, *purposefully,* as I followed Holly past the curved reception desk, to another door. She used her key card, again, and it worked this time. She inserted it once more at her office door and flipped a switch. Light flooded the office. Larger than Walt Meyer's and much more organized, her office still felt a little like a cell. No windows, and the L-shaped desk filled half the room. Holly closed the door and went straight to her computer.

I picked up a brief case from a chair and set it on the floor. "Let me know if I can do anything," I said, taking a seat to get out of her way. My eyes fixed on the door.

"I'm pulling up my letter of resignation," she said. "I'll let you read it and tell me—you know, is the tone right? I don't want to burn my bridges. If possible. Though I wouldn't ever want to come back here," she added, quietly.

"Do you think anyone's working late?" I couldn't keep from straining to hear.

"I doubt it. I could tell you who's already hitting the bars. If Sharla's here, she'll be bogged down in her own work. She's the only one who sometimes stays past five."

"And you."

"Sometimes. I tried not to make a habit of it. I didn't want anyone to see a pattern."

Smart girl I raised.

Holly tapped her keys, then stood up. "We have to print everything in the copy room."

"I suppose each person has a code to keep up with how much each one is printing."

"Right." Her voice echoed what I was thinking. How easily she could be tracked.

She took longer than I thought she should, simply to copy a letter. I rubbed the gooseflesh on my arms. Nerves, combined with the thermostat that must be set at sixty-five. Why waste energy to air-condition empty offices? It was a relief when Holly returned and closed the door.

"The copier had to warm up," she said. "Here's the letter. See what you think."

I read the hard copy while she worked at her computer. The letter thanked Tommy for the experience she'd gained, working with him. She gave no reason for leaving, just a vague mention that she would "*always be grateful as I pursue other opportunities.*"

"Brief and courteous," I said.

"Not one-hundred percent honest," she said.

"But not dishonest. The right tone, I think. I didn't even find a typo."

I handed the page to her. She folded it lightly and tucked it in her purse, a satchel handbag like mine, except that hers was a Kate Spade and mine was a designer knock-off.

Holly made a show of hitting the *Enter* key. "There. It's done. I thought it would be better to give it to him in person, but now I'm glad I won't be around when he reads it."

Time crept by. For ten minutes that seemed much longer, Holly was absorbed in her task. I kept thinking, "*Hurry!*" and "*Get out now!*" Wishing I didn't feel so useless, just sitting on the edge of my seat, trying to be patient.

"Printing as we speak," Holly said, finally. "Several short documents, twenty-two pages in all. I never printed that much at one time before, but I guess it's now or never."

What if someone came to the copy room and found the pages before she retrieved them? I didn't share my worry with Holly, but when she kept working, I asked, "What are you doing?"

"Deleting. Trying not to leave anything on my machine that I don't want to be found."

"You know deleted files can be recovered," I said.

"Yes, if they're looking for them. I have to hope I haven't given any reason to look."

She left for the copy room. Almost finished! I stood up, slinging my purse over my shoulder. Anxious to go. I cringed when the HVAC unit kicked on. I thought I heard another noise, but no, I told myself, it was just the system going through its cycle.

It took Holly just a couple of minutes, and she was back with the pages she'd printed. At her desk again, she powered off her computer and slid the printouts into a brown file folder.

She picked up a photo of her and Kyle on a ski trip and handed it to me, across the desk. "I think this is the only personal item I have left. I've been taking everything, a little at a time."

"Listen," I whispered. Now I was sure I heard footsteps. I put my finger to my lips.

She handed me the brown folder and pointed, jabbing her forefinger at the briefcase I'd sat on the floor, against the chair.

I turned and reached down for it.

The door opened.

"I wondered who was in the copy room," came the voice. Not menacing, but just short of.

I held my breath. I didn't have to look to know who it was. For one heart-stopping instant, I kept my back to Tommy Kahn while I did what I knew I had to do.

"Tommy, hi!" Holly sounded startled. A natural reaction, wouldn't he think? Grabbing her purse, she came around the desk. "I was just about to leave."

He'd stepped inside the room. Now I turned to face him, brief case in hand, and Holly was quick to introduce us. He was shorter than he'd seemed on television or from across the room at Sperry's. About my height. Up close, not even *that* close, I smelled his breath and knew he'd had a drink, or a few. The exchange of pleasantries between us lasted a minute, at the most.

Tommy turned back to Holly. "What're you working on?"

I've said many times that my daughter could put on a face, and if ever she needed to draw on her theatrics, it was now. Holly didn't disappoint. She pulled a paper from her purse and unfolded it. Her resignation letter, her excuse for being in the copy room.

"I decided to send this by email. Just did. But here's the letter I was working on."

Tommy scanned it so quickly, he couldn't have read much beyond the words "...*my resignation*..." He handed it back to her. "I never bargain with an employee that wants to go."

"I wouldn't expect you to," Holly said. "You know, it's just... time. Time to do something else. You've treated me well, Tommy."

I could almost see the wheels turning behind his keen dark eyes. He glanced at me, and I wondered if there was something he wanted to say to her. Maybe lash out. But he wouldn't, with her mother present.

"Looks like you're in an awful big hurry to get out of here. Good thing I don't believe in two weeks' notice."

"I knew you'd tell me to go on." Holly's smile seemed easy, not nervous.

"Nobody does anything but draw a paycheck after they give notice." He stepped into the doorway. Holly was close behind, and I was behind her. "I'll need your key card," he said.

"Of course," she said. She retrieved it from her purse.

It was almost over. Holly hadn't counted on meeting up with Tommy, but so far, so good. We were on our way out. But then, a slip. Holly glanced back at the brief case. Maybe she just had to make sure I had it before we were locked out. And then she fixed her eyes on mine for an instant, and I knew she was asking, *You got the folder, didn't you?* The first mistake she'd made.

And Tommy noticed.

"You're not leaving with anything confidential, are you?" he said.

Holly opened her mouth, but before she could speak, and possibly make matters worse, I opened the brief case and showed him the photo of Holly and Kyle.

"Nothing confidential about this," I said.

"A joke," he said. "It was a joke."

It wasn't, of course.

"I'll let you out," he said, and we headed for the lobby. "Don't think you can come back."

Someone was waiting for him, or so it appeared. A woman stood at the wall of glass, turned to the view so we could only see the back of her. Tall and curvy, platinum hair pulled up in a careless knot and fastened with a clip. Wearing athletic clothes, not dressed for a dinner if that was why she was there. Maybe there was a gym in the high-rise. Wife or girlfriend, I expected, though something about her, as she'd walked toward the window, seemed oddly familiar. I couldn't imagine why.

Tommy Kahn locked the heavy doors behind us, and I put her out of my mind.

On the elevator, I realized how pale Holly was, suddenly, how her shoulders sagged as if she couldn't carry the weight any longer.

Though we were alone, she whispered. "He knows something."

The elevator seemed to take forever.

We reached the ground floor at last. The doors opened and we couldn't get out fast enough.

"Where's the folder?" Holly asked.

I held my handbag close to me, and patted it.

Chapter 14

"I was wrong about Notorious," Kyle said.

"He confessed?" Holly asked, her eyes wide. My thought, exactly.

"No, not *that*," Kyle said. "I meant he *did* have a room somewhere near Shelby Park, but his landlady threw him out the last time he came in from a bender."

"And was that last night? And where did he happen to go?" Holly said, with a little I-told-you-so look.

Kyle groaned. "Yeah, OK. Sometime last night he wound up at the homeless camp."

A young server—weren't they all young?—this one with more piercings in the cartilage of her ear than she had fingers, came for our orders.

We were at Merchants, in the midst of all the Lower Broadway commotion.

After Holly and I had accomplished our mission at her office and were heading to her car, she'd texted with Kyle and they decided to grab a bite to eat. I offered to take an Uber to Aurora's, but now I was glad she wouldn't hear of it. I was finally beginning to unwind.

I had called Alex to let him know where I was. He and Aurora were just returning from a visit with Odelle. All good news there. Odelle had been moved from ICU to a room. Aurora was thrilled that her friend had recognized her.

"Merchants!" Alex said, and he'd wanted to remind me of its long and colorful history.

"I read your book, Alex," I told him.

Merchants was another Nashville tradition. The three-story building had stood for nearly 150 years, as so much of Old Nashville was torn down around it. Merchants, the restaurant, took its name from the Merchants Hotel that was once a staple of downtown. Upstairs, the dining room was more formal than the lively bistro at street level, with its black and white décor, where we sat in a booth. The third floor was reserved for private parties. All of this I knew from Alex's book. The thriving restaurant in the historic building had adapted, managing to co-exist on Lower Broadway with neighbors like Rippy's Honky Tonk, Nudie's Honky Tonk, and Honky Tonk Central.

"Have they charged Notorious?" Holly asked. A little distracted, maybe, but, considering what we'd just experienced at her office, she was putting on a good face.

"No, and they have nothing on him!" Kyle raised his voice. No one seemed to notice, amid the low roar of chatter and bursts of laughter around us, but he said, in a more conversational tone, "I talked with a sergeant and with Notorious. I got his story. I believe him."

Notorious admitted that he was so drunk, he had no idea what time it was when his landlady threw him out. He didn't remember how he made his way to the homeless camp, but it wasn't far. He had a buddy named Red, a man who spent a lot of time in the VA Hospital but had a tent in the homeless camp.

I couldn't help thinking about how caught up in Notorious's defense Kyle was. Maybe it was what Holly had said, that Kyle simply wanted the truth. Like Caleb. Holly was listening with noticeably less enthusiasm.

"Notorious made a lot of noise, trying to find Red's tent, so the police can probably nail down the time," Kyle said, "but it doesn't matter. Notorious doesn't deny that he went there and passed out. He says he didn't know anything till he heard all the disturbance. The sergeant said the call came in at 6:36 a.m. One of the homeless guys had gone over to the river to fish, and he saw a body, snagged on a tree that had fallen over at the edge of the water. It took a while for him to find a phone. By the time police arrived, seemed like everybody from the camp was there by the river, trampling the evidence. Including Notorious.

The server brought our drinks. It was hard to get the image of Caleb, once full of life, his body snagged on a tree at the edge of the river, out of my mind. I took a sip of wine. Kyle threw back a mouthful of beer. Holly stirred her cocktail, a peach concoction, looking into the martini glass as if she could find comfort there. Probably seeing the same image I couldn't shake.

"Did you find out the time of death?" I asked, after a long silence.

"Coroner estimated between four and six a.m."

"You say Notorious doesn't remember anything from the time he arrived at the homeless camp until the noise woke him that morning. That's a big gap," I said.

"He remembers he was passed out," Kyle said, sounding a little cross. "So was Red."

"Who might have been his alibi," Holly added.

"Well, yes. The thing is, Notorious didn't have a motive. That black eye? Nah. That's nothing. Notorious didn't know Caleb at all. Police can hold him for twenty-four hours, but unless they come up with some more evidence, which I don't think they will, he'll be out soon." Kyle took another drink. Another pause, and he said, "I don't know where he'll go."

"Don't even *think* of inviting him to stay with us," Holly said and we all smiled. A light moment, one we'd needed.

And then Kyle got a sheepish look on his face, as if he didn't really want to say it but had to. "I did promise I'd do something for him."

Holly touched her forehead. "Oh, God. What?"

"When the landlady threw him out, she said she'd hold the rest of his things for a coupla days. Notorious says she's been decent to him. He doesn't blame her for kicking him out."

"What did you promise?" Holly said.

"To go get his things and hang on to them till he gets settled."

Holly rolled her eyes. She might've been thinking that it could be worse.

Now our food arrived. Biting into my grilled chicken, I realized how hungry I was. Kyle, with his French dip, and Holly, who'd ordered a veggie burger, should've been starved. But neither showed much enthusiasm for their food, even though they'd barely touched the sandwiches I'd made for lunch.

Thinking back, it was hard to believe that was at noon, today. Alex's interview was just this morning. Holly and I had taken a huge risk at her office, only a few hours ago. Caleb was murdered in the early morning hours. All of it, today.

Kyle swallowed and wiped his mouth. To Holly, he said, "So what was it you wanted to tell me? What happened at your office?"

Holly glanced at me and took a long breath. The weight of it all showing in her eyes once again. "For a few minutes, I had stopped shaking," she said.

Me, too.

It didn't take much for Kyle to convince Holly that he should be the one to drive me to Aurora's. "You go on home," he told her.

"What a day," she groaned.

Tough day for both of them, but Kyle didn't have the same worn-to-a-frazzle look that hung in Holly's eyes.

"Go home, soak in a hot tub, and go to sleep," I told her. "Tomorrow will be better."

"Caleb will still be dead," she said.

Kyle and I didn't say much in the car, leaving downtown and all the merriment on the streets, even on a Wednesday night. It wasn't until we headed into Belle Meade that he said, "Holly did the right thing. *We* did. I was the one who said we should tell Caleb. I've never seen him so hyped about anything. Like he thought he was onto a Pulitzer-winning story. Caleb didn't care about things like awards, though. He was just excited to right what he saw as a wrong."

His quick glance at me told me he was carrying a load of guilt, just like Holly. *The right thing* might be what he was telling himself, and I wouldn't argue, but Caleb was dead. If it turned out that he was murdered because of the story he was working on, both Kyle and Holly would have a hard time forgiving themselves for getting him involved.

Alex opened Aurora's front door before the last bars of the UGA fight song had played. In a low voice, he said, "You can decide how much to tell Aurora. I haven't said *anything*."

I smiled at my uncle, at his good sense. Holly hadn't mentioned that we shouldn't tell, but of course it was all confidential. Tommy Kahn's PPP scheme might come to light in the papers, might result in something worse for the con man. I wouldn't share with Aurora, or anyone, and it was a relief that Alex hadn't inadvertently let her in on the story. As for Holly's part in all of it, not even Alex knew about the documents she'd removed from her office today. And I saw no reason for anyone else to know about that.

Aurora was in the media room, on the phone, the TV on mute. She said, "I have to go now," to the caller. Putting down her phone, she gave a careless wave. "An old friend," then proceeded in a squealy voice that reminded me of sorority days, "Oh, Jordan! Is Holly OK? Alex said she was completely *undone* over that young reporter's death!"

"I didn't *exactly* say—" Alex began.

"Such a terrible, terrible thing! So gruesome!"

No way she'd let me go up to my room, soak in a hot tub, and go to sleep, as I hoped Holly was doing, so I made myself a cup of tea and went back to the media room to join Aurora and Alex, with their brandy. And I told Aurora that Holly had been working for Tommy Kahn, until today. "She turned in her resignation this afternoon," I said.

I thought Aurora might be miffed that I'd kept that from her until now, but she said, "I'm *sure* Holly had no idea what kind of man she was working for until all of this came up about the Eagles Nest! And now, this reporter's death. After what happened at Sperry's last night with the reporter, I would think Tommy Kahn is a prime suspect. Did you tell Holly about that?"

"Yes." I paused to take in the aroma from the steaming tea. "They have a suspect. Someone they're questioning, a person of interest. That man who made a scene when Willow was singing at The Bluebird. The one they call Notorious."

Aurora was silent for a long moment. She sipped her brandy, then said, with a sigh, "I may as well come clean. I *did* know him. A long time ago, before Del—that's his name, Del Haskins—before whiskey got the best of him. I was embarrassed to let you know."

"Embarrassed *why*, Aurora?" I said.

"I was young and alone and wanting to be in the middle of it all. Everything about the music scene," she said. "That's how I met Del. I knew you wouldn't understand."

"You didn't give me a chance to understand," I said.

She made a gesture, trying to wave it all away. "Well, it doesn't matter. It was nothing."

Aurora clicked the remote, and the sound came on the television. I think she turned the volume up several notches, to drown out thoughts about Notorious.

I didn't believe for a moment that it was nothing.

Chapter 15

"You like *tahini*, yes? It is very good for you," Yazda said, pouring dark coffee for me.

After another restless night, I was wide awake at 6:30. The only thing predictable about my sleep since I'd been in Nashville was how unpredictable it was. Up earlier than Aurora or Alex, I went to the kitchen and took a seat at the table, while Yazda was making breakfast.

Yazda lived in Antioch, a community "far from here," she described it. How far, she couldn't say, but across town. "Many immigrants, Kurds and Hispanics, some Asians," she said. Far from Belle Meade, culturally, economically, and socially. Not just in miles.

She was married, with daughters who were nineteen and sixteen, a twelve-year-old son, and a grandson, eight months old. She laughed when I said I couldn't believe she was old enough to be a grandmother. "I was very young when I married. It was an arranged marriage," she said. "But my husband and I learned to love each other."

She surprised me, her intimate tone. "We had a son, Rihaan. His name means 'chosen one.' Our firstborn. He would be twenty-one next month. But… we lost him when he was seventeen."

"Oh, Yazda, I can't imagine," I said, groping for words. Feeling, as I always feel in these situations, that my response is so inadequate.

I thought she might say more, but she went back to making breakfast, talking about how much she loved working in Aurora's kitchen. I could see why. Every gadget imaginable.

I had the impression that Yazda was devoted to Aurora. She asked, "Do you know Miss Willow?" And then she said, "I do not trust her. She stayed here when she was sick with the virus. She is very... secretive." Surprising, and disturbing. I was stunned, hearing the sharp words from a person who seemed so kind, so gentle. I didn't know what to say, but I didn't have to respond. She made a gesture, waved the comment away.

Another dreary morning. No rain yet, but the sky was overcast, a blanket of ominous gray. I turned on the TV in the media room and flipped from channel to channel. All the weather men and women predicted rainy weather as the week went on, then storms, by the weekend. The forecast mirrored the gloomy feeling I had. Anxious for what was to come. Waiting for the bottom to fall out. Even though I kept asking myself, Something worse than murder?

Aurora joined me at the table, and we had breakfast together. It seemed Alex must have overslept. I knew he planned to go to Parnassus this morning, to be sure everything was in order for the book launch on Saturday. He was particular, like that.

I wouldn't have mentioned Notorious, but Aurora did. "I've been thinking about what you said, that Del's a suspect in a murder! Well, I don't believe it! He's a drunk, not a killer." Same words Kyle had said, but she'd called him by his real name. Something intimate about that.

We might have talked more about Notorious if my phone hadn't interrupted. Holly wanted me to come over. I told her I'd love to, but Alex needed the car.

"We can take mine," she said. "Nine-thirty OK?"

I'd expected Holly to be working while I was in Nashville. Now that she'd quit her job, we could spend more time together. Though she apparently had something particular on her mind this morning. Not just hanging out. And there seemed to be some urgency about it.

Aurora had a phone call, too, during breakfast. "Willow!" she said, beaming, and I knew from her end of the conversation that Willow was going to be performing somewhere. "Saturday night!" she told me. "A place called Bobby's. I may have to move heaven and earth, but I'm going!"

"Can you help with something—again?" Holly said, pulling away from Aurora's house.

"Whatever you need," I said. She put on the brakes as a runner edged into the street. I wished I'd managed to get in a run before the rain that seemed certain to set in, but this *something*, whatever it was, was a priority. My self-sufficient daughter didn't often ask for help.

"You might be sorry," she said.

"Well, not yet."

Kyle had talked her into picking up Notorious's belongings. "He called the landlady before he went to work," Holly said, "and she blew up when Kyle told her Notorious was in jail. She threatened to put his things out on the street!"

"Maybe this was just the last straw," I said. "I remember Kyle saying that Notorious didn't blame her for evicting him. Sounds like he'd been trying her patience for a long time."

"But she promised to hold his things for a couple of days."

I didn't mention that, technically, this was the second day.

"She told Kyle that somebody'd better show up this morning because today is garbage pick-up day and the truck comes around noon. I'm not a fan of Notorious, but that's cruel."

Long-suffering did have its limits, and dealing with a tenant who was perpetually drunk couldn't be easy. Still, putting someone's things on the garbage truck seemed unnecessary.

"She wanted to know what he'd done to get himself in jail," Holly said. "Wasn't he just sleeping off a drunk? Kyle told her the truth, which was probably a mistake. Then she *really* went ballistic. She said, 'If the garbage truck gets here before noon, it's on you!' and hung up."

Holly turned onto Harding Road, which I'd learned became West End Avenue and then Broadway, if you took it east to downtown, or changed to Highway 70 if you followed it west and didn't split off to Highway 100. We were traveling east.

"Kyle knew he couldn't get there before noon. He has some meetings that were postponed from yesterday when he left work," Holly said. "He has to leave early today, anyway. He wants to meet Caleb's brother who's flying in from D.C."

We caught a red light and stopped. Sitting at the light, we were quiet, Caleb looming large in our minds. Then Holly said, "Kyle means well. His father was an alcoholic, you know."

"I didn't know."

"He died before Kyle and I met. Kyle doesn't talk much about what his life was like growing up. He says his dad was sober the last couple of years, and he tried to make amends."

"Sounds like Kyle believes in the possibility of redemption," I said. "So do I."

Holly glanced my way, then said, grudgingly, "Yeah, I guess I do, too."

"You're doing a good thing. Notorious might be redeemable," I said.

"*We* are doing a good thing," she said. "You don't mind too much?"

"No." I couldn't help being curious about Notorious. I didn't mind at all.

The classical features of the three-story-brick on South 14th Street suggested that this once had been a nice house. Poor maintenance was evident from a distance. Some roof shingles missing and paint peeling. At the entrance, the mailboxes told the rest of the story. The house had been cut up into rooms. Some of the rooms must have had more than one occupant, from the number of mailboxes, at least a dozen.

Holly had dropped me off at the sidewalk and was trying to find a parking place on the street. I stood on the small porch, examining the mailboxes, without a clue which one belonged to the landlady whose name I didn't know, when the heavy front door opened.

"What do you want?" came a harsh voice. A cigarette dangled from the fingers of the large woman in jeans and a Titans sweatshirt, untamed hair, smooth dark skin.

"I'm here to see the landlady," I said.

"You're looking at her."

The word that came to mind was *lioness*. Statuesque, straight-backed, with high cheekbones and huge, almost-black eyes. I sensed a kind of weariness about her that runs deep, yet there was something fierce about her. And wary.

"Who are you?" she asked.

I thought about the times I'd been asked that question, recently. The woman with owl glasses at the emergency room. The detective, outside Odelle's room in the ICU. I kept getting myself into these situations where I didn't really belong. Meddling in other people's business, Alex had said many times, a caution that didn't seem to work.

"I'm Jordan Mayfair," I said. "My daughter and I are here to pick up Notorious's things. She's parking the car." The woman's gaze shifted, and I turned to see Holly, crossing the street. "I don't know your name," I said, partly making conversation, but it would be nice to know.

She scowled, as if my question was inappropriate. Then, hiking her chin, "Theodora."

"A noble name," I said, still not able to get a smile, but a softer look came into her eyes.

Holly joined us. Theodora tossed her cigarette butt into the yard and took us inside, with smells of coffee and bacon hanging in the air. Up a flight of rickety stairs. With some difficulty, she unlocked a room. I could imagine all the noise Notorious would make, dragging himself in, drunk, wrestling with the lock. The room was barely large enough for a small chest with two drawers, an old-fashioned banker's chair, and a pull-out bed that probably stayed pulled out. It was a mess, smelling of the take-out cartons strewn across the floor. Along with beer cans, whiskey bottles, and unwashed clothes. Holly opened the drawers and found, in one, a few socks, jockey shorts, and wrinkled shirts, presumably clean but not necessarily. In the other were half a dozen spiral notebooks and an old cassette player.

Nothing had been rounded up to put out for the garbage truck. Probably Theodora was just venting when she threatened to get rid of everything.

"I didn't think about bringing boxes," Holly said.

The landlady crossed her arms and stood tall.

I spotted a well-worn duffel bag in the corner. Some wadded up shirts and pants spilling out, but there was room for more. We crammed the clothes and notebooks from the drawers into the duffel.

"Maybe I can find some trash bags for all this crap," Theodora said, finally, kicking a dirty T-shirt across the floor.

I picked up the cassette player. Out of curiosity, I punched the ON button.

Someday I'll be a whisper in the wind, the song began.

With all my washed-away forgiven sin.

I held my breath. I couldn't stop listening.

Chapter 16

Someday I'll be a whisper in God's ear,
A broken prayer that only He can hear,
And I'll ask him, What was all this suffering for?
When I don't have to love you anymore.

An elegant instrumental finish, and the music died. I punched the OFF button.

"Was that Notorious?" I asked Theodora, who had returned with black trash bags.

She nodded, handing bags to Holly and me. She kept one for herself and began to fill it with bottles and cans. "I didn't know him when he could sing like that. But that's him."

Whenever Notorious made the tape, apparently long before whiskey got the best of him, he'd had a deep, resonant voice, full of feeling. Was he the songwriter? Did that graceful melody and those lyrics that spoke of a great, once-in-a-lifetime love come from the man who wound up living in this filthy room, surrounded by empty bottles and cans and reeking cartons?

Holly began picking up dirty clothes, cramming them in the bag. I took on the worst of the take-out rubbish. "How long has he lived here?" I asked.

"Going on two years. Mostly drunk, mostly trouble," Theodora said, bending for an Early Times bottle under the edge of the bed.

"But you let him stay."

"He's a vet. He was Special Forces. Fought in Desert Storm." She straightened up. "I've got a brother in Houston that did three tours in Afghanistan. I can see him ten years from now, same as Notorious. *If* he lives that long. He's in bad shape already. All the times I was 'bout to throw Notorious out, I'd think of my little brother and change my mind."

I wondered if she was changing her mind now, but there was a sudden shift in her voice. "I'm worn out with Notorious! I can't keep on with him and his demons. I have single women living here. One's expecting. Most of the men are down and out, but they don't get crazy drunk like he does!" She dropped one last Budweiser can in the bag and looked around the room. "I'm trying to run a decent place here. Not everybody in this town can afford an apartment that rents for a thousand dollars a month."

"Or a lot more," Holly said.

Another few minutes, and we finished picking up. Holly and I weren't leaving with much. The remnants of a musician's life. A duffel, a bag of dirty clothes, and a cassette player. Theodora took a ratty blanket off the bed. "He might need this," she said, handing it to me. Something sad in her eyes, as if she could picture him on the street, or in a homeless encampment.

In the car, I played the tape again and thought of Kyle's description of Notorious.

He was almost somebody once.

Holly's house was no more than fifteen minutes from where we'd been, but it was a world away. East Nashville was like that. As we passed Rosepepper, a lively Mexican restaurant that already had a busy lunch crowd, Holly remarked, "That was Caleb's favorite. Whenever we went out with him, that's where he'd want to go."

Outdoor seating was popular at the restaurant, even though the overcast sky looked like it could open up and drench everyone, any minute. Mostly youthful, laughing diners. Strollers and highchairs, even a black Lab leashed to one table leg, with a bowl in front of him.

Mixed as this East Nashville district was, with its hodgepodge of original and gentrified properties, Holly's neighborhood felt safe. But there was no guarantee of safety, not in Holly's neighborhood, not even in Aurora's. As we turned into Holly's driveway, a wrinkled old woman flagged us down.

"My neighbor, Miss Miranda," Holly whispered. "Kind of a Miss Havisham character. Remember *Great Expectations?* She's lonely, I think. Keeps up with what *everybody's* doing."

Rolling down her window, Holly called, "Good morning!"

Miss Miranda moseyed over from her mailbox. Gray hair that hadn't seen a comb today. She wore an old-fashioned housecoat and orthopedic shoes, untied, that she might have slipped into just to go outside and check the mail. Looked like one envelope was all she got.

"Were you expecting somebody from the gas company?" she asked in a high, thin voice.

"No," Holly said. "We don't have gas. Just electric."

"That's what I thought! I *knew* Ethan and Pam didn't put in gas when they fixed up their house." Miss Miranda raised a crooked forefinger. "That woman said she was looking for the gas meter around your back door. She said she was a new meter reader. But she wasn't even wearing a uniform. I guess she didn't count on me watching from my kitchen!"

"Maybe she got the wrong house," Holly said. "What time was she here?"

"A few minutes after you left. Made me wonder if she'd been watching your house and waiting until you left."

I leaned toward Holly and her window. "Could you describe her?" I asked.

Miss Miranda ran her arthritic hand through her wild hair. "Tall, for a woman. Light-colored hair, best I could tell, but she wore a cap. And sunglasses."

"How was she dressed?" Holly asked.

"Like I said, not a uniform. I guess you'd call it running clothes. Not shorts. Long pants. A T-shirt. Black. Solid. All of it black. And tennis shoes."

"Did you see what she was driving?" I asked.

If Miss Miranda was tired of all the questions, she didn't show it. Quite the opposite. Her pale hazel eyes were round with eagerness, like a child wanting to please. "She took off, not running, but in a hurry, and by the time I got to the front window, she was out on the street, walking fast. Might have parked somewhere on the next block. I thought about calling the police, but whenever I call to report something in the neighborhood, they just say, 'Yes ma'am, we'll check it out,' in that put-on voice, you know, like they're thinking, 'That old woman again, crazy as a loon.'" A smile crossed her lips, and her dentures clacked. "I *did* call police when that man moved in on the corner, and boys kept going into his house, and that amounted to something!"

"Yes, it did," Holly said. "We're lucky you keep an eye on things."

Miss Miranda stepped back. She looked at the envelope she was holding. "Electric bill. Can't be good news. March was awful. I turn off the heat at night, just pile my mama's quilts on the bed, but still…" The old voice trailed off.

Both the storm door and the wooden door were locked and intact.

"No signs of anyone trying to break in. I don't know what to think," Holly said.

"Your neighbor was convincing," I said.

The small back yard was enclosed in a six-foot fence. Good for privacy and protection, but only Miss Miranda, looking out her kitchen window, could see the back door. A large, leafy maple tree obscured the view from the neighbor on the other side. Straight back was an alley.

"Good thing Miss Miranda was being watchful," I said. "Nosy neighbors come in handy." I'd been called *nosy*, myself, especially by Alex. I liked to think the word was *curious*.

"Oh, she's watchful, all right, and gossipy. But maybe she did scare off an intruder." Holly unlocked the doors and we went into the kitchen.

"Do you remember the woman standing at the big glass wall in Tommy Kahn's office when we were leaving yesterday?" I hadn't thought of her again until I heard Miss Miranda's description of the person posing as a meter reader.

"I didn't see anyone. I was thinking about getting out of there." Holly gave me a suspicious look.

"I didn't imagine it, Holly," I said. What I didn't say was that there was something familiar about the woman. Because it seemed impossible that I would've seen her before. Maybe she reminded me of someone. "Tall, platinum blonde. Does Tommy have a wife or girlfriend?"

"He's married. Dee Dee's her name. Tommy calls her Double D." Holly rolled her eyes. "Medium height, and she has long dark hair. If he has girlfriends on the side, I wouldn't know, but it wouldn't surprise me." She washed her hands at the sink and opened the refrigerator. "Let's have lunch. I'm in the mood for a grilled cheese sandwich. Comfort food. I can make a salad, too."

It hadn't been long since breakfast with Aurora, but I can usually eat. I washed my hands, too. "Yesterday I saw that woman at Tommy's office, and today, someone resembling her was snooping at your back door. That seems like too much of a coincidence."

Holly assembled bread, several cheeses, and butter on the counter.

"It's a little creepy," she said, then stopped short. "The documents I took from the office... they're in my brief case, in the bedroom. That's what you're saying, isn't it? Somebody connected with Tommy tried to break in and get those documents?"

"It's a thought," I said, then reconsidered. "I don't know, Holly. Probably my imagination's working overtime."

"I should check my brief case, anyway," she said.

It took her just a minute. "Everything's there. I need to make copies this afternoon, before I hand them over to Walt."

Holly's phone rang. Kyle was asking if we'd retrieved Notorious's belongings. A good time to bring in those sad possessions from the car.

Holly's neighbor waved to me from her porch swing. The kind of neighbor that the transplants from California and New York, in their sterile, multi-million dollar homes, would probably never have the pleasure of knowing.

Chapter 17

Something in Holly's eyes and voice lingered, the way sadness holds on in spite of all you do. But for a while today, in her cozy kitchen, there were no tears, only smiles.

It was the first chance we'd had to just hang out, Holly and me.

She sat down across from me at her kitchen bar and asked, "How're my sibs?"

As it turned out, she knew as much as I did about Julie's homesickness and as little as I did about Claire. Catherine found time from her pre-med studies at Emory to text with everyone in the family, as often as we'd keep up a running conversation with her. Michael at Georgia Tech, not so much. But he'd spent a night at home on Spring Break before joining his buddies at Hilton Head. He gave my waffles as his reason for the stopover.

"He still knows how to play you," Holly teased.

"It works! You'd think my other children would take a lesson," I said.

It was like that, plenty to smile about, even laugh a little. We talked about the family, our hopes for Thanksgiving or Christmas this year, though the holidays were months away, and we ate Holly's gourmet grilled cheese sandwiches. So nice, a few minutes of unwinding.

Not that we hadn't spent time together. We had, and some of the time we were by ourselves. At Radnor Lake, in the car, at Holly's office smuggling confidential documents. Just that all of those times were dominated by something serious, even tragic. Like Caleb's death.

A call from Walt Meyer interrupted, and I knew it was the end of hanging out. Holly said, "Yes, I have everything… Come on over. I'm just across the river," and she gave her address.

Walt knocked, and I answered the door.

"Holly ran out to make copies of the documents," I told him, inviting him into the living room. He looked more stoop-shouldered than I remembered from yesterday. Almost as if his navy jacket was pulling him forward. I motioned to the big comfy chair that seemed to fit his frame. "She was going to some place on Gallatin Road. It shouldn't take long."

"No problem," he said, filling the chair. "I was downtown and thought it was a good time to drop by and take care of this." He studied me, and I wasn't sure he remembered who I was. Maybe he thought I was someone who shouldn't know anything about the documents.

"I'm Holly's mother. Jordan Mayfair. I was with Holly yesterday at your office," I said.

"Of course. I'm sorry." He made a fist and tapped his forehead. "I'm still reeling over what happened to Caleb. Yesterday's kind of a blur."

"Please don't apologize," I said. "It has to be overwhelming."

"He was like a son. Not just an employee. We're a small outfit. A family." Walt looked uncomfortable. Shifted, swung his ankle over his other knee and pulled down his pants leg. "I intend to finish the work he did. That's all I can do for him now."

He gave me a quizzical look, and I figured he was still wondering how much I knew.

"Holly told me all about the PPP scheme. And I was with her yesterday when she printed the documents at her office," I said. "We thought we were alone, but Tommy Kahn appeared as we were about to leave. It was a little unnerving."

Walt's bushy brows arched. "She didn't tell me that. I don't want her to get into trouble."

"Me, either," I said, and before I could help myself, I was telling him about the woman I'd seen at the glass wall, possibly the same woman who posed as a meter reader today. I suppose I wanted to be sure he appreciated the risks Holly had been taking, all along, for this story. And the sacrifice she'd made, quitting her job, though that seemed like a very good thing. Even if she hadn't given information to Caleb, she had lost respect for Tommy Kahn. And trust.

"Tommy Kahn may have smelled a rat," I said. "He knew Holly was in the copy room, and if he'd checked her code, he'd know how many pages she printed. Considerably more than the one-page letter of resignation that she showed him."

Walt nodded, slowly, thoughtfully. "I was just now at a Chamber of Commerce lunch, and one of the guys there, I've known for years. He's in insurance. Friendly fellow. Always working the room. But today it was pretty obvious he was keeping his distance from me. And I'm afraid I know why."

"Something to do with Tommy Kahn's scheme?"

"Bingo. His name's on one of the fake companies Kahn created. Caleb's story describes fraud that reaches way beyond Tommy Kahn."

Through the front window, I saw Holly's car turn into the driveway. "Looks like she's back," I said. "I hope this is the end of it for Holly."

He nodded. "I'd like to think so." And then he gave me an earnest, straight-on look. "But to be honest, a story with a reach like this, well, it's probably not the end for any of us."

Holly and Walt sat on the sofa, with the documents spread in front of them.

I busied myself in the kitchen. Not trying to eavesdrop, trying *not* to, trying to pretend they were simply having a friendly conversation, but the house was small. I couldn't help overhearing names of individuals and companies that I didn't know and didn't need to know. A glance at them, and I saw that Holly was as absorbed in the papers as Walt was.

I made coffee for her and sweet tea for Walt, who'd said he was not a coffee drinker. I'd thought all hard-core newspapermen thrived on strong black coffee, but so far most of what I'd learned about Walt and the *Nashville Voice* didn't match the TV or movie stereotypes.

"Police didn't find Caleb's laptop in his apartment," he said, almost whispering, as I delivered their drinks and a few Fig Newtons I'd found in the cabinet. His quiet voice might've had something to do with my presence, but I didn't think so. In fact, he looked up and gave me quick nod. I had the feeling he was hearing himself talk about this for the first time. Trying it out, so to speak. "A detective came by this morning. Wanted to take look at Caleb's office," he said.

"Was his laptop there?" Holly asked.

"Not anymore. Strangely enough, it disappeared. Only to reappear in my locked cabinet."

She bit back a smile.

"You don't happen to know his password, do you?"

She shook her head.

I left them to it, more uneasy by the moment. It probably was *not* the end for Holly.

Nothing more to do in the kitchen, trying to stay out of their way, I picked up my phone. I had silenced it this morning while I was in Notorious's room and hadn't thought about it since.

I had missed a call from Paul Broussard.

I clasped my phone in both hands and held it against me. What do you do with a man like Paul Broussard? And how many times had I asked myself that question?

Paul, charming patron of the arts, had first dazzled me in Provence. We flew to Paris in his private plane for dinner. He'd flown to Dublin for a few hours with me when I was in Ireland and spent a week in Florence, a time that was supposed to be just for us. It was not one of those whirlwind romances, passion so intense that it quickly burns itself out. Nor was it love that will survive the storms and take you across the desert. It was a kind of love, but complicated.

Miles have a way of changing feelings. Through the pandemic, unable to meet in exotic places, we had texted, called, zoomed, but what happened in Florence was hard to get past. The daughter Paul hadn't known about when we met, Bella, was desperate to drive a wedge between us. I was lucky to be alive. Paul, being a father, just trying to figure out what that meant with an adult daughter, had not believed what I knew to be true about Bella.

And so, during the dark time of virus and isolation and uncertainty, the other side of the world, where Paul Broussard resided, became so far from Savannah that I didn't know if we could ever find a way to be close again. I listened to the message he'd left on voicemail.

"Jordan, call me if you will. I have something to tell you, something you need to know."

The sound of his voice was always like one of those unforgettable old songs that still sends your blood surging, still makes your heart remember.

But Paul did not sound well.

Walt left, and Holly received a text from Kyle asking if she wanted to go to the airport with him later that afternoon, to meet Caleb's brother. It was time for me to leave.

Kyle would be coming by their house for Holly soon, so for this trip across town, I called an Uber.

A light mist had started when the driver put me out in Aurora's driveway. I hurried to the door. Aurora was standing there. I didn't have a chance to hear the UGA fight song.

No leaning on her quad, this time. She was standing straighter than before. "Jordan," she said, business-like, "I need to tell you something. As you know, this is a large house and I have plenty of rooms. We have another houseguest. I promise, he won't inconvenience you and Alex."

He? I was thinking of Willow as Aurora started her speech. But no. Booming voice. "Who's this?" He came in with a guitar in one hand and a bottle in the other. "I'm Notorious!"

Chapter 18

"Two questions, Aurora," I said. It was the first chance I'd had to speak to her, alone.

I had already been upstairs to Alex's room and failed to get the response I expected from him when he answered my pounding on his door. A suspect in Caleb Hunter's murder was a guest in Aurora's house. The man who made a scene when Aurora's niece was singing. Didn't Alex find that troubling? Or, at the very least, peculiar?

Apparently, not as much as I did.

He peered over his glasses. "I'm a guest in Aurora's house, too. As you are, Jordan."

"Are you saying I should keep my opinion about this person to myself?" I said.

"You can have an opinion, yes, but I don't see the cause for outrage. Notorious was released. He said he was cleared. Aurora believes in his innocence, and I... he doesn't seem like a bad fellow."

"*He* said he was cleared. Maybe police just don't have enough to hold him yet. Yet!"

Alex raised his palms to the heavens. "What are you suggesting we do?"

"I'm not... suggesting. I'm not outraged. Oh, I don't know!" What *was* the word that described what I was feeling? I turned on my heels and headed back downstairs.

Quiet strumming on a guitar came from the sunroom. I found

Aurora in the kitchen making a roast beef sandwich. Presumably for Notorious. If she'd prepared any food for herself since the problem with her back, I wasn't aware of it. Miraculous recovery, to care for Notorious.

"Just *two* questions?" she said. That tone, familiar from college days when we had disagreements. Never a serious argument that I could remember. I couldn't even recall the substance of those minor skirmishes, but her tone hurtled me back to those times. A gloss of humor in her voice—she hated confrontations—but underneath, undeniable irritation.

"I have a boatload of questions about Notorious," I said, "but for starters, why is he here, and why is he drinking?"

She slathered mayonnaise on the toasted bread. "Well, he has nowhere else to go. Can you imagine what that homeless camp must be like? In the rain? And storms on the way." She glanced at the window, at the mist that made her backyard look like it had been painted with watercolors. "The other question, why's he drinking?" She sighed. "Because it's what he does."

I considered that. "It's your house," I said. "Shouldn't you have some… expectations?"

"House rules? Oh, Jordan!" She laughed and shook her head. "You don't know anything about Del." Taking a jar of pickles from the refrigerator, she said, more earnestly, "I tried. Believe me, I did. He's an alcoholic. I can't save him from himself, I know that, but here I am with a house full of bedrooms, so I can damn well give him a place to sleep."

Neither of us seemed to know how to go from there. Everything I wanted to say sounded so judgmental. Aurora cut the sandwich in half, added a kosher dill to the plate, and left the kitchen. From the sunroom came Notorious's voice, gratitude for the sandwich, calling her an angel. Everyone seemed to give him a pass. Aurora, Kyle, even Alex. Why couldn't I?

In Paris, the time would be 10:35 p.m. I don't make a habit of calling people at that hour, but it was probably not late for Paul Broussard. A notable figure in Parisian society, he might not even be home for the night. He might be with a woman, dining at Lasserre, dancing to that magnificent music. I could almost hear his charming, slightly accented words, words he'd once said to me: "*The night doesn't have to end yet. Paris is full of delights.*"

I'd heard something else in his message today. Something that worried me. I had to call.

Paul answered straightaway. "Ah, Jordan," he said, clearing his throat, "It's so lovely to hear your voice."

"Did I wake you? I know it's late."

"No, no, I was not sleeping. I was catching up on some much-neglected work." I could see him in my mind, the silver in his dark hair, lean face with strong jawline, his intense blue eyes. "I'm getting over COVID, and I don't quite have my voice back." He may have heard my intake of breath because he hurried to say, "I'm much better now."

"Are you sure, Paul? You sound… not well," I said, stumbling over the words.

"Well enough to dismiss the nurse my doctor sent. I let her go this morning. She was, as you might say, a Nurse Ratched." I laughed at his allusion to *One Flew Over the Cuckoo's Nest*, and he laughed, too, the familiar ring of it that always cheered me.

"How long were you sick? It must have been serious for your doctor to send a nurse." Though even as I said it, I knew that Paul Broussard had resources most of us did not have.

"My doctor said he would go to great lengths to keep me out of *hopital* where people were dying." Paul explained that he'd tested positive fifteen days ago, with the usual symptoms, fever and congestion. He took the antiviral medication, but recovery was slow. "The worst was difficulty breathing. It felt as if a heavy creature sat on my chest. That was frightening."

I had never heard Paul Broussard admit to being frightened.

"And the persistent lethargy, so frustrating," he said. "Lying in bed, thinking of all the things that needed my attention, but Nurse Ratched refused to bring my laptop, and I did not even have the energy to get up and walk to the next room."

"I wish I'd known. I wish you, or Nurse Ratched, had called to tell me," I said.

"That's kind of you, Jordan," he said. I could hear the smile in his voice and missed him more than I had realized. "There was nothing you could do. But I did not want you to worry."

"You promise you're going to be all right?" I said.

"Yes, I promise." A long breath that might have been labored, or it might have been my imagination, and he said, "There is another reason that I wanted to talk to you. It's… Bella."

Paul's daughter had spent close to a year in a psychiatric *hopital* in Geneva. Upon her release, Paul had gone to meet her, to bring her to Paris, but she'd wanted to stay in Switzerland. The reason she gave was the psychiatrist she'd been working with, who could continue treating her as an outpatient. Paul thought it was a good idea, and perhaps it was. Being Paul, he'd believed her. Being Paul, he'd found a place for her in Geneva. Something on the order of a villa, I suspected, though he'd downplayed it when he told me about it several months ago.

"I talked with her every week. I thought she was much improved," he said. "But Dr. Hauser telephoned a few days ago. Bella had not shown for her appointment, twice. He'd tried to find her… I won't go into all of that. Suffice it to say, he took steps that he was not obligated to take. I tried to reach her myself. Having COVID made it impossible for me to travel to Switzerland, but I had contacts." He paused. Again, I thought he sounded a little short of breath, but maybe he was thinking about how much he should tell me. When he spoke, I knew he'd skipped over the part about his methods for finding her whereabouts.

"She is somewhere in the States," he said. I let that sink in. "Just this morning, I received that information," he continued. "I was able to talk to her half-sister, Jessica, in New York. Bella did not go to New York, or if she did, she hadn't contacted Jessica."

Now I was the one whose breathing was labored. My throat wanted to close up. A long space of time passed, until I could speak. "Where do *you* think she might be, Paul?" I asked.

He gave the answer I expected. "Possibly Savannah."

"If Bella is looking for me in Savannah, she won't find me," I said, and I explained why I was in Nashville. "I won't be going back home until next week."

"Ah." Relief sounded in his voice. "That will give me time." He didn't have to say more. He'd do whatever it took to find Bella. To keep her from finding me, if it was possible.

"I cannot tell you how sorry I am, Jordan," he said. "I would never have imagined something like this could happen."

I could have reminded him that he didn't believe me when we were in Florence and I told him what Bella was capable of doing, but the sadness that lay beneath his words made me sad, too. Paul Broussard was many things, and one of them, the part he didn't know until recent years, was a parent. He was overly indulgent. But I could imagine the worry of a parent whose daughter was missing. It didn't matter that she was an adult. "You'll find her, Paul," I said.

"*Oui.* I will let you know. Though I cannot believe you are in any danger."

Probably not.

For a while I lay on my bed, just thinking. Was it possible that the woman I'd seen in Tommy Kahn's suite was Bella? The thought of it was simply too far-fetched.

Bella was tall, though in my memory, she was not as tall as *that* woman. Her hair was more honey-blonde than platinum, but hair color could change. Still, how would Bella know I was in Nashville? She couldn't. Even if she knew Tommy Kahn, and that was doubtful, though both had lived in New York some years ago, Tommy didn't know me or know I was in Nashville until yesterday, just moments before I saw the woman at the glass wall.

All of it, so implausible, that in the end, I tried to find some comfort in Paul's words: *I cannot believe you are in any danger.* Not from Bella, maybe. But who was that woman?

I joined the others in the sunroom, where Notorious was wailing a twangy tune about broken strings on a guitar and the broken strings of his heart.

Chapter 19

Notorious held up his empty bottle. "That's a mighty good tastin' brew."

He'd had a few beers, singing and playing his bad country songs, line after line of clichés and melodies that sounded mostly alike, but it didn't seem that the beer had much effect on him. Maybe because he was so used to the hard stuff, cheap whiskey that tasted like gasoline.

I expected Aurora to bring him another, as she'd done before when he held out an empty bottle to her. Remarkable how well she was managing to get around now. But this time she didn't take the cue. "It's a craft beer. I like to patronize the local microbrewery," she said. "Go on, Del, play something else."

Remarkable how much she seemed to be enjoying the concert. Or putting on a good act.

I could've excused myself. Maybe I was thinking too much about the song I'd heard on the tape this morning, wanting to know if it was possible to reconcile that powerful, elegant music with the wreckage of the man before me. Maybe I was hoping he'd say something that would give more insight into Caleb Hunter's murder.

Notorious strummed some chords, frowned, his bushy brows pulling together. Black brows, contrasting with his gray ponytail and gray beard. At The Bluebird, his beard was scraggly, but he'd shaped it up a bit. The gray T-shirt and jeans looked nothing like the clothes

I'd expect him to be wearing, having gone from the homeless camp to jail and straight to Aurora's house. Notorious had told Alex that Aurora sent a car to the jail for him after he'd called her, that he called Aurora because hers was the only number he had engraved in his mind, that she was an "angel." That conversation took place before I'd arrived. I would've asked more questions, but Alex presumably behaved like the gentleman he was and did not interrogate.

So Notorious must have cleaned up here, at Aurora's. Which made me wonder where the change of clothes came from.

That prompted me to bring up the subject that might be touchy. His eviction. While he was still humming and fooling around with one riff and another, I took the opportunity to say, "I met your landlady this morning, Notorious. My daughter and I packed up your things and took them back to her house. Hers and Kyle's. You know Kyle."

He frowned again, seemed to be thinking hard. Then one sound lick on the strings, and he stopped. "Kyle, yeah, the boy works at the Hall of Fame. Always asking me for a new song."

That was not Kyle's version, but there was no point in arguing.

Facing the wall of window panes, he seemed to be studying the rain, a slow drizzle now. The sky had turned from a chalky white shade to the color of clay. I wondered if Notorious was thinking about the homeless camp. Aurora's words, a kind of gentle scolding, came back to me. He was here because he had nowhere else to go.

Alex said, "Kyle visited you in jail, too. He believes in your innocence."

Words that took me by surprise. Alex had been so quiet. Seemed so deep in thought. It was a relief that I wasn't the only one refusing to overlook the obvious. Aurora stiffened and I knew *she* wanted this line of conversation to stop, but Notorious didn't seem to mind.

He said, "Yep, that boy came down to the slammer and told me if I needed a lawyer, he'd get me one. Said I prob'ly wouldn't have to pay, which he knew I couldn't. Turned out the police couldn't keep me. The whole thing was all a big mistake. I shouldn't a gave that boy a black eye but I didn't kill him. The boy they pulled out of the river."

The image made my heart clench. Or maybe it was the word *boy*. Caleb was not a boy, but twenty-something or thirty is young, and I thought of the long life he should've had ahead of him. The way the honest inquiry in his eyes would've aged into wisdom.

"Somebody had to go and say they saw me down by the river," Notorious said.

"Are you saying you *didn't* go to the river?" I asked.

"I mighta gone down there to take a leak is all. I can't say I remember. But I know I wouldn't do that around where people were sleeping. That'd be just plain uncivilized."

"If somebody saw you, what was *that* person doing?" I was musing, more than anything, thinking about other possible suspects. I hadn't meant to say it out loud.

Notorious pointed his forefinger at me. "You are one smart cookie! Why didn't the police think of that?"

"I'm sure they've thought of it," Aurora put in, suddenly. "If you ask me who the murderer is, my vote's Tommy Kahn. Not that *he* would dirty his hands, but there's a dirt that comes off of him. He'd hire somebody to get rid of Caleb Hunter. I don't know why a piece in the newspaper would cause such hatred, but the look in Tommy Kahn's eyes, when he threw his drink in Caleb's face at Sperry's, it was murderous!"

"What about Sperry's?" Notorious said, and Aurora told him what happened. Then her voice changed. She might have been speaking to a child. "But let's not talk about that young man's death. It's too sad. Play something else for us, Del. Play something that will remind us what happy is like." She'd managed, cleverly, to steer the conversation from Notorious. For now.

I was given a reprieve from Notorious's nonsense when my phone rang.

"It's Holly," I mouthed, leaving the sunroom, perhaps too gladly. Notorious was deeply into a ballad, wailing, "*You turned on the electric in my heart,*" his eyes closed. He might not even miss me.

"Where *are* you?" Holly asked. I was in my room now, door closed, but she'd had an earful before I escaped to upstairs.

"Hold on to your seat," I said. "That's Notorious you heard. Aurora is letting him stay here at her house."

Holly caught her breath, noisily. "What are you saying? Aurora knows Notorious?"

"Knows him, yes. Seems they meant something to each other, a long time ago, and she still feels some obligation."

"Aurora and Notorious?" She was aghast. A little laugh, more disbelief than mirth.

"He's been *entertaining* us the last couple of hours," I said. "Nothing like what you and I heard on that old tape. It's hard to listen to his caterwauling now, knowing what he used to be, what he might've been."

"I wonder if Willow knows," Holly said. "Her aunt, someone she loves and admires, and the drunk that accused her of stealing his song—how ironic is that?"

"Roll the years back far enough and they might not seem so mismatched," I said.

"Still… I can just imagine how it would all go over with Willow."

I remembered Willow had called Aurora to say she was singing somewhere Saturday night and asked Holly if she knew anything about it.

"I got a text from her, too, asking me to come to Bobby's," Holly said. "Just like before, I tried to reach her, left a message, but she hasn't called back. Sure, she may be busy. But she could text. Even when we talked with her after she'd sung at The Bluebird, I got the feeling she was, I don't know, not the Willow I remembered. Everything she said, she was so *vague*."

It was the same word Aurora had used about Willow. "Are you and Kyle going?" I asked.

"Not sure. Are you? Isn't Uncle Alex's event at Parnassus Saturday afternoon?"

"Two o'clock. It wouldn't keep us from going to hear Willow that night. Aurora really wants to go." Now that Notorious was in the picture, I wondered how she'd manage. Would he insist on going? Would he behave? And what would Willow think, seeing him there?

"We don't know what Caleb's brother is planning," Holly was saying, "but we want to be available for him. He's so much like Caleb, it breaks my heart. His appearance, anyway. Not in his manner. They're twins, you know."

She and Kyle had met the brother at the airport and dropped him at his hotel. "We wanted to take him out to dinner but he wasn't up for it. He said he'd like to go to breakfast, though. Do you want to meet us at The Pancake Pantry in the morning?"

"The Pancake Pantry? Definitely," I said.

"Uncle Alex, too," she said. "I think he'd like to meet Caleb's brother."

"I'll ask him and text you." Yes, Alex would want to meet the young man, and I couldn't imagine he would say no to The Pancake Pantry, another icon of Old Nashville.

I dashed off texts to my children in Atlanta, Santa Fe, and Chicago. Trying, as texts do, to say what was going on without giving away what was actually happening.

The rain, drizzling now, made it hard to judge the time. I thought it had to be much later than six o'clock. The Notorious show had made for a long afternoon.

Now the sunroom was quiet, empty except for Notorious, either napping or passed out. Legs stretched out, head thrown back, mouth open and eyes closed, he cradled his guitar tenderly, like a baby.

Aurora was in the media room, watching the news. As she straightened up in her recliner, the doorbell rang. "Oh, that's Door Dash," she said. "I ordered from P.F. Chang's."

Whatever else Aurora was, she knew how to play the part of a perfect hostess.

"I'll get it," I said.

I went to the door, but not before the chimes sounded again, and then another time. The delivery girl, wearing a rain slicker, smiled, looking a little sheepish. "I like your doorbell," she said.

I heard Notorious's boisterous belly laugh. "Still playing that old Georgia song!" he hollered, stumbling from the sunroom.

Carrying the bags of food, I followed him into the media room. He headed straight to the liquor cabinet and began to shake the door handles. "Aw, Rora, you didn't go and lock up your good stuff, did you?" he moaned. "Why'd you do that?"

I caught the tail end of the weather forecast: "*The unsettling atmosphere continues to bring precipitation, increasing over the next forty-eight hours, with storms moving in on Saturday. Severe weather is possible.*"

Chapter 20

"I'm a terrible niece," I said to Alex, the next morning.

"Not *terrible*," he said. His teasing smile was genuinely full of affection, and I knew we were all right, but I was still ashamed that I'd forgotten all about the podcast he was recording today. Until last night, when I'd mentioned breakfast at The Pancake Pantry.

The first time we traveled to Provence, I was worried about my uncle's health, so I went along to keep an eye on him, to help him out as he researched his first travel guide. During our travels in Ireland and Tuscany, for his second and third travel guides, I came to realize that my uncle looked out for me as much as I looked out for him.

On this trip, I'd left him too much on his own. Not that he wasn't capable of driving around the city or making his scheduled meetings, but I hadn't been the *support* that I think he counted on. And his age was finally showing. Yes, I'd waited in the green room while he held his own with the piranha who interviewed him on her TV show, but I couldn't promise I would have been there if he hadn't asked, "*You will go with me, won't you, Jordan?*"

I pushed the cup of steaming coffee toward him. "I've been too distracted. How could I have forgotten the podcast?"

He patted my hand. "You're getting a little forgetful. It comes with age." He laughed. "Holly has been on your mind. And it's not as if you have to sit beside me. I would *not* want that. I'll be having a conversation by phone, upstairs in my bedroom."

Yazda, tending to something on the stove, spoke up. "Podcast. I don't know podcast."

Alex explained in his teacherly manner. "So there will be a recording, and we can listen to it anytime," he said. "I can show you how to find it on your phone. If you have an iPhone."

She patted the hip pocket of her jeans. "Oh yes. iPhone 14."

"Newer than mine," Alex said.

"Aurora needs to tell Notorious that he can't start making noise until you're finished. Or maybe he'll be sleeping off his hangover," I said. Aurora had given him the second bedroom on the first floor, across from hers. Maybe she'd worried about his ability to climb stairs safely. But it made me wonder if she had another reason for keeping him close.

"Where *is* Aurora?" I asked.

"She was up early but went back to bed," Yazda said. "She took a painkiller."

"I guess she overdid it," I said, thinking of how accommodating she'd been to Notorious.

Alex pushed his glasses up on his nose. "I was having trouble going to sleep, so around midnight I came downstairs and made myself a brandy. Notorious and Aurora were still in the sunroom. I didn't *see* them, but from what I could hear, it sounded as if they were—" I could tell he was choosing his words, carefully—"having a good time."

"The liquor cabinet was unlocked?" I asked.

"Yes." Surprise in his voice. He hadn't been in the room when Notorious was shaking the doors on the cabinet, whining that Aurora had locked them. Guess she changed her mind.

I checked the time. "I'm supposed to be at The Pancake Pantry at eight-thirty. I wish you could go, Alex, and I'm sorry—"

He raised a flat palm like a traffic cop and shook his head. "No worries, Jordan. Please be careful in this weather."

I had to go upstairs for the raincoat I'd almost talked myself out of packing, to go with the umbrella Aurora had loaned me. Downstairs again, as I passed Aurora's room on the way out, I saw that her door was ajar and heard Notorious's voice. Wearing only white boxers, Notorious was standing just inside Aurora's room. I could tell his back was scarred. Shrapnel scars? I remembered Theodora's words. Special Ops. Desert Storm.

"Where'd you put 'em? I know you have 'em!" Notorious bellowed.

"Stop it, Del," came her voice. "You're talking *years* ago. You've got it all mixed up."

"No! I mighta forgot at first, but it's all come back. I put my *soul* into them songs!"

As I let myself out the front door, he was saying, "I never woulda thought you'd do that to me. Not you, Rora. Not you."

Long lines were one of the things I remembered from my visits to The Pancake Pantry, several times with Holly, once with Aurora when she first came to Nashville, another time with my parents when I was a senior in high school and we were checking out Vanderbilt, my mother's alma mater. Excellent university but without an architecture program, and I was already sure I wanted to be an architecture major.

The Pancake Pantry dated back to the 1960s. Even this morning, there was a line, though it didn't wrap around the building and up the street, as I'd seen on those other visits.

Holly waved at me from the door. She and Kyle, along with Caleb's brother, had waited in the rain for a table. When my eyes met those of the hopefuls in line, drizzled on but not deterred, they didn't seem as cross as I would've expected. Their gazes seemed to say, *Lucky you.* If I'd seen anyone without an umbrella, I would've offered mine.

From a distance, the young man at the table with Kyle could've been Caleb. Though I'd seen him only once, there was such a resemblance that I felt my breath catch. A closer look, as the brother stood and we shook hands, and I noticed small details. That his hair was cropped shorter than Caleb's, his clothes exquisitely tailored, and the most striking contrast of all, the expression in his gray eyes that made him seem years older than his twin. Grief, maybe.

"Joshua," I said, my hand over my heart. "I can't tell you how sorry I am." Words that always seem vastly inadequate, but what else do you say?

"I appreciate it, Ms. Mayfair."

"Please, call me Jordan," I said.

A fresh-faced college-type young woman arrived with coffee. She'd already left menus. "Back in a jiffy for your order," she said. Efficiency was a priority, especially if you had a dozen customers waiting in disagreeable weather for tables.

The awkwardness of the first moments disappeared when Kyle steered us to the menus. "Everything's great, but I highly recommend the first one under Breakfast Favorites. Eggs, biscuits and gravy, bacon. You can add two buttermilk pancakes, and I will, definitely."

"…and add a huge load of guilt," Holly said, giving him a scolding glance, followed by a smile. "I'm going for the Small Appetite Plate."

The server came back and took their orders, then mine. I asked for the Small Appetite Plate, too. Joshua looked up from his menu and said, "Small order of silver dollar pancakes."

Not sure why, but I had a feeling that what he really wanted was fruit and yogurt.

Another awkward moment. Holly, Kyle, and I reached for our coffee.

"I understand you're from D.C.," I said.

"Joshua works for the Department of Justice," Kyle said, and then, with a grin, "That's not confidential, is it?"

"No, of course not."

And I realized the expression I'd tried to identify was not grief. It was something weighty that didn't come about these past few days. The weight of his job? Or a heaviness that reached back even before that?

"I knew what Caleb was working on, and I begged him to give it up," he said, startling me, and I could tell that Holly and Kyle were startled, too. The suddenness of his words. Getting right to it. "I told him to let the DOJ do its job. Justice can be slow in coming, but the arc of the moral universe bends toward justice. Caleb wouldn't listen. He'd listen to others but not me." Joshua fixed his eyes on Holly, and I couldn't help thinking it was an accusatory look.

"But it's *long*," she said. Her eyes were wide, her voice just a notch below angry. "Dr. King's quote. 'The arc of the moral universe is *long* but it bends toward justice.' Caleb was one of those journalists who cared about justice, about shining a light on the truth. Sometimes the DOJ takes too long. Or even lets things slide. Caleb thought he was doing the right thing."

Remembering what Alex had said after meeting with Caleb, I spoke up. "Your brother told my uncle that he felt a burden, I think that's how he put it, to tell the truth and be fearless."

"I know he did." Joshua finally picked up his coffee. "Our parents had to give us those names from the Bible story. It was just a name to me, but Caleb took his to heart."

"You work for justice, too," I said. "Maybe if you were named Bob, you'd be a stockbroker."

"Or a truck driver," he said. "Our uncles, Bob and Joe, drove eighteen-wheelers cross country." For the first time, Joshua managed a smile, just as our orders arrived.

Conversation with Joshua was easier over food. I asked where he and Caleb grew up, and he said Kentucky. A car accident during a heavy snowstorm took his father's life when the boys were ten, and his mother, diagnosed with multiple sclerosis shortly after that, died when they were nineteen. "Caleb was at Georgetown, but I'd stayed home after high school. I commuted to Murray State, to be there with her, at the end. After she died, I went to Georgetown, too."

I was beginning to understand the weight he'd been carrying, and he confirmed what I was thinking when he said, "I always had my brother's back, when I could. Even at Georgetown. These last years, though, with him in Nashville and me in D.C., we hardly ever saw each other."

"But he called you," Kyle said. He'd picked up half a biscuit and held it now in midair.

"Yes, when he started working on his big story, and then he called several times." Joshua looked down at his plate and cut off a piece of pancake. "I don't like to think he was trying to pump me for information."

"Maybe he just wanted your advice. Or support," Holly said, a hard look still in her eyes.

"My advice was, '*Give it up*,'" Joshua said, no mention of support. "The last time we talked I tried to put the fear of God in him. I said, 'You're not dealing with some mom and pop outfit that inflated a few numbers. These guys have a great deal to lose, and they play hardball.'"

"When was that last time you talked with him?" I asked.

"About ten o'clock Tuesday night."

The sounds around us, voices, laughter, flatware clinking on plates, filled our silence. All of us knew that Caleb was murdered in the early hours Wednesday, maybe six hours after that last conversation.

Joshua wiped his mouth and put his napkin down, leaving one of the silver dollar pancakes on his plate. "I could tell he was up to something. I could always tell." He frowned, tried to sound infuriated, but I knew he was masking the guilt he felt. "He said he had to meet someone. I assumed it was about the story. Wasn't *everything* about that story? But I never imagined that he was going to a meeting on a riverbank at four a.m."

Another pause, silence at our table, making all the other noises seem louder.

"Have you told the police?" I said, finally.

"No, I haven't had a real conversation with police. Just their call, the notification. But I will. I'm going to the station this morning."

His gaze was fixed on the middle of the table. The maple syrup? Salt and pepper? Not on anything, really. Holly and Kyle seemed to know, as I did, that he wasn't finished with what he wanted to say.

"Caleb told me something else that I should've read for what it was, though I couldn't have done anything to change his mind." Joshua finally looked up, looked at each one of us in turn. Did he wonder if we were judging him?

"'You remember my password, don't you?' That's what he said, like he was joking. But there was a message there. I can see now, he knew he was in danger, but my brother, my fearless brother, tried to make light of it, and I let him get away with it." I could almost feel the crushing regret that made his shoulders slump.

The air around us seemed to go still. "You know his password?" Kyle said.

"Numbers thirteen," he said. "The password he'd always used."

I folded my napkin and wrote numbers13 on it. I showed it to Joshua.

"Just like that," he said, nodding.

"The chapter in the Bible with the story of Caleb and Joshua," I said.

Again Joshua nodded. "Caleb put way too much stock in that story."

Kyle made plans with Joshua to go to a bar that night, some place Caleb had liked. "It's a cop hangout, too," Kyle said. "Maybe we can find out how the investigation's going."

It sounded like a guy-thing. Holly had just picked at her food. I tried to raise her spirits, asking her, "If you're not busy, why don't you go to the symphony with Alex and me?"

She attempted a smile, something resembling a smile. "I'll let you know," she said.

Chapter 21

The rain had slowed to a mist, not substantial enough to bother with the umbrella, but there was something sharp about it. Like minuscule shards of glass.

Detective Slater and I narrowly avoided colliding at the front door of the hospital's main entrance. I was hurrying through the door. The detective stepped back quickly to let me pass. He recognized me and said, "Well, good morning."

"Detective Slater!" I said. "So sorry."

"No harm done," he said, moving out of the way of the foot traffic at the door.

"You've been to see Odelle?" I said, stepping over toward him.

He nodded. "She couldn't give me anything, I'm afraid."

"Told you so."

A reluctant smile made its way into his eyes. He was quite good looking when he wasn't as grumpy as he'd seemed at our first meeting.

"I heard she's doing better, and they've moved her to a room," I said.

"I think they're going to send her home today," he said.

"You can't mean it! She's barely out of ICU."

A woman rushed by me, on her phone, half-talking, half-crying. Reminding me that there were worse things than getting sent home from this place earlier than might be prudent.

"The girl that was with her was up in arms, saying it was too soon.

Young woman, I should say. Friend, maybe a colleague," he said. "Name of Skye. Very protective. She was there at the Eagles Nest but not with Ms. Wright, so she wasn't much help."

"I would've told you, Detective, if Skye had been with us when Odelle was hurt. It was just Odelle and me, and we didn't see who threw the brick." I caught myself before too much *I told you so*. I had to admire his determination to get to the bottom of things, though his visits to Odelle were obviously a waste of time.

"Point taken." He produced a card from inside his jacket. "If you think of anything that could help, or if Ms. Wright does, give me a buzz."

He pulled out a ball-point pen and was wrote on the back of it. "Here's another number. I'll be off the next two days, so this is the best way to contact me."

"You're very dedicated," I said, taking the card. "Working on your days off."

"Detectives aren't really ever off, not when something comes up about a case," he said. He gave me a little salute and walked away.

"But I *want* to leave this place," Odell was saying when I opened the door of her room. Shaky voice, but she was sitting up, on the side of her bed, dressed in emerald green sweatpants and sweatshirt that set off her white hair.

Skye, in pink tennis shoes again, was packing up a bag on the end of the bed. "I'm just afraid you're not ready, Odelle." Looking up at me, then, she said, "Oh!"

I couldn't say she sounded glad to see me. More like she'd spotted a bug in her soup.

"Jordan! How good of you to come!" Odelle stretched out her fragile arms and I hugged her, as carefully as I'd cradle a newborn.

"Looks like you're flying the coop," I said.

"None too soon," she said.

"Medicare runs this place," Skye said. "It's all about the bottom line."

"Oh, it's not like that, Skye." Odelle gave a little laugh. She had color in her cheeks and a twinkle in her eyes. So much improvement since I last saw her. "Jordan, sit down, please," she said. "A detective was here. I don't remember what happened at the Eagles Nest. Do you?"

I told her all that I could. She had a vague memory of seeing me there but did not recall the signs being distributed by Tommy Kahn's people, or bricks flying, or being struck down. She drew a blank on Aurora's visit to her when she was in the ICU.

A male nurse who looked too young to shave came in as we were talking. "The doc says you're one lucky woman, Ms. Wright, to have as much of your memory back as you do. And you'll probably be remembering more, gradually." He came to her with papers to sign, talked to her about what to do and not to do, and gave her instructions about following up with the neurologist. "I'll get a wheelchair now, and you'll be outta here soon," he said.

Odelle wanted to go to the bathroom before leaving. Skye tried to help her to stand, but Odelle shooed her away. We watched Odelle walk across the floor, unsteadily, but with a straight back, and into the bathroom.

"She's a determined woman," I said. "Patients with her grit get along much better than those who lie back and let people do things for them."

"So I've heard," Skye said. She snapped the small bag shut and gave me a hard look. "Has your daughter told you the latest about Tommy Kahn?"

The latest that I knew about Tommy Kahn would not be something Skye knew. "I'm not sure what you mean," I said. "Holly quit her job on Wednesday."

Skye took a moment, looked like she was letting that register. When she spoke, there was a kind of warmth in her voice that I'd never heard. At least an absence of irritation. "Good for her," she said. "Maybe I misjudged. I apologize."

"She's probably a lot like you, Skye. Tries to do the right thing. And fearless." Skye laughed, and I asked, "So what is it about Tommy Kahn?"

"He was on Presleigh Deere's show this morning. She's usually bitchy." Skye raised an eyebrow, and I wondered if she'd watched the interview with Alex, and if she knew of his relation to Holly and me. But that didn't matter. "Maybe she has the hots for Tommy Kahn," Skye said. "It was like his speech in front of the Parthenon times ten. She didn't cross him once. Softball questions, that kind of thing."

We heard the toilet flush and Skye lowered her voice. "I don't think Odelle knows. I was watching it at the office, and I didn't mention anything to her. But I'm afraid there's no way to keep it a secret, once she gets home."

"Keep *what* a secret?"

"That bastard is making sure we don't have time to save the Eagles Nest. He says he's scheduled the demolition for Monday."

Something made me want to see the Eagles Nest again. I can't say what. But it wasn't far from the hospital, and I had nowhere to be until tonight. Alex had tickets for the Nashville Symphony, and I hoped Holly would go with us.

No sign of protesters today. The rain must have sent them home. Or the passion for their cause may have dwindled, but Tommy Kahn's announcement on Presleigh Deere's show might bring them back. Skye said preservationists would be burning up the telephone lines trying to get local politicians to put pressure on Kahn. She mentioned applying for an injunction but doubted that would work.

My experience told me it wouldn't.

This was Friday. Not much time to get anything done before Monday.

I drove past the front of the Eagles Nest, turned down the side street, and parked. From there, I could see how far back the building extended, house with the studio that had been attached. Tacked on. That much was clear, even from my car. I snapped a photo, curious about the haphazard addition. Odelle and The Coalition were trying to get the Eagles Nest declared a historic landmark. Surely they'd examined it carefully, the 1920s house and the studio that was added much later. Having worked on historic buildings in Savannah, I knew how surprises could crop up. One time we found a plaque that proved the property had belonged to the City before the private owner bought it. City records, which no one had thought there was a reason to check, showed the property had been designated a historic landmark in 1950 because it had been a location where slaves were auctioned.

I decided to take a closer look, though I couldn't imagine the exterior would yield any new information. The mist seemed to envelop me. It felt like I was walking through a cloud. I raised my umbrella, but it did no good, so I put it back in the car. On impulse, I took the brick from my purse. Maybe I should've given it to Odelle today. On the other hand, it might've upset her if the memory came rushing back all at once.

The ground was soggy. I made my way to the studio from the side street where I was parked. Brick and cinder block on this addition. Seemed no one had taken care to make the studio compatible with the original house. The brick that I'd been carrying around ever since the protest matched up with the bricks on the studio, not with those on the house itself, and I realized that all the bricks that were flying around that day came from back here.

I noticed something else.

These were very old bricks. I had enough experience with historic architecture in Savannah to recognize historic bricks. Why hadn't I paid more attention to the one I'd been carrying around for days? I thought of it now as Odelle's brick. Had she been trying to tell me that this was not a modern brick? Would that be important?

Though bricks nowadays could be produced in various sizes, I knew that historic bricks were generally longer and wider, more irregular than those made after brick sizes were standardized in the 1920s and 30s. Rock and iron fragments made historic bricks more porous than modern bricks fired in kilns at a much higher temperatures, giving them a harder compressive strength. The color of historic bricks was noticeably lighter than dark red contemporary bricks. All of these features were there, in Odelle's brick, but it didn't all synthesize until I saw the old bricks laid in courses on the exterior of the studio.

Construction with old materials wouldn't qualify a building for historic designation. Odelle would know that. But seeing the studio up close made me even more curious about what Odelle wanted me to know when she insisted that I take the brick. Twice.

Where the studio and house adjoined, there were gaps. Dead spaces where the floors didn't line up. Several bricks were scattered around. An easy find for protesters, that day.

If I'd been brave, I might have tried to investigate further. Some of the plywood, an attempt to cover the gaps, had rotted and might come off without too much effort. But my phobia of dark places would not have allowed me to get inside, even if I could. The memory of a black priest hole made my heart race, even now. Just remembering.

Quickly, I took some photos and went back to the car. Before I put Odelle's brick away, I examined it carefully, which I hadn't done before, and I noticed a word on one side, the letters almost unrecognizable.

Wolford.

I'd known of brick-making companies that imprinted their names on their bricks. With all that I'd waded into, here in Nashville, I didn't have time for research, but I Googled the name from my phone. Nothing remotely related to bricks.

I pulled away from the Eagles Nest, not hopeful. Thinking it would be the last time I'd see the structure, the house and studio, that had meant so much to Nashville's music industry.

On Monday, Tommy Kahn would take it down.

Chapter 22

Alex and I were alone in Aurora's kitchen when Alex said, "I was an enabler."

From somewhere else in the house, probably Notorious's bedroom, came humming and strumming.

"I didn't mean to be, but I suppose enablers never realize what they're doing."

He opened the refrigerator. Two twelve-packs of Coors, front and center. Clearly, Notorious had already been into one of them.

I took our tea to the kitchen table, set his cup down and then mine. "How did that happen?" Trying to keep scolding out of my voice. I could see Alex felt bad enough.

"It started this morning when I came downstairs, after I'd done the podcast."

I wanted to ask about the podcast but that would have to wait.

"Aurora was on the phone with Willow. I suppose Aurora and Notorious had talked about going to hear Willow tomorrow night." Alex settled at the table and reached for his tea. It fascinates me how people look into their teacups when they're thinking. As if they can see wisdom there. "It sounded like Aurora was trying to calm Willow down, trying to convince her that it would be all right for Notorious to be there. I heard her say, 'He wants to apologize!'"

"Ah," I said, all of it beginning to come into focus. I had wondered how Willow would take it when she learned that Notorious was staying with her aunt. Now, not only that, but he wanted to go with Aurora, with *us,* presumably, to Willow's show. Not too surprising that Willow hadn't taken it well. "So where do you come in, being an enabler?" I said.

"I'm getting to that." Storyteller that he is, Alex wouldn't want to be hurried. "Aurora must have persuaded Willow. Her voice was soothing. 'I promise you,' she said, 'He will not be a problem.' I don't know how Aurora could make such a promise."

Alex doctored his tea with cream and sugar, stirred it, and said, "A few minutes later she called an Uber and left the house. She told me she had an appointment to get her hair fixed, manicure, pedicure, all of that business that occupies so much of women's time. I can only imagine it will take hours. Aurora seems like a, what do you say, *high-maintenance* woman?"

That was the right term.

"Wasn't long before Notorious knocked on my door. He asked if I could drive him to Walmart."

"To buy beer?"

"No! I wouldn't have done that, Jordan, and that's not what he said." Alex was sounding impatient with me, so I let him take his time. "Notorious told me he needed some decent clothes to wear tomorrow night. He said, 'I have those old clothes in the foot locker, but I want something nice when I see that girl.' He said he'd had no idea she was Aurora's niece, at The Bluebird, and that he had to apologize for the way he behaved. 'I don't remember much about it,' he said. 'I just know that when I heard that song, it did something to me.'"

Old clothes in the foot locker confirmed what I'd believed, that at one time Notorious must've lived here with Aurora. And something was missing, if I'd understood what he was saying to Aurora this morning. Notebooks with songs in them? The notebooks Holly and I had found in his room when we packed up his things at Theodora's?

Aurora told him he was mixed up about it. And it was certainly possible. That he just didn't remember taking them with him.

"He told me he had money. He gets a VA check. He wasn't asking for a handout. I thought he sounded sincere." Alex took a sip of tea and looked into the teacup again. "So I agreed to give him a lift to Walmart."

I hadn't meant to chime in again, but I couldn't help myself. "Let me guess. He didn't buy clothes. He bought beer."

"Both," Alex said. "He came out with several bags, bragging about the good deal he got on a denim jacket. I didn't have a clue about the beer until he put it in the refrigerator."

"It's not your fault," I said. "Enablers often have the best intentions."

Alex said he was pleased with the podcast. "I think it was a success. Certainly not like the fiasco with Presleigh Deere," he said.

"It wasn't a fiasco," I said. "You held your own."

"I suppose I did manage to get some of my talking points in," he agreed.

Notorious came into the kitchen and helped himself to another beer. It was lunch time. I wasn't hungry, after The Pancake Pantry breakfast, but Alex, who'd had only a bowl of cereal, said he could eat something, and so did Notorious, who'd had nothing he couldn't drink, without foam on it. Good to get food in him. I settled on omelets.

The secret to my omelets is to put everything I can find into them. I found a carton of eggs and scrounged in the refrigerator, where Yazda, presumably, had organized leftovers in zipper bags and Tupperware. Several kinds of cheeses, ham, turkey, chicken, onions, rainbow-colored veggies, including red, green, and jalapeno peppers.

Putting it all together, I gave Notorious a quick glance and said,

"My daughter and I packed up your things at Theodora's. Holly and Kyle have all your belongings at their house."

I had the feeling that if he'd brought his guitar into the kitchen, we'd hear a few licks before he answered, but he threw back a swallow of beer instead. "Yep. You told me."

"Did I mention that we found some notebooks and papers in your room? And a tape player?" Another glance, and I saw that he was paying attention now. "We listened to the tape. It was really something. A beautiful song."

For a moment, his eyes seem to fill with confusion. And then a light came through. He began to sing: "*Someday I'll be a whisper in the wind… With all my washed-away forgiven sin.*" He blinked, as if he'd been lost in a memory, and now he was back. "My voice ain't what it used to be," he said.

I was shocked that he remembered the words.

"Not bad, Notorious," Alex said. "Are the lyrics yours?"

"Yeah." Another long pull from the bottle.

Standing over the stove now, with the egg mixture beginning to sizzle, I said, "You could do it again, Notorious. Even if you didn't get back to performing, what about writing songs?"

"Nah, too much water under that bridge." He drummed his fingers on the table. That tune still playing in his mind, perhaps. He said, "You know about me and Rora."

"A little," I said.

"I was spiraling down fast when she couldn't take it no more," he said. "But I still had something in me, that… I don't know… like what's left of a blazing fire. The embers, I guess you call it. That's when I wrote that song, 'When I Don't Have to Love You Anymore.' I bought a tape player and recorded it cause I wanted to remember. Remember I *had* it, once. I did. After that, I wasn't worth a damn. But for a time, I was almost there."

Almost somebody.

"I'll make sure you get those notebooks we found," I said. "You never can tell what they might trigger."

He gave a little laugh. "Yeah, well, my mind's too muddled to do much anymore. But I'd be glad to see 'em." He shook his head, scowling. "I was so sure I left them songs in that foot locker. I woulda bet my old Martin…"

"I'll make some coffee," I said.

Notorious paid no attention. I could see in his eyes, he was still puzzling.

"Rora's right, though. Sometimes I get things all mixed up," he said, before polishing off his beer.

I served up the omelets and suggested that we listen to the podcast Alex had recorded.

Norman's Nashville was more Norman than Alex, but he gave Alex's book a nice shout-out. According to Alex, the show had a loyal audience who loved to hear Norman slam developers and city leaders. Like cable news channels. A good ol' boy, or that was his persona, he lamented taxes "out the wazoo," the loss of Nashville "treasures" like Exit/In and Rotier's, "progress for the super-rich on the backs of the poor," and the Lower Broadway "vulgar circus."

Alex made some good observations. Norman said he was driving behind a "raising hell on wheels" bus and "a drunk stood at the back, unzipped right there before God and let it rip!"

Alex said, "Maybe the City should offer free car washes to drivers on Lower Broad."

Toward the end of the thirty-minute segment, the conversation turned to the few "authentic" venues still around. Old Nashville. Cheekwood, a historical estate with botanical gardens and art museum. Norman mentioned Bobby's, where Willow would be singing, Saturday night. The old Bobby's had been demolished, apparently, but a new one still offered music on Music Row.

Top of his list, The Bluebird Cafe. Norman mentioned "the girl that brought down the house the other night." Alex made sure he got her name, Willow Goodheart.

Notorious had cleaned his plate. He closed his eyes. Remembering, seemed like. Maybe he'd played The Bluebird, long ago. A good memory, from his expression. Or he was thinking about Willow's performance, when he accused her of stealing his song. The podcast ended, and Notorious opened his eyes.

"A hundred singers come and go, but every now and then, it just feels right. It's like the distance between the singer and the audience closes in, and everyone in that tiny space knows it." Trace of a smile. "They say people are stars, but it ain't about light. It's about sound. About the echo you've been searching for in the back of your mind, and when you hear it…" His chest lifted as he took in air, then let out a long slow breath. "When you hear it, it's undeniable."

I could not for the life of me come up with anything to say.

Alex and I watched in stunned silence as Notorious went to the refrigerator for another beer.

Chapter 23

Aurora had gone for a short feathery style and a lighter shade of blonde. Cut and color, along with what appeared to be a professional make-over. All of it designed to take years off her façade, but there were still those cautious steps as she bent over her quad.

No one would mistake her for thirty.

From the upstairs hall, I saw her make her unsteady way through the foyer toward the media room. Notorious hollered, "Rora! You gotta hear this," as he came from the sunroom, picking on his guitar, none too steady on his feet, either. I opted to miss out on a tune he must've just composed, after a few beers, and turned back toward my room.

It was after three o'clock, and I hadn't heard from Holly, so I called her.

"Everything all right? What did you decide about the symphony?" I asked.

"I guess I'll go," she said. "Why not?"

Mothers can always hear what lies under the words, and this was no exception. Even as we made plans for the evening, I could hear that *something* so close to despair in Holly's voice. Then she said, "It was my first time at a funeral home with someone making arrangements."

She and Kyle had met Joshua at the funeral home, after we'd left The Pancake Pantry. "Joshua said Caleb wanted to be cremated. I never heard him say anything about that," she said. "But it's what

Joshua wants. Cremation. A private thing, tomorrow morning. Joshua said he'd come back to Nashville soon for a memorial service that Caleb's friends could attend."

Our call was cut short. "Gotta take this. It's Walt. I left a message for him." I could hear her voice waver as she said, "I need to tell him what Caleb's password is."

My consolation, as her voice faded, was that the symphony might be a distraction for her, a brief distraction from the overpowering grief. And guilt.

Paul's text came as I was laying out clothes for the evening.

> No sign of Bella in Savannah. My contacts
> are confident she has not been there. Search
> continues in the NY area.

So impersonal. If he'd called, I would've answered, but maybe there was really nothing else to say. He was sorry. He did not think I was in danger. He'd said it all.

I thought I should call him. The text had just come in. He'd surely answer, though it was midnight in Paris.

But I didn't. There was really nothing else to say. Not yet.

The off-and-on rain throughout the day was *off,* for the time being, as we headed to the symphony. I was driving. I could've swung around the city on I-440 to East Nashville, to get Holly, but instead I took Harding Road toward downtown. A straight shot, the street name changing to West End, then Broadway. Alex wanted to make notes about all the new buildings, to be sure he had accurate information if he was asked at his Parnassus event tomorrow.

It started to feel like we were going down into a canyon, walled in by towering buildings. New construction all around, evidenced by cranes, silhouettes against the sky. With more skyscrapers going up, would these blocks of Broadway eventually be a shadowy place, no sun, except for high noon? Old and New Nashville stared at each other as we came to Union Station—the once-upon-a-time Gothic train terminal, now a magnificent hotel. Across Broadway, the sleek Grand Hyatt. Steel and glass, with its neon blue strip, top to bottom.

Past Bridgestone Arena, Nashville's premiere entertainment and sports venue, Lower Broadway felt claustrophobic, the Nashville Ultimate Party Bus crowding on one side, Big Drag Bus coming toward us. Tourists in their new cowboy hats spilled off the sidewalks. Loud music blared into the streets from one honky-tonk, competing with the next.

"Are you and I simply out of step with the modern world, Alex?" I asked.

"Not *you*. You're thoroughly modern, Jordan," he said.

I made a sweep with my hand. "All of this… progress. If that's what it is." I sighed. "Is the same thing happening in Savannah? A vulgar circus, as Norman called it? And I'm just blind to it?"

Alex raised an eyebrow. "You can find whatever you're looking for in every city. Certainly in Atlanta, and, yes, Savannah," he said. "But it seems to me that the citizens of Savannah place a far greater value on history than Nashvillians do. It's not *just* about tourism dollars in Savannah. I wish Nashville could be more like that."

Suddenly he pointed to the open-air bus in front of us. "I wouldn't get too close to those young fellows. Remember the hood of Norman's car." Packed in at the rail of a Rowdy Bus, the twenty-somethings, wearing baseball caps and cowboy hats, pushed at each other, waved, and yelled something unintelligible. I let them get a safe distance in front of me.

As we turned onto historic Second Avenue, we talked about the bombing on Christmas Day, 2020. The vibrant street life made it seem that activities had returned to normal, or nearly normal, around the shops and bars and restaurants housed in the buildings that dated back to the late 1800s.

"I never understood why he did it," I said, referring to the man who detonated the bomb in an RV, killing himself. Miraculously no one else died.

"The FBI report could only speculate that his intention all along was suicide," Alex said. "A man who suffered from paranoia, too much exposure to conspiracy theories, without close relationships that could've provided support."

"So much of that in the world now," I said.

Moving on north, we saw that life had not returned to normal in all of the historic district. Scars remained, shells of historic buildings with uncertain futures, fenced off and dark. More collision of old and new.

Across the bridge, past the Courthouse, Main Street took us to East Nashville.

Holly served us smoked salmon canapes and crudités, a fancy arrangement of veggies, served with little toasts and a caramelized onion dip. Alex and I were probably overly complimentary. So unexpected. "It helps to do something productive," she said. Though I yearned for the spirited daughter I knew she would be, again, I was encouraged by her effort.

Kyle grabbed a couple of canapes before he left to meet Joshua. "I don't think we'll be late," he told Holly. "Unless I'm reading Josh wrong, he's wiped out. Hard day."

Not only the hour at the funeral home, Holly told us, uncorking a white wine, but another hour at the police station, and then this afternoon at Caleb's apartment. "Kyle and I didn't see him after the funeral home," she said. "Kyle offered, but he said no."

Some things you can only do by yourself. Holly would understand when she had more experience with losing people close to her. I prayed that would be many years in the future.

"Kyle talked to him, a little while ago," she said, pouring wine. "Joshua told him there was a new development in the murder investigation. Police were questioning a man from the homeless camp, the one they called Red. He'd tried to use a credit card to buy beer at a market, and it was Caleb's card. Naturally, he claimed he'd found it. Stupid, thinking he could get by with using it."

"Found it down by the river?" I asked.

Holly nodded. "That's what Joshua said."

"Anyone could've dropped it," I said, imagining someone finding a wallet, taking the cash and cards, and throwing the wallet far out into the river. Anyone. Including Notorious.

Alex said, "Police told Caleb's brother that they'd brought in this man… Red?"

"I'm sure the locals take note of Joshua's DOJ connection," I said. "Gives him clout ordinary citizens don't have."

"Joshua said a detective accompanied him to Caleb's apartment and stayed for a while," Holly said. "Plenty of time to talk. Then he left Joshua there to do whatever you do when you have to go through things where your brother lived." She took a long breath, as if trying to imagine. "Police had already looked high and low for some clue about what Caleb was working on. They found an empty shredder. Thank goodness Caleb put everything on his laptop! His phone was recovered from the river, but it was ruined."

"Did you tell Joshua where the laptop is?" I asked.

She shook her head. "Kyle and I talked about how much we should tell. Joshua has good intentions, but I can't see him withholding information like that from the police."

"Walt's taking a big chance," I said.

Alex chimed in. "What do you mean?"

Holly and I exchanged a glance. "I probably didn't tell you everything, Alex," I said.

"Well, don't you think it's about time you did?"

Over the wine and hors d'oeuvres, Holly filled him in on all of it. He knew about Tommy Kahn's scheme but didn't know about the close call we'd had in her office, when she was confiscating documents. Or about her cooperation with Walt Meyer. Predictably, Alex shook his head, said to me, "You should know better, Jordan," and scolded Holly for being "just like your mother."

"I take that as a compliment," she said. It touched me to see a brief smile, the first time in a while. But the smile faded. Holly took a drink of wine. With a sigh, she said, "I regret more than I can say that I got Caleb involved. I don't think I'll ever forgive myself."

The Schermerhorn Symphony Center sits on a full city block. This was my first visit, so I wanted to see it from every angle. Alex placated me, driving all around. I was intrigued by everything, from the bronze angel statue at the corner of the property, to the fountains and formal garden, to the building itself, with its impressive neoclassical elements. Colonnaded portico, the balanced structure, the pristine white limestone with granite and marble accents.

The Schermerhorn is a short walk from Lower Broad, but it could have been a world away. All so civilized, I thought, watching attendees arriving in business attire, some in cocktail dresses, speaking in soft to moderate tones. A valet took Alex's keys and gave him a ticket. Other parking options within a few blocks of the Schermerhorn might be fine on a clear night, but the weather was too erratic tonight. We didn't want to be running to the car in a storm.

Inside, I wasn't inclined to hurry to our seats, so much for an architect to appreciate. Alex seemed glad to linger, too, but Holly urged us on. The concert was going to begin soon. We entered the spacious concert hall, took our programs, and examined our seating arrangements. We had two seats together. Alex took the single in another section that I'd reserved when I knew Holly would be joining us.

Before we started into the aisle, I was staring up at the elaborate chandeliers, like sparkling upside down wedding cakes. I couldn't help myself. So I missed the moment when Holly and the person she recognized first made eye contact. But when I noticed, I had the feeling neither of them quite knew what to do. Holly touched my arm. "I'll just be a minute," she said. I stepped out of way, best I could, and waited while she headed toward a young woman. Short, black hair. Rimless glasses. Sharp nose. Curvy figure in a black suit, maybe a few pounds too curvy. She spoke to Holly, not anything close to a minute. Holly returned, then, her face ashen.

The aisles were no longer crowded. Reasonable guests of the symphony were already seated. We found our seats and settled in just as the lights went down.

"That was Sharla, from Tommy Kahn's office," Holly whispered. Leaning closer, she spoke so softly that I could barely make it out. "She said, 'Tommy knows.'"

Chapter 24

The Mexican Tenors was not the program Holly would've chosen. I was able to lose myself in the performance. Almost. But I couldn't help noticing that each time we applauded, Holly blinked, as if she'd been startled out of a daze. The moment the lights came up for the intermission, she stood up. "I need to find her," she said. A continuation from before the concert began. As if she'd thought of nothing else during the music.

I stayed in my seat, looking all around the spacious Laura Turner Concert Hall. I'd read about its thirty soundproof windows running along two long walls, that allowed natural interior light. Something I wished I could experience in daytime. I'd read about how the orchestra level of the concert hall, with fixed theater seats, could be transformed to a flat floor, for other uses. A few minutes into intermission, though, the elements of design couldn't keep me from thinking about what the woman from Tommy Kahn's office had said to Holly: "*Tommy knows.*"

There was still time to stretch my legs. Maybe find Alex. I would tell him about the woman's warning, and maybe he'd persuade me that everything would be all right.

I went to the West Lobby, closest to his seat in the Loge, and he was there, nursing a drink. Holly beside him, with a water. "In pleasant weather, it's just lovely, sitting out there in the courtyard," he was saying. "You could be in a European city. Vienna, yes. You could imagine you're in Vienna until the raucous party buses pass and the woo girls start acting out."

Holly handed me her water. "Now I really *do* have to go to the bathroom."

"Do you know what this is all about, Jordan?" Alex said, as she turned away. "Holly said we need to go to Loser's Bar later." He looked a bit horrified.

"Loser's Bar? I don't know anything about that."

"Holly said she met up with someone named Sharla, who works for Tommy Kahn. The woman was in line for the ladies' room, and all she would say to Holly was that she'd meet us at Loser's. A dive bar, between here and Broadway." His expression the equivalent of an eye-roll.

I thought about it. "I can only imagine Loser's is a place they can talk without worrying about being seen. Tommy Kahn would never frequent a place called Loser's."

My theory was correct. "Tommy hangs out only in high-end places," Holly said.

She and I had walked to Loser's, just north on 4th, just half a block from the symphony, while Alex took care of the car. Finding parking in downtown Nashville was always a pain, but it would be easier now to get into one of the pay lots, since people were leaving the symphony.

Loser's was packed. We were lucky to get a table when two couples left, with one of the noisy women, apparently overserved, supported by the men. We ordered beers. Not my drink, but we were not here for the beverages.

"Except—" Holly took up where she'd left off about high-end places, "Déjà Vu. Rumors are, Tommy doesn't mind hanging out in Déjà Vu."

"The gentlemen's club," I said.

"You know about it?"

"Alex mentioned it in his book but didn't write much. I can't see Alex in the company of scantily-clad women, even if it was for research." I raised my eyebrow. "Though I suspect if he'd wanted to know more, there are plenty of men who'd give him eyewitness accounts."

"Including Kyle," Holly said.

I opened my mouth. "Oh" was all that came out.

She laughed. It was good to see her laugh. She said that Barry Blake, Kyle's former employer on Music Row, used to take them to Déjà Vu. Barry, a Tommy Kahn wannabe but without the same slick veneer. Married to Felicity, who had killed him, or was an accomplice. And could have killed me. My old sorority sister, like Aurora. I felt my pulse start to race.

"Kyle said one time was enough," Holly went on. "Said it was the saddest thing. There was this one coked-up girl that he finally gave some money. She was bumping and grinding, trying everything in her playbook that usually worked with customers. Kyle was embarrassed for her. When he was leaving, she followed him and said, 'What'd you want, anyway? What'd I do wrong?' Turned out, she was only twenty and had a little girl, four years old. She said, 'This is all I know how to do, and I'm not even any good at it.'"

A young man, one more cowboy pretender trying to make it in Nashville, stepped up on the stage and started in on a Texas-swing song. Not bad. But it was hard to hear. I saw Alex at the door and got his attention. He made his way, threading through the customers who were swaying, calling for drinks, not many listening to the singer. Someone spilled beer on Alex's sleeve. He reached us, finally, looking a little like a shell-shocked soldier returning from combat.

"Weren't you supposed to meet someone?" he asked Holly. No mistaking his irritation.

Holly said, "She probably had to move her car." But she didn't sound confident.

The set seemed to take forever. The singer was already taking a break, a few songs in, when Holly perked up. "There's Sharla," she said, waving to the woman at the door. The noise all around intensified and enveloped us as the singer left the stage.

The man who was with Sharla at the symphony came in behind her and went to the bar. Bespeckled, stoop-shouldered, he looked like an older Tuck Meyer. I could imagine this was how Walt's son would look in another decade. Sharla joined us. We'd managed to save her a chair. Not an easy thing in this crowd, as other customers kept asking for it.

Her obligatory smile was weak and quick. "I can't stay long," she said.

"Thanks for coming," Holly said. Sharla darted a glance at Alex and me, and Holly said, "My mom and uncle. They know about Tommy. All of it. We can talk."

The mention of Tommy seem to jolt Sharla. I could almost see the spark. Spark of fear.

"I'm quitting, too. And I'm leaving," she said. She shook her head at the server, who was coming our way. It was a look that said more than a polite *No*. More like *Get lost!*

"Leaving… Nashville?" Holly asked.

Sharla nodded. "I'm in too deep. I let myself get drawn in, and now… Miller, that's my husband, back there at the bar, he says it's all gonna come crashing down, and Tommy will make sure I'm implicated."

Holly looked like she was having trouble getting her breath. I felt something tighten in my chest, too, thinking about what this might mean for Holly.

"Miller's wrapping up things here. He's leaving a good personal injury practice," Sharla said. "We're pretending everything's just peachy for another few days. And then we're outta here."

"Where will you go?" Holly asked. "Can you tell me?"

"Canada. Miller actually has relatives in Ontario that can help us. I probably shouldn't be more specific." She gave a twist of her lips, meant to be a smile. "Sorry to be so cryptic."

"Maybe you could talk to the DOJ. Be a whistleblower," I put in, thinking of Joshua.

"We don't trust the system," she said. She gave Holly a hard, straight on look. "But I couldn't leave without telling you. Tommy knows everything. Knows you gave information to the reporter, who, by the way, probably wasn't careful enough when he went digging for dirt on the other crooks. It's not just Tommy, you know. A banker you've probably met came in the day before the murder, and I heard them arguing. The reporter had contacted him, wanting his side of the story. Dillon Lowe. Ring a bell?"

"The lender that approved the PPP application." Holly shook her head and took a deep breath as if all of it was too heavy, too much. "I can't believe this is happening," she said.

"I didn't want to believe it." Sharla looked down at her nails. "Now I know too much. I knew when he was building low-income houses, before the pandemic. He'd accuse the owners of breach of contract, of interfering with construction. The banker, Dillon Lowe, would freeze the construction loan. The owners couldn't hang on until it was all untangled. They lost everything, and Tommy was there to sweep it up, pennies on the dollar. Of course, Dillon Lowe got his share. Lowe was hot when he came in. Hot, like, mad as hell that Tommy hadn't managed to keep everything under the radar."

She leaned forward, her voice so low I could barely hear above the noise around us. "Don't know which one did it, but one of them killed Caleb Hunter. Tommy or Dillon Lowe, or maybe they did it together. I heard them talk about how to get rid of him."

I exchanged a glance with Alex and saw the worry in his eyes, matching mine. Again, Holly looked like she could hardly breathe.

"There's more, but you don't need to know." Sharla scooted her chair back. "I have to go. Miller's not too happy that I'm talking to you."

"Sharla," I put in. "I saw a woman looking out the glass wall, when Holly and I went to her office for the last time. Do you know who she is?"

"I don't know her name. She's been around for months, comes and goes like a pesky rash. Tommy's very secretive about the women in his life. He needs to stay in Dee Dee's good graces. She has family money." Sharla stood up. "I really have to go now."

Holly reached up and squeezed her arm, whispering, "Be careful, Sharla."

I'd wanted to ask, and this was my last chance. "You said Tommy knew what Holly was doing. She thought she'd covered her tracks. How'd he find out?"

Sharla looked down. Bit her lower lip. "I figured he'd find out anyway, and maybe I could save my skin. Or buy some time. I had to throw you under the bus." She glanced up, briefly, then turned away, and her words were almost drowned out by the clamor around us.

"I'm sorry, Holly. I didn't have a choice."

Chapter 25

No one spoke as we took Woodland Street Bridge across the dark water of the Cumberland River. All of us, I suppose, thinking the same disturbing thoughts.

Passing Nissan Stadium, Alex finally broke the silence with small talk. "Do you and Kyle go to the Titans games?" he asked Holly.

"Can't afford it," she said. Her voice sounded far off, much more distant than the back seat of the car. "We watched all the games, though. Most times with Caleb."

Quiet again. I contemplated her use of the past, *watched*. No doubt they would watch football again, but like so many pivotal events in our lives, Caleb's death would always be a dividing line for Holly and Kyle. The before and the after.

Traffic picked up as we approached Five Points, where Clearview Avenue and 11th Street intersect with Woodland. Historic and eclectic, the spirited district is home to trendy cafés, antique stores, art galleries, and the likes, but tonight the bars dominated. Five Points was as lively as Lower Broad, with noisy crowds pouring out onto the streets. Alex, white-knuckled at the wheel, was leaning forward a bit, hyper-focused. Like the rest of the traffic, we were barely crawling, but already a pedestrian with a Duck Dynasty beard and Titans cap had darted in front of our car and slapped the hood.

"I should've told you how to avoid Five Points," Holly said. "I wasn't thinking."

Alex's brow was furrowed in deep concentration until we were traveling east on Woodland, passing the post office. "No harm," he said, finally. "We're in no hurry."

Alex just wasn't up to driving in situations like this, I thought. Nighttime, with craziness going on all around. I'd offered, but I wished I'd insisted.

A couple of turns and we were in Holly's neighborhood. Quiet, the streets empty.

"Do you want us to come in with you?" I asked. "We can stay till Kyle gets home if you feel… like having company." Feel anxious about being alone, I was thinking.

"Are you kidding? The guys might close down the bar."

"Kyle mentioned he wouldn't be late," I said.

"MO-ther." So familiar, from her younger years. From all the girls, when they thought I was being ridiculous. Not Michael, that I remembered. I turned around and saw Holly's mock scowl. "It wouldn't be the first time I've gone to sleep before Kyle came home. Don't worry."

"I can't help thinking about what Sharla told us," I said.

"Yeah. I thought she was a friend, but she's scared—" Holly's house came into view, lights on, Kyle's car in the driveway. "Oh. Kyle's home," she said.

No mistaking the relief in her voice.

We waited until we saw Kyle let Holly in and wrap her in his arms.

Alex took the interstate around the city to the West End exit. On Harding Road, not far from Belle Meade Boulevard, I answered my phone. "Me again," said Holly. Joshua was coming to their house for brunch at eleven tomorrow, and would we join them? And maybe I could come early to help.

"The book signing is at two, you know," Alex said.

"And Willow is singing at seven."

All of that on Saturday. And the rain had started again, in earnest this time.

Still steady, Saturday morning. Creeks rising, all around Nashville, and heavy storms on the way.

Holly was mixing batter for blueberry muffins when I arrived to help in the kitchen, leaving Alex in the living room with Kyle, with mimosas that Kyle had made.

My job was watching the bacon sizzle, turning it as it browned.

"We met Joshua and Walt at the funeral home," Holly said. "Walt had something going on with his family so he couldn't come to brunch. Joshua should be here soon. He had to check out of his hotel, and he wanted to go by the police station again."

"What was the service like? I don't know much about cremations," I said.

"It wasn't really a service, and yet…" Holly looked up, a sad smile, then continued pouring batter into the muffin tin. "We went to support Joshua, to be there when the funeral director gave him the urn with Caleb's ashes. But after we'd sat, mostly quiet, for a few minutes, all at once, Walt stood up and began to speak. Like he was giving a eulogy."

She hurried to put the muffins in the oven, washed her hands, and went to get her phone from the bar. "What he was saying was so… appropriate. So sweet. I recorded it."

Walt's voice came on. "…a newspaper man for twenty-plus years. The thing about ink is, it gets on your hands and somehow, for a few of us, it gets in your heart. Every once in a great while you come across someone who has that kind of ink in their blood. Someone who has a need to tell stories about a wicked world slowly wending its way toward justice. Caleb's story ended suddenly, tragically. Only God knows why he was taken so young. But it's left to those of us who loved him to find the justice that he chased with every byline."

She clicked off her phone and laid it back down, her eyes jewel-bright.

"Beautiful," I whispered.

"And that's not all. Kyle—I couldn't believe he did this. He took his phone out and read the Twenty-Third Psalm. '*The Lord is my shepherd…*'"

"Surprises me, too," I said. Holly had stopped going to mass years ago, but she'd been raised Catholic. You don't get that out of your blood. I could testify to that, lapsed Catholic that I was. Kyle had never mentioned anything to make me think he had a religious background.

"It all felt so comforting," Holly said. "Without even thinking, I started singing "*Amazing Grace.*" And the men joined in. At the end, the funeral director was standing there with an urn. Caleb's ashes."

I turned to smile at Holly. She was smiling, too. Memory in her eyes. "I can't help thinking those few sweet moments would mean more to Caleb than a memorial service with a church full of people," I said. "All of it had to mean a lot to Joshua."

"I don't know about Joshua," she said. "He's hard to read."

Brunch, set out on the kitchen bar, looked like Holly had prepared for twice as many as the five of us, but it was late morning, all of us ready for food. Hors d'oeuvres were all that Alex, Holly, and I had eaten last night. Kyle's plate was piled high. Even Joshua, who had only picked at his food when we were at The Pancake Pantry, ate like he was hungry.

It was the first time Alex and Joshua had met. Alex was quieter than I'd expected. Maybe he was sizing Joshua up. Comparing him to Caleb, the one time they had met, when Alex was so impressed.

Kyle, scooping fruit from a big bowl, asked Joshua if he'd gone to the police station.

He nodded. "For all it was worth."

"Did you tell them that Caleb was meeting someone at the river?" I asked him. "A source for his story?"

Joshua paused, laid his fork down. "I'd already told them he was meeting someone Tuesday night. Caleb didn't say where or when, but if he thought someone had information for him, he'd meet them anytime, anyplace. The detective said, 'If we can find his computer, maybe we can get some traction on this case.'"

He looked at Holly, then Kyle. "If I knew where it was, I would tell them. No question. I would do whatever it takes to help them find my brother's killer." He picked up his fork and speared a strawberry.

All of us busied ourselves with our food.

I was probably the one who steered the conversation to earlier that morning, at the funeral home. As Holly had said, Joshua was hard to read. Nothing from him about the spontaneous outpouring of emotion from Caleb's friends.

Kyle spoke about Walt's "way with words," and then he said, "I hadn't meant to read a Scripture, but I just had this feeling Caleb would want me to do it."

"Holly said you read the Twenty-third Psalm. Perfect," I said.

He explained, "Caleb and I went to a funeral once. A woman who worked at the Y. The preacher invited people to speak, anybody who had something to say. Everybody liked her, so several people spoke, and then Caleb stood up." A grin crossed Kyle's face. "Damn if he didn't recite that Scripture. The whole thing, from memory. Later, people asked him about it, and he just said, 'I memorized the Twenty-third Psalm when I was six years old. Never forgot it.'"

"True," Joshua said, a smile trying, but never quite happening. "It was for something at church."

"Caleb had a phenomenal memory," Kyle said. "He had a playlist of hundreds of songs and knew all the words to every one. Out of the clear blue, he'd come out with something like a speech from one of Shakespeare's plays. He could remember thirty years of baseball stats."

"Back in the winter," Holly said, "January, I guess it was, it was snowing, and Caleb came in the kitchen reciting 'Stopping by Woods on a Snowy Evening.'"

The room grew silent. All of us had to know that poem. All of us had to remember those lines. "*But I have promises to keep, and miles to go before I sleep, miles to go before I sleep.*"

And I thought how Caleb, running with Mr. Frost now, couldn't have known how few miles he'd have left.

Chapter 26

Stopped at Hillsboro Road and Woodmont, on our way to Parnassus in Green Hills, I asked Alex, "What's your take on Joshua?"

Anytime I'd ever been in this part of town, traffic was heavy at this intersection. Today, in the insistent rain, we were in a line of cars that backed up almost to where we'd exited I-440, coming from East Nashville. I was driving. Alex had persuaded me to leave Holly's house well before one o'clock, and now I was thinking he'd been right about getting across the city.

He made a sound, a little thoughtful groan, a lament. "Joshua is nothing like Caleb."

"I wonder if he really appreciated how much Caleb's friends loved him," I said, moving us up a few car lengths as the distant traffic light changed.

"Joshua carries a lot of baggage," Alex said. "I could see it in his eyes, just from the short time we spent together. Growing up, he must have been the twin who was supposed to protect Caleb. As adults, they went their separate ways, but it's clear he still felt that obligation."

I told Alex what Joshua had said at The Pancake Pantry yesterday, about their names, their parents, how Joshua stayed at home to see his mother through to the end, while Caleb went to college. It all fit with Alex's assessment. And mine.

"Here's my take on Joshua, on his behavior toward Holly and Kyle," I said. "He knows they were Caleb's closest friends, closer than he and Joshua were, in recent years, and he can't forgive them for involving Caleb in something that most likely got him killed."

I glanced at Alex and saw him nod. "And yet, at the heart of things," he said, "Joshua believes *he* could have saved Caleb."

"Caleb called him about the PPP fraud, wanting his help," I said. "Joshua had to keep DOJ investigations confidential, so all he did was try to steer Caleb away from the story. But could he have done more? If he had, would Caleb still have put himself in such danger?"

We were moving, but the light would have to change at least once more before we made it through.

"Joshua must be asking himself those questions," Alex said.

"Blaming Holly and Kyle is his way of avoiding his own guilt," I said.

As we stopped, one more time, Alex said, "They'll be all right, Jordan. Holly and Kyle."

"Kyle will. But Holly is having the same trouble as Joshua. Trouble forgiving herself." I glanced at Alex. Not sure what I wanted him to say, but he simply let the silence answer for him.

Aurora took an Uber and met us at Parnassus. "You're by yourself," I remarked, as we made our way to the chairs, approximately thirty, the front rows already filled.

"Notorious said he wasn't much for books." She gave a little laugh. "Fine with me."

We sat about half way back, the first row that had empty seats on the end.

"He's at your house by himself?" I asked.

"I know what you're thinking, Jordan," she whispered. "Del knows I will absolutely refuse for him to go to hear Willow tonight if I find out he's been keeping company with Jim Beam or Jack Daniels while I'm away."

The bookstore was filling fast. A diverse group of customers that made me think of the crowd outside the Eagles Nest the day of the protest. I felt anxiety coursing through my blood. Thinking of that brick I still carried around. Trying to determine whether these were all friendly faces, or if some were here with confrontation in mind. New Nashville promoters, intent on taking down a defender of Old Nashville.

Alex had the hang of book events by now. He went around, speaking to people as they arrived, thanking them for attending. Relaxed. Watching him, I tried to relax, too.

It was a lovely bookstore, the kind that actually had more books for sale than coffee mugs and trinkets. The chairs filled, and I looked around to see a row of people standing in the back, including Holly and Kyle. Not everyone in the store was there for Alex. Customers moved around at the shelves, looking at books, some herding children who were also looking at books. A perfect pastime for a rainy afternoon. Bookstore or library, where I used to take my little ones.

Promptly at two o'clock, a young woman with a pretty smile and a pink streak in her hair stepped in front of the crowd, welcoming everyone to Parnassus, thanking us for coming out in this weather. She said, "We're so fortunate to have Professor Alexander Carlyle as our guest. His book, *Rise of the New Nashville,* has created quite a stir in our city." Applause and smiles. Alex stood and greeted what appeared to be a gracious audience, and he began to talk about writing. Completely at ease, doing what he'd done for many years. Talking, explaining, connecting with his listeners.

As he told about what had led him to write his first travel guide about Provence, my mind wandered. Provence was where I'd met Paul Broussard. Where he'd swept me off my feet. Romance in the air, but there, as always, something got in the way. The last obstacle, Paul's grown daughter, who had tried to get rid of me on the trip to Florence. Bella. Where was Bella now? I felt a stitch of guilt that I hadn't called Paul to get an update, to show some empathy for what he had to be feeling, worried about his missing daughter.

Alex had moved on to his decision to write about Nashville. "I've been coming to this city for many years. The first time, I traveled by train." *Ah*s and soft laughter rippled through the crowd. Several white-haired ladies and gents nodded. "Coming to Nashville was always like visiting an old friend. And then as the years went by, you know how it is, you begin to realize that so many of your old friends are gone." He paused to let that sink in. "I suppose I began to have that feeling, driving into the city. It's easier to drive from Atlanta, a city with its own problems, mind you, than to get to the airport, park, wait, fly into Nashville, and get transportation to wherever you're going. I keep remembering the trains. Wouldn't passenger train service in Nashville be a *real* sign of progress?" That earned him a big round of applause.

On like that for another few minutes. Alex had an easy way of drawing you into his reflections and carrying you along. He also knew when to quit, and he did, leaving his audience with a final thought. "I would never have written *Rise of the New Nashville* if I didn't care deeply about this city, about its character, and its future. Some of my observations are criticisms. Yes. But I like to think of my book as a love letter to the town that Nashville once was."

Much applause, then Alex said, "If there are questions..." and hands flew up all over the place.

He answered some easy questions, responded to a few that were not questions as much as agreement with his book. What a congenial audience, I was thinking when a man's voice sounded from behind me. I turned to see who was cutting off the college-student type Alex had just recognized.

"I moved here from California. I'm in residential real estate," the man said, stepping out into the aisle, maybe to flash his cowboy boots with their store-bought shine. "If you're selling your house, I can be your best friend. Nashville's a hot ticket. You all should just go with it. Enjoy the ride. You all act like Californians and New Yorkers are the enemy. We're not."

"You mentioned selling. True, it's a seller's market," Alex said. "Teachers, policemen, firemen can't afford to buy houses in the city where they work. But are you asking a question?"

"Yes, I do have a question," he said. "It's about the Eagles Nest. I saw the owner making a speech in front of the Parthenon this week. He made a lot of sense to me. What do you think, Professor? Should someone who owns an old building be free to do whatever he likes with it, without the kind of flack you all are giving him? Seems you all want to take away his rights."

I flinched, worried for Alex, but he thought for a moment, then said, "You should get to know the members of the Nashville Coalition for Historic Preservation. Get their perspective. I'm a big believer in talking things out." He made a gesture toward Aurora. "One of the members happens to be here today. Right here. She's a lovely woman, and I'm sure she'd talk, and listen, to you."

"Sure!" Aurora called out, looking up at the man, "but sweet mother of God. You need to learn to say y'all."

The line ran through the store to the table where Alex was signing books. I left Aurora in her seat, in case the man from California wanted to talk to her, but he was nowhere in sight when I went to find Holly and Kyle.

Kyle was buying a book. Holly was examining new titles, without much enthusiasm.

She didn't have a good look about her. No spark in her eyes. A mother knows things, and I thought if I were to run my hand across her heart, I could feel the desolation that she was trying to push into a corner. I asked if she was all right—foolish question—and she said, "Not really. I can't… can't keep from thinking… about what I've done. Maybe I just need some time."

I touched her hand. "Let the people that love you help you through this, Holly."

"Maybe I need some sunshine. God, will this rain ever be over?" Holly cast a wistful gaze toward the parking lot, where puddles were beginning to turn into a lake. Still looking out there, she said, "I thought it would help, being around Caleb's brother, but it made me feel worse. Made me feel even more responsible for getting Caleb involved. It feels… so heavy."

Remembering what Alex said, I told her, "Joshua carries some heavy baggage of his own."

I would have said more, but Kyle returned. He held up a copy of the *Nashville Voice*. "It came out late this week," he said. "I wonder what Walt wrote about Caleb."

"Let's go, Kyle," Holly said. To me, then, "Tell Uncle Alex he was great."

"See you tonight then," I said.

She nodded. "If it was anything else, I'd probably bail, but for Willow, yeah. I'll be there."

Chapter 27

Pretty eyes, pretty eyes,
Can't disguise your pretty lies.

Three major chords. Notorious said, "Nah," and tried again.

Pretty lies, pretty lies,
I can see 'em in your eyes.

Eager as a puppy-dog, Notorious had met Aurora, Alex, and me in the kitchen. Seemed he was sober. That was a good thing. His songs had kept him occupied while Aurora was away.

"Which do you like best?" he asked, repeating the lines.

I made a face, *Hm-m-m*. I could've said I liked the space between the two best.

"Oh, I can't really say," Aurora poured from the teapot, three cups. Notorious had scowled at the mention of tea. "You know, Del, you should really try to rest up before tonight."

"Rest up? Shoot. What have I done to rest up from?" His brows pulled together like a peevish child, and I couldn't keep from feeling a twinge of pity. He was used to roaming around the city all day, playing his songs and maybe even getting a smidgen of approval here and there. Making his own choices, good and bad. And now, here he was, a "kept" man, it would seem, having to take it easy on the booze so he'd be allowed to go out at night. And nobody caring about his songs.

With no answer to his question, he said, "Guess I'll go on and get myself cleaned up."

"I might take a nap," Alex said, pushing back his chair.

"I was thinking the same thing," Aurora said.

I picked up my tea. "Good idea."

In my room, I texted my children, trying to make my words cheery. Trying to not reveal how I really felt—anxious, gloomy as the weather. Finally, I dashed off a text to Paul Broussard. "I can't imagine how worried you must be about Bella. Hope you get good news very soon," I wrote. Bella was a damaged soul, but she held her father's heart.

I didn't nap. I lay on the bed for a while, listening to the crushing rain.

Wishing we could all stay in tonight. Safe from the storm. Knowing it was only supposed to get worse.

Time came to head out into the blustery night. The winds had picked up, whipping the rain against the windows so hard, it was a wonder they didn't break. I caught the end of a weather report Aurora was watching in the media room. All around Nashville, there were streets closed due to flash flooding. Severe thunderstorms moving up from the Gulf were expected to reach Middle Tennessee around midnight and continue throughout the early morning hours.

I thought of what Holly had said. If we weren't doing this for Willow, we'd cancel the night out. It was tempting to cancel anyway, but no one suggested it. At least we'd be home long before midnight.

Alex joined us, then turned suddenly, and a smile broke on his face. "Well, look at you!" Notorious came into the room. His hair, slicked back in a ponytail, looked clean. He'd trimmed his beard by an inch. The white shirt appeared new, and he carried the new denim jacket he'd told Alex about. His jeans were worn. Probably they came from the foot locker, washed, then put away. He was wearing the same heavy hiking boots, but it looked like he'd tried to clean them.

Aurora and I complimented Notorious, too, just as the oversized TV brought up Tommy Kahn's unrealistically large face. "My intentions are unchanged," he said. "First part of the week, assuming the weather's good, and it's supposed to be, we'll be bringing in the bulldozers."

The camera switched to a young reporter, bald, with a goatee. "So there you have it. Tommy Kahn hasn't changed his mind, in spite of tireless efforts by preservationists to save the building with a history many believe should qualify it as a historic landmark. It seems certain that the Eagles Nest is going down next week."

Aurora switched off the TV. "Sonofabitch," she muttered under her breath.

"The Eagles Nest going down?" Notorious said. "You mean, the wrecking ball?"

"You were at the protest, Notorious," I said. "You gave Caleb Hunter a black eye, remember? I thought you were there because you didn't want the building to be demolished. Don't you remember?"

"Oh, yeah. I remember."

I wasn't at all certain I believed him.

But then his eyes lit up. "I went to that old Eagles Nest with a woman that worked there when it was a massage parlor. Now, poor girl's on the street." He stuck his arm in a sleeve of the denim jacket. Getting hold of his thoughts, I suppose, while he wiggled into it. "Name of Chloe. Pretty name, ain't it? Chloe. I been known to curl up with her, back there in that old studio."

Aurora rolled her eyes and sighed, noisily.

"She wasn't nothing to me, Rora, just a little warm on a cold night," he said. I was surprised that he'd noticed Aurora's reaction. "Long as she brought along a bottle. That was before I got a good room to go to, at Theodora's." He blinked, maybe remembering why he didn't have the room at Theodora's anymore.

"Are you saying you and this Chloe woman went to the Eagles Nest the day of the protest to rekindle all those happy memories?" Aurora said. Almost spat it out.

"Nah! Chloe was mad cause she'd heard they were tearing it all down. She said it had been a good place for her to crash, in the cold. Better'n anything at the homeless camp, she said. I just went along. Nothin' better to do." Notorious scratched his head. "We went back there where we used to get into the old studio. Picked up some of the bricks laying around."

I took a deep breath. "You and Chloe were the ones that started throwing bricks?"

"I wouldn't say we *started* anything," he said. "I might've tossed a couple out into the crowd is all. You know how it is when you get into the spirit of things. All the yelling and such."

We were standing now in the middle of the media room, looking at each other. The more Notorious talked, the more I wanted to know.

Alex said, "Shouldn't we be leaving?"

Bad timing, Alex, I thought. Just when Notorious was telling us about the bricks. I intended to bring up the Eagles Nest again in the car, but Notorious kept talking as we made our way through the house.

"We been all through that echo chamber. That's what they call it. Echo chamber. It's like a concrete tunnel. Like a silo on its side, maybe fifty feet long. That's how they built 'em to get the reverb. Kinda spooky, the way it is now, 'cause they just closed it all up and left everything. Microphones and speakers and all kinds of drug paraphernalia. Wasn't just mixing sounds that went on down there. Some of the walls still covered with blankets and carpet. Nasty. But better'n sleeping out in the cold."

Alex had stopped and turned around at *paraphernalia*. "You are a remarkable man, Notorious," he said.

He was, when he wasn't drunk.

Notorious looked down at his boots. Embarrassed.

Bobby's was a modest stucco building between 16th and 17th. Bobby's Idle Hour Tavern, with a big plywood guitar hanging under the Welcome sign. Alex parked in the last available space, next to the building, thank goodness, and we sloshed through a sea of water, getting to the door.

A sizable crowd had already assembled in the dim bar, though it was early yet. The tables next to the stage were taken, but the one we found, big enough for six, had a good view of the stage. From the seating arrangement, it looked like Bobby's was a place where the music was actually given a priority. People actually paid attention. A whole wall was devoted to head shots of country music legends.

While we waited for Holly and Kyle to arrive, Alex filled us in on Bobby's history. "Bobby's was a big, older building, leased on 16th," he said. "Any newcomer with a guitar came through there for decades. A few years ago, the lease ran out and the bulldozers rolled in, and now there's a sleek black glass building where all those dreams are buried. But some old-timers didn't want to lose the last place to hear country music on Music Row. Investors scraped up money for this place. So here you have it, a collection of the gonna-be's and the never-will's."

"First time I been here," Notorious said, "but I played at the old Bobby's some." He kept gazing at the photos, searching the faces of the hopeful and forgotten, among the stars. Maybe thinking his face should be up there. Thinking about how he was almost somebody.

Our drinks came. "Want something to eat?" the server said. She was young, piercings all around her face, ears, nose, above one eye, and a stud in her tongue that seemed to be uncomfortable when she spoke. Her teeth didn't show an orthodontist's care, which you see with so many her age.

Aurora, Alex, and I exchanged glances. I said, "We'll wait till the others get here."

The server had just left us when Alex looked up, at the door. "There's Kyle now," he said.

I turned to see Kyle shaking the wet off of him.

I watched him cross the floor. Not his usual long-legged, ambling walk. More deliberate. Just Kyle.

And I felt something uneasy in my bones.

Chapter 28

Kyle greeted us and scraped back one of the chairs. "Is Holly here?" he said.

"We thought she'd be with you," I said.

"I guess she's taking an Uber," he said. It sounded more like a question than a statement of confidence.

Then he brightened. "Notorious! Man, I didn't expect to see you. You're looking good."

"I guess I clean up pretty good," Notorious said. His demeanor, when he wasn't drunk, was a little sheepish. Trying hard to do and say the right thing but it didn't come naturally for him. Alcohol fueled his certainty that he was smart and funny and likeable. His unease made me think of that new kid in a sixth grade school yard. So far he'd ordered one beer and was taking it slow, nursing it under Aurora's watchful eye.

"Holly *is* coming, isn't she?" Aurora said. "I know Willow's expecting her."

"Oh yeah, Holly's counting on it. I guess we got our wires crossed. I was waiting for her to text me, but she didn't, so I thought she probably decided to call an Uber." Kyle must've seen that I wasn't following, and maybe the others weren't, either.

"She went to church," he said. "To pray."

Something crumpled inside me. Nothing wrong with praying. Who couldn't use more prayer? Maybe it would give Holly some peace. But I knew her desire to go to church and pray was all tied up with the guilt that was gnawing at her, and seemed to be getting worse.

Kyle said he'd been watching a game, half asleep, and he thought Holly was taking a nap in their bedroom. She'd said she was exhausted. He didn't know she was going to the church till she was leaving, and her Uber was already pulling into the driveway.

"I told her to text me when she was finished at the church. I'd pick her up and we'd come on over here. The Cathedral's just a few blocks away."

"The Cathedral of the Incarnation," Alex said. "On West End. A beautiful church."

"Yeah, it is. We've been there for weddings," Kyle said. He motioned to the busy server who came right over and gave him a big smile, exposing her crooked teeth. He ordered a beer.

"I prob'ly should've gone to the church with her tonight," he said.

You can't ever tell about young people, their relationships, the dynamics. There was an underlying concern in Kyle's voice, but nothing alarming. Maybe he wasn't telling the whole story. Holly might have *wanted* him to go with her. Maybe they'd even argued about it, and now this was a kind of payback. Let him worry a little. Don't be too available for a while. That didn't seem like Holly, but she hadn't been herself since Caleb's death.

"Her phone could've died," Aurora said. "I forget to charge mine sometimes, and then, just when I need it…" A little gesture, a shrug and palms turned up.

Kyle nodded. "But you'd think somebody at the church would've let her use a phone."

Notorious said, "Maybe she's still praying. Sometimes what you want to say to God, what you're asking for, takes a long time. It don't seem like anybody's up there listening. Or maybe God's got a busy signal. You keep on till you feel like you're getting through or you get plumb wore out trying."

He looked down again, as if he wished he hadn't spoken.

"It's possible she's still there, still praying," I said, for his benefit.

The server came back with Kyle's beer and asked if we wanted anything else. We ordered some bar food. A few minutes later, Willow came by. All made up, her long blonde hair freshly styled. Dressed in skinny jeans and a sequined, form-fitting top. Her eyes glittering. I didn't want to think it was anything but excitement, but there was something about Willow that I couldn't put my finger on.

"Willow!" Aurora raised her arms and Willow bent down to hug her.

"Thanks for coming, everybody," she said. "Where's Holly?"

I excused myself. Kyle would repeat what he'd told us about Holly, then Aurora would orchestrate an apology from Notorious for his behavior at The Bluebird. I didn't need to be at the table for all of that. I found the small bathroom and tried to call Holly. Not expecting an answer, after what Kyle had said, I was still disappointed when I had to leave a message: "Holly, we're at Bobby's, wondering where you are. A little worried. Well, you know how I am. Indulge your mother. Let me know you're on your way here. Or if someone needs to meet you somewhere. Just call. We'll come and get you. It's such an awful night out there."

I was at the sink trying to tame my damp hair when Willow came in. She wore a pouty face. When she saw me, she said, "I don't know why my aunt insisted on bringing *him*."

"Did he apologize for crashing your performance at The Bluebird?" I asked.

"Yeah, he did. It just… messed me up." She shrugged and seemed to shake it off. "I hope Holly gets here before I go on."

"Me, too," I said.

"I've missed her. I know it's been my fault, not keeping in touch." Willow took lip gloss out of the pocket of her jeans and put it on at the mirror. "She still working for Tommy Kahn?"

The expression in her eyes was hard to read, but there was something. That glittery look had turned hard. Tommy Kahn's name was not one I expected to hear from Willow.

"She turned in her resignation this week," I said. "Do you know Tommy Kahn?"

"No," she said quickly. Maybe a little too quickly. "Saw him on TV one day, making a speech in front of the Parthenon, and it made me think of Holly. She went to work for him while we were sharing an apartment, so his name rang a bell."

It was a plausible explanation.

Pushing the lip gloss back into her pocket, she flashed a fake smile and said, "Gotta go. I'll talk to you guys later. Wish me luck."

"Break a leg," I said. And I thought of so many things broken, all around me.

A four-piece band was playing that evening. Willow was supposed to have a few minutes during their first break. "You take what you can get," she'd told us.

Their songs were a mix of country, pop, and rock, it sounded to me, but I was no authority. The drummer banged out a frenetic beat, and the lead guitarist's fingers flew up and down the frets at breakneck speed. The lyrics, hard to make out except for repetitive phrases, didn't seem to be the point, but I wasn't paying that much attention. The audience cheered and whistled after each song.

I kept checking my phone. Kyle was checking his, too. Aurora and Alex darted puzzled looks at me now and then. All I could do was shake my head and, I suppose, look helpless. I couldn't come up with a reason why Holly was not here. Notorious was antsy, drumming on the table. He motioned to the server for another beer.

After forty-five minutes that seemed to go on forever, the band went on their break, and Willow took the stage. Sitting on a high stool, playing softly on her guitar, she said, "I'm Willow Goodheart, to those of you that don't know me." She thanked the owner and the boys in the band for giving her these few minutes. "I wrote this song about a storm, and I guess tonight's a good time to play it," she said, voice so soft, you could barely hear her over the chords.

But then she leaned into the microphone and began to sing.

> *There was lightning in your eyes*
> *And I felt a storm rise in my heart.*

It was reminiscent of that night at The Bluebird. Her voice, so expressive, so full of feeling. She had a way of capturing the audience, holding them in the moment. And yet... I kept waiting for the song to climb into something thrilling. It never did.

The first song ended and the crowd was mildly appreciative, clapping, respectfully. The appreciation from our table was, predictably, the most enthusiastic. Willow went straight into another song and ended with another. Each time the applause was polite, and it might have been sufficient if it hadn't been for that night at The Bluebird. The night she experienced what it was like when the crowd loved her. This crowd liked her well enough, most of the audience. But where she'd given an unforgettable performance at The Bluebird, tonight, it was forgettable.

Her time was up. She thanked everyone, disappeared from the stage, and the noise ratcheted up for the band as they returned for another set. A drunk at the bar howled, "Now! Something I can tap my foot to!"

Aurora knew what I knew. She'd heard what I'd heard. In the same way that there's no missing greatness, there's no escaping mediocrity. I could see it in her face as she turned to the rest of us at the table and said, "Well! She was good, wasn't she? What a voice that girl has!"

Before I could say anything, and I'm not sure what I meant to say,

Notorious declared, "That voice will take her places, if she sings the right songs." He'd spoken a hard truth.

None of us commented, but I was certain we all remembered that song at The Bluebird. With a song like that, her voice could take her places. But not the songs we'd heard tonight.

After the band's first tune, Kyle stood up and reached for his wallet. "I'm gonna drive over to the Cathedral. Maybe somebody there knows something about Holly."

He didn't say she might still be there. I didn't think she would be, either.

"We'll take care of this," Alex said, waving him off. He nodded and put his wallet back.

"What time did Holly leave the house?" I asked him.

"Five minutes past six," he said. The strength of his answer made me believe he'd already been thinking about how long it had been. Two hours and then some. Not such a long time, I tried to convince myself. Except that Holly would know we were waiting, and Willow was performing, and Kyle was expecting her text. And it wasn't Holly's nature to let people down when she knew they were counting on her.

"Let's get a pizza to share," Aurora said.

We'd ordered some other bar food earlier, and no one had seemed too hungry. Pizza was a good idea, so we didn't look like campers who held a table for hours without spending money. Alex ordered another beer. Notorious might've wanted another, but his bottle wasn't quite empty yet. I tried to imagine how hard it was for him to practice restraint, after a lifetime when a dozen beers would normally be nothing to him.

Time inched by, as the band belted out songs about small town life, dirt roads, and whiskey. Though it seemed much longer, no more than a half hour passed before Kyle returned. Leaning in, so we could hear over the music, he seemed not to notice how wet he was, his clothes dripping. "The priest said there was a young woman at the altar, earlier," he whispered. "I described Holly and he remembered the color of her hair. But he couldn't say how long she stayed. No one else came to the church tonight, not that he saw."

Where *is* she? My heart pounded. We had to do something. I thought of Caleb, and as I looked into Kyle's eyes, I saw the same quiet alarm.

I said, "Let's call the police. Holly could be in real trouble."

Chapter 29

Sure, I knew. Police wouldn't put out a missing person's report on an adult after two hours. I was just grasping at straws.

"You don't *really* think something... bad... has happened to Holly," Aurora said. "Do you?" She reached for my hand and patted, her diamond rings sparkling.

In that moment, I wavered. Did it make sense to go to the worst-case scenario? Struggling with growing panic, I told myself, Don't assume the worst. There might be some perfectly innocent reason we can't locate Holly. But what possible reason? Unless Kyle wasn't being absolutely truthful, and I didn't believe that for a minute.

"I just can't imagine where she is, why we've heard nothing," I said. Sounding like a worried mother, which was exactly what I was.

"I'll call the police. It can't hurt," Kyle said, and he got up and went toward the bathroom. For a few minutes, though I tried to listen to the band's music, my mind wouldn't stop spinning a web of terrible what-if's. Finally, I glanced toward the back of the room and saw Kyle on his phone. A moment later I received a text from him.

> Police say wait 24 hrs but they took her name and description. Gonna drive around, make calls.

Looking up again, I met his gaze and we nodded at each other. Kyle slipped out the door, out again into the hammering rain.

It was an interminably long set. I nibbled on pizza. We whispered back and forth, Aurora and Alex asking if Kyle had called the police and where he was going now. Making calls would be easier from his car, without the high-decibel band in the background. Calling Holly's friends, probably. If she and Kyle had fought about something, maybe she'd go to a friend. I couldn't see it, though, couldn't see anything wrong between the two of them. Everything he had said rang true to me. I wondered if he'd thought of calling Walt. I texted, and Kyle replied, **Good idea.**

The set ended at long last, and Willow slid into what would've been Holly's chair at our table. Aurora clasped her hands in a gesture of joy. "You were fabulous, sweetheart!" she said. Willow put on a grateful smile, but her eyes said she recognized the kind lie for what it was.

She didn't look to Alex or me for confirmation. Or Notorious. "So I guess Holly didn't show," she said to no one in particular, an irritable note in her voice. "Did Kyle leave?"

"Kyle went out to look for Holly," I said. "We're worried. I'm sure she didn't just *not show*."

Willow's expression changed, her eyes suddenly full of concern. "Omigod! What are you thinking? Like, she was in an accident?"

"I guess we should call around to hospitals," I said. That wasn't what I was thinking, but what I was thinking, I hadn't said out loud.

Notorious turned up the last of his beer and when the server came by, he motioned for another, but Aurora intervened. "I'm calling an Uber for us, Del. My back's killing me." She looked up at the young woman and said, "Sorry, honey. That's all for him tonight."

"I'd like to stay here a while," I said to Alex. "If it's all right with you."

"Absolutely," he said. Neither of us believed Holly would show up here, not now, but we'd wait for Kyle and figure out our next move.

"The Uber's five minutes away," Aurora said. She and Willow

talked quietly for a moment, their heads bent toward each other.

I heard Willow say, "It means *so much* that you came."

As Aurora and Notorious stood to leave, Aurora said, "You have such a gift, Willow."

"Voice of an angel," Notorious said, "needs a good hymn," before Alex helped them to the door, into the rain, and into the Uber.

The band started up again. Willow scooted over next to me and whispered, "What do you *really* think? About Holly? I know she wouldn't just… not show. Holly's not like that."

"I think something's wrong," I said. I didn't even try to keep the anxiety out of my voice.

"How long has she been missing?"

"More than three hours now."

"Well, that's not such a long time," Willow said, but her withering look didn't inspire confidence.

Willow stayed with Alex and me, something I hadn't expected. I could tell she was genuinely concerned. She leaned in now and then to whisper, "Anything from Kyle?"

Kyle and I kept texting. Walt hadn't heard from Holly. Kyle had tried calling around to hospitals. **Hard to get info**, he texted. He'd been driving all around Music Row and West End and Lower Broad. Talked to an officer in a patrol car near the Cathedral. No luck. Called a few of Holly's friends and left a message with another. More than anything, that indicated to me the depth of his worry. If Holly was missing because of something he'd done, he might be ashamed to call her friends and admit he couldn't find her.

Kyle believed, as I had come to believe, that Holly was in trouble.

Alex and I tried to keep our whispers between songs. Bobby's was not just any honky-tonk dive bar. The audience was here to listen to the performers.

At that point in the night, we were bona fide campers; our server wasn't coming around anymore. It was our habit for Alex and me to split the check. I'd leave a generous tip, and I was sure he would, too.

My nerves were jangling by the time the set ended and the band finally said their goodbyes. Another act was coming on for the late show.

As people moved around, a drunk stumbled to the stage and began singing "Take Me Home, Country Roads." The room quieted. A hush, for a moment, while he bellowed a few more lines. The microphone was turned off, but we had no trouble hearing him. His voice, full of longing, began to crack. And then a bartender came around, touched him on the arm, and led him away.

I blinked back tears that had been welling up behind my eyes all night.

Would Holly ever find her way home?

I didn't feel bad keeping the table a little longer, during the lull between performances, because the crowd was thin. Not at all what I figured it would be on a clear, starry night. Sane people were staying at home tonight.

"Are you still waiting for Kyle?" Willow said.

"I guess so," I said, looking to Alex.

Palms up, Alex said, "I'm not sure what we can do here."

Or anywhere, I thought.

"I wonder if Kyle knows how to get in touch with Sharla," I said and began to text him.

"Who's Sharla?" Willow asked.

I suppose it was the anguish in her face and the helplessness I felt that made me say more than I might have, otherwise. "Sharla works for Tommy Kahn. She and Holly both know too much about him and his business. Sharla's quitting, too. She's leaving town."

"Omigod! You think Holly's missing because… you don't think Tommy Kahn has done something to her, do you?"

Alex tried to reign me in. "I think what Jordan is suggesting is that Holly could have been in touch with Sharla." But Alex had been at Loser's with us. He'd seen the fear thrumming through that young woman. He added, "Not a bad idea to talk to her, though, if Kyle knows how to contact her."

"Kyle's texting now," I said, looking down at my phone. "No clue how to reach Sharla except at office Monday," I read. "Don't know what else to do. Going home to wait. You should go. We can keep in touch."

Just go to Aurora's and wait? My throat tightened. How could we just give up?

"He's right, Jordan," Alex said. He got the server's attention and called for the check.

"I suppose Holly might've gone home," I said. Wishful thinking. Just musing, really. In any case, we couldn't sit here all night.

Willow said, "If there was anything I could do… but I don't… I just…"

"I know," I said, touching her arm, giving a squeeze. I didn't have words, either, for my helplessness. "You can't do anything. Unless Holly happens to get in touch with you. You'd let us know. But I'm not expecting that."

"No," Willow said. "I don't think she'd call me if she needed something. I haven't been a very good friend."

"Do you mind driving?" I asked Alex, before we made a run for the car. "I've thought of someone I can call." It was a long shot, but it was something. I didn't know what else to do.

By the time I found the card with the number on the back, we were moving down West End like an ocean liner pushing through the water. The traffic lights were out, some dark, some blinking. I was surprised the road wasn't closed. As we passed the Cathedral of the Incarnation, I whispered once more, "*Please, God.*"

The voice that answered my call sounded like gravel, and I knew I'd pulled him from a deep sleep.

"Detective Slater?" I said. He grunted. "This is Jordan Mayfair. I apologize for waking you."

"You have some new information?" he said, his voice suddenly clearer.

"This is not about Odelle Wright or the Eagles Nest. And I know you're off duty," I said. "But I need your help."

Chapter 30

Aurora was a welcome sight, holding the door open, as Alex and I hurried through the blowing rain. She didn't ask if we had news about Holly. Our faces must have told her we didn't.

Inside, we both came out of our shoes, our feet soaked.

Aurora's face showed the strain of her back ache, as she made her way to the kitchen, leaning forward on her quad. But she had prepared a tray of sandwiches, along with coffee, caffeinated and decaf, a bowl of grapes, apple slices, and a plate of chocolate chip cookies. She'd also set out a bottle of Courvoisier and a couple of brandy snifters.

"Yazda must have been here," I said.

Aurora smiled. "You hurt my feelings, Jordan. I'm not *totally* helpless in the kitchen."

Alex went straight for the brandy.

I wasn't hungry, but I took a cookie and poured a cup of decaf.

From the sunroom came Notorious's strumming and humming. Surprising that he wasn't in the kitchen, but maybe he needed time by himself. Going to Bobby's must have triggered memories. Shined a light on the reality of his shattered dreams. And if he didn't use alcohol to keep all of that from hurting so much, he could only retreat into his music.

"Speaking of Yazda. She's a jewel," Aurora said. "I called her. She was awake, waiting up for her husband to come in off his shift. He's a night watchman at some factory. I told her about Holly. I knew we'd need food in the morning... unless, of course, things change before then."

It made me think of other times people gathered around food, waiting. Waiting in the kitchen while someone was dying. Or after a death. A visitation. A wake. Waiting for it all to be over. Something knotted inside me. I laid the cookie on my napkin, my stomach churning.

"You always think of the little things," I said.

"Food is no small thing!" Aurora gave me a bright smile. "That's all I can do, provide a gathering place, and food. I have to do something."

I put my arms around Aurora and held on for a minute. Like we were in college again, and something had happened that seemed like the end of the world, as it did, at least every semester. The world had never ended with any of it, though. The world hadn't even turned upside down. Not then. Would I be so fortunate now?

The doorbell rang, and I remembered Aurora didn't know the detective was coming over. Heading toward the door, I called back, reminding her that Detective Slater had been at the hospital, wanting to see Odelle. "He said he could help us." Actually, he said he'd try.

Since my call dragged him out of bed, I expected him to look a little disheveled, like Columbo. But he looked and smelled like he had showered, and his salt-and-pepper hair was combed. He wore khakis, button-down shirt and jacket, not rumpled at all. He'd even taken time to shave. I wondered if he kept an electric razor in his car to use while driving to work a case. But for the first time I noticed the furrow in his brow that looked like it had become permanent, over the years. And there was something about him, an air of perpetual disappointment about the world around him.

Without any niceties, he said, "I made some calls on the way over. No reports of anybody like your daughter at area hospitals."

He didn't mention the UGA fight song that surprised everyone else who rang the doorbell and caused them to smile. No smiling tonight.

I introduced Aurora and Alex, and he nodded as we made room for him at the table. Aurora offered food. He said, "Maybe later," and directed his gaze at me. "So now, let's just talk. You have some ideas about what might've happened, don't you, Ms. Mayfair? Jordan."

When I called him, figuring the detective's mind would fly to domestic issues, first thing, I had told him I was certain Kyle knew nothing about Holly's whereabouts. Now I repeated everything Kyle had said about the last time he'd seen Holly and how he'd expected her to text him from the Cathedral. I added what the priest had told Kyle when he went to the church. Detective Slater made notes on his phone.

"You said she went to the church to pray. What's that all about?" he said. "Is that something she does, routinely? Is she a church goer?"

I shook my head. "Caleb Hunter, you probably know he was the reporter whose body was found in the river this week, Caleb was a close friend of hers." I added, emphatically, "Kyle's friend, too, his best friend. Both Holly and Kyle are torn up about his death."

"I'll talk to Kyle. Boyfriend, right? Or fiancé? I'll need his number."

"Serious boyfriend." I checked my phone and provided his number.

The detective looked at me, a look that waited for something else? And, yes, there was more. I had to lay all the cards on the table if I thought this off-duty detective could do anything for us. I let it all spill out, how Holly had fed information to Caleb for a big story he was writing about Tommy Kahn's PPP scheme. Caleb might've been murdered because of that story.

"So she was a whistleblower," he said, "and she felt responsible for what happened to Caleb Hunter?"

"That's about it," I said.

Aurora didn't know any of this. Well, now she did. The shock on her face would've made me laugh under other circumstances. I knew what she and Alex were both thinking. How did a nice girl like Holly get herself mixed up in some covert operation? I didn't care that I'd told everything. Not anymore. I just needed to find my daughter.

"You think Tommy Kahn has something to do with Holly's disappearance?" Detective Slater gave me a piercing look. "And he's involved in that reporter's murder? Because, I've gotta say, Jordan—" he sounded a little uncomfortable using my name—"guys that commit white-collar crimes are usually not murderers. Not even violent, usually. Corrupt? Yes. But they pay hefty fines, may even serve some time in a country club prison. But a financial crime, it's just a stumble. That's happening all over the country with those fraud cases. It's a shame, but what I'm saying is, would a guy like Kahn risk a murder charge or a kidnapping charge?"

He shook his head slowly, answering his own question. "It's a long shot," he said, and something sank in me like a life raft with a hole in it. If not Kahn's doing, I had no other theories.

The detective kept probing. Good at his job, I could tell, because I wound up telling him everything. Almost everything. About the woman I saw at Tommy Kahn's office who was probably the same woman who posed as a meter maid at Holly's house. About Sharla, who said she was leaving town because she was afraid. About the documents that I hid in my purse that last day at Holly's office, and how she said, "He knows," after our close call with Tommy Kahn.

I held back one piece of information that could've related. Walt had Caleb's computer and his password. Actually, two pieces of information. I didn't mention the brick I was carrying around, either. That couldn't possibly have had anything to do with Holly's disappearance.

Around eleven-thirty, Detective Slater put his phone away. He said, "There's not much more we can do tonight. I'll make a few inquiries, get a few winks before daylight and start again—"

A sudden burst of wind blew a branch against the window and the lights flickered. "Oh, Lord!" Aurora cried. "What an awful night!"

"—in the morning, after the storm has passed," the detective said, standing.

"Holly is out there in that storm. I can feel it," I said, pushing out of my chair. "I know about the twenty-four hour thing, and it's just been… not quite six hours, but don't you have enough to go on? Don't you see that Holly didn't just walk away?" I said, my voice rising.

His expression was sympathetic, but I knew he didn't really understand the urgency. He didn't know Holly. She would never just *not show.*

I walked through the house with him. "Maybe you can beat the worst of it," I said, as I opened the door, and he braced himself to go out in the fierce rain.

And then he said, "Get some rest, if you can. For tomorrow."

And it made me think that he *did* know something awful had happened to Holly. The worst was yet to come.

I didn't rest. How could I? A mother knows things, and I knew something was terribly wrong, whatever was keeping Holly from communicating with us. *Someone has taken her.* I hadn't said those exact words out loud, but they echoed in my head. *Someone has taken her.*

I showered, changed into sweatpants and a T-shirt, comfortable clothes I could wear out, should I be called on to go somewhere quickly.

Waiting is excruciating, and waiting alone is worst of all. I climbed onto my bed, then, shivering for no good reason, scrambled under the covers. I didn't switch off the lamp beside my bed. The dark was too terrifying. I had to stay awake, be alert.

I called Kyle.

"Hey, you know anything?" he answered.

"No. Do you?"

"No. A detective called me. Slater."

"He's someone I met this week when I was visiting Odelle Wright. He's off-duty this weekend, willing to help, unofficially, since *officially*, the police won't look for Holly for twenty-four hours."

"Yeah, maybe he can light a fire," Kyle said. "But he wasted his time with questions about Holly and me, whether anything was wrong between us. No. But I guess he had to ask."

"Every couple quarrels sometimes," I said. I remembered their disagreement about Notorious, when Kyle was going to see him at the police station, but that was nothing, really.

"I can tell you this," Kyle said. "If Holly and I had a fight, she wouldn't just slither away to some dark corner. She's not like that. She'd raise holy hell. You oughta know, Jordan."

"I do," I said. "I believe you."

The wind, already loud, began to howl with a force that made me wonder about a tornado. Tornados weren't in the forecast, but thunderstorms and straight-line winds could be devastating, too.

I thought of the homeless camp, the flimsy tents that gusts like this could take down.

A thunderclap that sounded like an explosion shook the house.

"Damn! I heard that!" Kyle said.

It was not a safe thing to do, but I couldn't keep from looking. I climbed out of bed, pulled back the drapery, and peered out into a night I would never forget. The thunder rolled, and lightning bolts cut across the sky, illuminating trees bowed over in the driving rain, a yard strewn with branches. The wind sounded like the rush of a locomotive.

And somewhere, out there in the storm, was Holly.

Chapter 31

And it went on and on and on.
Not like so many other storms that gradually build to a crescendo, do their damage, and pass on. Not this chain of never-ending thunderstorms.

Over and over, strikes of lightning with thunder that clashed like cymbals, all of it at once, the storm *right over us,* a roar that kept accelerating until... the deafening noises began to weaken, a gradual retreat of sounds except the battering rain... and then... gathering once more. And the whole thing started all over again.

On and on and on.

I closed my eyes and tried to pray. *Please, God, let her be safe and dry. And not afraid.*

Over and over, the same silent prayer echoed in my head, and my faith rose up against the storm. A mother's faith, trying to beat back the doubt. Which would quit first, and which would prevail, the storms or my prayers? Through the clamor of the pounding rain and the violent winds, through lightning flashing like strobe lights and thunder crashing, through my paralyzing fear.

It went on and on and on.

A memory, still raw after nearly twenty years, found its way into my fear for Holly. Michael was a toddler, two-and-a-half. He and

Catherine, his twin, both probably too young to be left in the back yard with just their sisters, but I was watching from the kitchen window. The phone rang, my brother, something about work, and I let my attention turn from the back yard, just for a minute.

All of them playing happily. My husband, their father, dead just a few months. Life was not easy. But sometimes it would be like it was that morning, no fussing, all of them playing, and my heart would take the first few tentative steps, trying to remember its way to happiness. Holly would've been eight, Claire seven, Julie five. Holly and Claire, both so responsible. On this day Claire was doing cartwheels, showing off for Julie. Holly was pushing her toddler sister in the swing. Michael was playing with the neighbor's dog, a gentle, though energetic, Cocker Spaniel named Patience.

It was a cloudy day, and then, suddenly, one of those summer rains. The skies opened up, a downpour that came without warning. I told my brother, "Got to get the kids inside!"

The rain had sent them running to the house. All the girls.

"Where's Michael?" I called out.

They seemed to bump up against each other at the back door. I ran outside, shouting, "Michael? Where are you?" I went to one corner, then the other, calling, "Michael? Michael!"

Claire had come back outside to help. Like me, she was drenched in the rain. I faced her, met her anxious eyes, and scolded, "Weren't you watching him?"

Something in her seemed to turn to stone.

But I couldn't worry about that. In a panic, I ran around the house, into the front yard, looked down the street. I went to the neighbor's house. The dog's owner, a SCAD professor named Cecilia, wasn't at home. I knew Patience wasn't allowed to run lose. She'd gotten out of the house somehow. I should've known, when I saw Michael playing with her.

I went all around the neighborhood, begging other neighbors for help, and they dropped whatever they were doing. One of them, an older man, said, "Have you called the police yet? You know there are bad people out there."

I didn't need to hear that, or maybe I did. "Please!" I said. "Can you call 9-1-1?" I had left my phone in my kitchen.

Because Michael was two-and-a-half, the response of the police was immediate. A patrol car pulled up to my yard in about three minutes.

But as I hurried to meet the officers, I heard Holly's frantic voice. She was sprinting across the yard, holding my phone, shouting, "Mom! Mom! They found Michael!"

The story could've ended tragically, but my silent prayers were answered.

The call was from Cecelia, at SCAD. Someone in Forsyth Park had found Patience and Michael and realized there was no adult with them. Boy and dog had made their way across Abercorn and Drayton, two busy streets. Cecelia's number was on the dog tag.

Somehow Patience had slipped outside when Cecelia had left to go to work that morning.

They were safe.

Terror still coursed down my spine when I remembered the feeling. The feeling of a lost child.

And even though Holly was an adult, the same terror gripped me now.

The storms went on and on and on.

Another hour of the same, except, as the night crawled on, there seemed to be more time between each chain of thunderstorms. Even as the rain kept pummeling the roof, I convinced myself that the storms were letting up. And I convinced myself that I should go out to look for Holly.

I knocked on Alex's bedroom door and was not surprised that he answered promptly.

"Any word?" Alarm in his eyes and his voice as he opened the door for me.

"I haven't heard anything."

Alex's robe looked like a 1940s dressing gown that Cary Grant might've worn at breakfast with Doris Day. "Come in," he said. A book lay open on the desk beside his bed, a bed that did not look slept in.

"I'm guessing you haven't slept, either," I said.

"Not at all."

"Do you think Tommy Kahn is behind all of this?" I asked.

Alex ran his fingers through his hair, some of it standing up, I suppose, from doing just that. Like a yard gnome. But nothing funny about the look tonight.

"The detective made a good point, Jordan. Kahn may be rotten to the core, but kidnapping is quite another thing."

"I suppose that should give me some consolation," I said. "But who, then? What about the woman who posed as a meter maid, the one at Tommy Kahn's office?"

Alex held up a forefinger. "We don't know for sure that's the same woman."

I rubbed my face, closed my eyes, and thought some more. "I read in the *Voice* about an attempted kidnapping on Lower Broad by sex traffickers. Could this be something like that? Holly's a beautiful young woman."

"Human traffickers, abducting someone from a church? It's possible, but…"

"We know she was at the Cathedral," I interrupted. "The priest saw her. Something happened while she was inside the church or while she was outside waiting for the Uber. She was *taken*." It was the first time I had said that word.

"She wouldn't have waited outside in the rain," Alex said.

"Is there any way to check, to see if an Uber driver has a record of her call?"

"There might be, but I wouldn't know how."

"Alex! Stop *doing* that! I don't know if anything I'm saying makes sense, but I have to try to think of *something!*" I cried. "I can't just sit around and not even *try* to come up with an answer!"

My outburst had landed hard on him, I could see. He took a deep breath, and what I saw in his eyes was not alarm as much as sorrow. "I've become an old man, Jordan. I feel so powerless," he said, finally. "So useless. Useless to Holly. Useless to you." He blinked, and his voice began to grow more resolute. "Yes, I expect Detective Slater can check about the Uber. Police track down taxis all the time. And he can find the woman in Kahn's office. Tommy Kahn will know who she is. I don't know whether she's the woman who posed as a meter maid, or whether the meter maid had bad intentions, but I think the detective will agree to follow up with Kahn. We can go over all of this with him in the morning."

In the morning. Nothing was happening until morning. And then it would still be hours before police would consider Holly a missing person and put their resources into a search. But would that be too late?

I stood up. "Alex, I need the car keys."

"Jordan!" he gasped. "You can't go out in this storm!"

"Yes, I can. I have to do *something*."

He reached for my arm. Not just a reassuring squeeze. I could feel he wanted to hold me back. "You're not thinking clearly, Jordan. Where would you even *begin* to look?"

The car keys lay on the desk, beside his wallet and his book.

I pulled away, as another line of thunderstorms moved in. "At the last place Holly was seen," I said, as I reached for the keys. "The Cathedral."

Chapter 32

Only one driver was brave enough or foolish enough to be out on Belle Meade Boulevard. The Boulevard was passable. I couldn't have met a car, for all the water coming up on the sides, but I didn't have to meet anyone. The Boulevard was four lanes, with a grassy median, teeming with flowers that the rain was beating down.

Harding Road was in worse shape, the street closed around Belle Meade Plaza. A police cruiser with blue flashing lights was parked next to orange and white barriers, blocking Harding. I had to turn at Lynwood Boulevard. I imagined the policeman was cursing the idiot who was driving in this weather.

All through Belle Meade, the streets had rivers flowing on the side. I was able to find a path in the middle, to straddle the center line, and no one else was challenging me for that lane. My wipers were barely keeping up with the insistent rain.

Slow-going on Estes, Woodmont, down to Bowling, and finally I was back on Harding. Or West End. I never knew where the name changed. Traffic lights swaying, blinking, some dark, but no traffic. I couldn't have said what, exactly, I expected to find, out here, tonight. Certainly Holly would not be walking along the street. All I knew was that the Cathedral was the last place where anyone had seen her. That's where I had to go.

I met an ambulance, its siren shrieking even through streets that were clear except for me. I passed the tall dorms of Vanderbilt

University, windows lit up. College students staying in on a Saturday night. Better judgment than mine.

Not far from the Cathedral now.

The rain and wind picked up, announcing more thunder and lightning. The downtown skyline barely visible as the windshield wipers made an arc, clearing a space for just a moment.

And then, something I could scarcely believe.

Directly in front of me, above downtown Nashville, a sudden flash, the largest bolt of lightning I had ever seen. The street seemed to shake. Before my eyes, like a scene from a movie played in slow motion, a building began to fall.

My scream was louder than a siren as I watched it happen. A high-rise collapsing like a house of cards. It was all over before I could wrap my mind around it.

I pulled off the road, fortunate to find a place on an incline, where the water was still flowing instead of pooled on the side. The building that rose above downtown Nashville just moments ago was no longer part of the skyline. The latest creation of New Nashville, simply… simply gone. I could almost persuade myself that it was a mirage, a figment of my imagination. Of my fear. My heart raced, as if I'd been sprinting. I waited, put my head down on my steering wheel. A minute later, I knew it wasn't a dream. New sounds began to rise and gather into the noise of the storm, sounding like dozens of sirens heading into the center of Nashville.

For a moment, I thought I wouldn't be able to drive. I was trembling, caught in a nightmare. I might've given up, turned, and headed back to safety had I not been so close to the Cathedral. What I'd seen had shaken me, but my thoughts turned again to Holly.

No, I would not give up.

I pulled out into the street again, and minutes later, the dark church came into view.

There was too much water to park in front. I turned at the corner and then into the empty lot behind the Rectory. Water, yes, but not high enough to keep me from parking.

Looking up at the bell tower, I considered, for the first time, what I could do here. Go to the Rectory and beat on the door until I roused the priest who'd seen Holly? And what could he tell me that he hadn't told Kyle? For the first time since I'd made up my mind to head into the storm, I had the sinking feeling that I was a fool on a fool's errand.

As I sat in the car, the storm all around me, I thought I saw, even in this dark night, a light from the Rectory. A pale light, but enough. Someone was awake. It seemed like a sign. Something telling me that a knock on the door of the Rectory would not be unwelcome, even at this hour.

But I didn't get that far.

I opened the car door, pushing against the heavy rain, and stepped out. One foot into water that nearly covered my shoe, then the other. A few quick steps, and I felt something underfoot that made me stop. In the water lay a curl of rosary beads.

This was a Catholic church. A rosary was not entirely remarkable. But even before I picked it up, I knew.

Something can make a young woman reach for her rosary, even if she hasn't touched it in years.

On the back of the center silver medallion was the name I'd had engraved for Holly's confirmation when she was thirteen years old.

I texted Alex. **On my way back.**

He texted back. **Thank God.**

Letting me in Aurora's front door, he looked at me as if he was seeing a drowned kitten that might not survive. I handed him the rosary.

His face flooded with dread. "Where?" he whispered.

I told him. The rosary only confirmed what I'd known in my

heart, but maybe it would convince the police that Holly was taken.

"You should get into some dry clothes," Alex said.

"After I make a couple of calls," I said.

"You've been out in this storm?" The detective's response was generally the same as Kyle's, though Kyle had gone on scolding, with no shortage of swearing. Detective Slater might've been shaking his head as he listened to my frantic voice. A deep sigh came across the line. "So you found a rosary. You think it's Holly's."

"I *know* it's Holly's. Her confirmation name is engraved on the medallion! I gave it to her when she was thirteen!"

I was shouting, but his voice was calm. "All right. Yeah, sounds like she may be at risk. I'll do what I can to move things along."

"Will police get on it immediately?"

"As soon as possible, Jordan, but you have to know what kind of night it is," he said. "You've been out there."

"Yes. And Holly's still out there, too," I said.

"I'm aware." There was a note in his voice that struck me as kind. After a pause, he said, "The storm took a building down in the Gulch. Police are all over downtown. Rescuers are getting people out of their houses, all over the city. Lots going on. I'm not saying Missing Persons won't take Holly's disappearance seriously, Jordan. Just that tonight the thin blue line is stretched even thinner here."

I let that sink in. *Here.*

"You're at the police station, aren't you?"

"I am. Everybody that's available is on the job. But I promise, I'm not forgetting about Holly."

A hot shower eased some of the tension in my arms and back. I dried my hair and put on clean dry sweatpants and T-shirt.

All at once, I realized that I hadn't heard thunder in a while. The only sound I was hearing was a soft pulse of rain that felt almost comforting.

The storms had finally passed.

They always do. But the trouble they leave behind was just beginning.

I listened to the sirens and imagined the rescue efforts in progress around the city. Houses flooded. Fallen trees that had crushed roofs and blocked streets. Cars swept into ditches or, God forbid, into creeks, by flash flooding.

I climbed onto my bed. Just to let my body rest. Clutching my phone in one hand and Holly's rosary in the other.

Like other Catholic children, Holly chose a confirmation name, the name of a saint, when she was confirmed at thirteen. From the time she could read, Holly was enamored with Joan of Arc because she was brave. Now, as I touched the medallion, with the word *Joan* on the back, I whispered, "*Stay brave, Holly.*"

Sirens kept wailing. On and on and on. Just like my prayers.

Chapter 33

Everything's always worse in the dark hours before dawn. At 3:42, I opened my eyes.

And listened. To the silence. The sirens had gone quiet.

I must have dozed. How was that possible?

More than nine hours now since Holly left her house.

I needed coffee. No more dozing off. I couldn't have explained why I believed I had to stay awake. For Holly. Something told me that wherever she was, she wasn't sleeping, and I knew if I closed my eyes and surrendered myself to sleep, something terrible would happen.

It made no sense, but a mother's worry is not a thing of reason. There's no battering down the possibilities that creep from your worst imaginings, into what is likely.

On my way down to the kitchen, I heard what sounded like a distant siren. It came from the media room. I saw a light and went toward it, expecting to see Aurora.

It was Notorious, reclining in her chair.

He jumped and gave a little grunt when he saw me. He punched the remote, and the chair straightened up. "Just watching a little TV," he said, as if I'd caught him in a nefarious activity.

I put my finger to my lips. "We don't need to wake up Aurora," I whispered.

"I was trying to keep it quiet."

"I know you were."

He turned the volume down even more, so low I could barely hear the voiceover, as the cameras panned over a strip of houses that looked like they were sitting in the middle of a lake.

"O-o-o-oh no." I had no other words. Hearing about it was not the same as seeing it.

"They say as many as 2,000 houses flooded, just like that," he said. "All over the place. Bellevue, Hickory Hollow, Joelton, I forget where else, and 23,000 without power. We got lucky here, I guess. Funny how Belle Meade is always lucky."

"What about deaths?"

"Haven't heard of any. I guess that's kind of a miracle."

The camera had captured the rescue of a family, through the blur of rain. Woman grasping a baby in her arms. Man with a little girl in pajamas riding on his back, while he helped a bent old woman with her cat climb into a boat.

For an instant, the images took my mind away from Holly. Now everything came back to me. Bad enough that Holly was missing. Worse on a night like this. But I wanted to believe in miracles.

"You won't believe what happened downtown," Notorious said. "One of them steel and glass buildings under construction fell down."

I believed it. I didn't tell him I was a witness.

"Sixteen stories. Toppled right over I guess. Steel beams and all. Good thing they'd just started up with the glass, but what they'd put up already flew everywhere."

What kind of winds would it take to make a building like that collapse? A tornado, maybe, but this wasn't a tornado. Was it simply that the building had weak bones?

I sat down in the wing-back chair across from the recliner and watched with Notorious. All the wreckage I'd anticipated. And houses sitting in lakes that I hadn't even imagined.

After a while, the news report returned to downtown, to the construction site where the building fell. Sheets of glass had flown like missiles, causing extensive damage to a nearby high-rise, a condominium complex. Residents were evacuated to at least a dozen hotels. Because the hotel occupancy rate was so high in the downtown area, the reporter said, some of the residents were still on the sidewalk, blankets around their shoulders like refugees, waiting to be taken to hotels around Opryland and the airport.

The building collapsed, over and over again, courtesy of someone from a nearby high-rise who happened to be getting a video of the storm.

"Betcha somebody was taking shortcuts with that building," Notorious said. He gave me a knowing look and shrugged. "Just sayin'."

The reporter, a bald man with a goatee that I remembered from a piece about Tommy Kahn, looked earnestly into the camera. His tone somber. He might've been talking about death and dying. In a way, maybe he was. Some families might never recover from the loss. And not just victims of the storm. Something in the city itself seemed like it was mortally wounded. Notorious had said we were lucky. Would we be lucky enough to find Holly, and soon?

My attention was fixed on the reporter's background, the gray stone building with the words Customs House inscribed in the arch over the central door, its massive clock tower rising into the dark sky. The magnificent Gothic structure on West End that had withstood over a hundred years of storms.

"Look at that. Makes me think about the old Eagles Nest," Notorious said. "Been standing through storms for near a hundred years."

"Old buildings seem to find a way to endure, even as a new one falls," I whispered.

"Betcha that old girl stood this storm tonight, too," he said. "Like she don't even know the bulldozers are about to take her down anyway."

I said, "Notorious, this may be the only time I ever ask, but I could use a song."

He nodded and went to get his guitar.

Notorious played a few plaintive chords and a melody began to rise.

> *You can't unfeel the hurt you been feeling,*
> *I can't unsay the words that brought you pain*
> *But here we are tonight next to each other,*
> *Let's just close our eyes and listen to the rain.*

I had the feeling I'd had when I heard the song he'd recorded, the one I heard at Theodora's. The poet in him, rising from the ruin of a man.

"Did you come up with that, right now?" I asked.

He gave a little shrug. "Sometimes it just comes at me. Just feels right. Sometimes nothin' I do can will ever make it feel right."

I was surprised when he laid his guitar down, as if he knew he couldn't do any better than that one, not tonight, anyway.

Once again, we witnessed the moment when the downtown building collapsed. A closer view this time. Something like a fine cloud of dust seemed to rise up from the rubble.

And then, even in the night sky, light from somewhere seemed to cut through the particles. Dust turning to shards of light, shimmering for just a moment before settling into the shadows. I asked Notorious if he saw it, too.

"Yeah. Ain't that something?"

"The death of a building," I said. "Like any death, I suppose. Dust becomes light."

Notorious grew silent for a moment, like he was listening to a voice no one else could hear.

"Sounds like a song," he whispered.

We watched the news reports for a while. Holly was never out of my mind, but this was better than lying up in my room with no distractions. Counting my troubles and forgetting my blessings.

Notorious said, "Well, I ain't doing anybody any good, watching all this misery." He stood up and took a few steps, then stopped. "I been thinking about her song."

"Willow's song?"

"That song she sang at Bobby's. The hook wasn't bad. '*Love ain't blue skies. Love's a storm.*' I could sure do something with that. The rest of it was just ordinary, you know, one of them milk-songs that lasts about ten days before they go bad. Songs that don't have an expiration date are about things you know are true. Old things, but you say 'em in a new way." He kept standing there, looking like he was puzzling over something.

"Notorious," I said, "why did you think the song she sang at The Bluebird was yours?"

That embarrassed, hangdog expression came to his eyes. "I don't even remember what it was now," he said. "Maybe it reminded me of something."

"There was a line about things that don't fade away," I said.

"*...some things will vanish but they don't fade away*," he repeated. "I might've had something like that in one of my songs. Seems familiar."

Notorious frowned, like he was trying hard to dredge up a memory. There was something painful about it, I could see. The synapses *almost*, but not quite, connecting.

He shook his head. "I can't remember. Guess it reminded me of who I used to be, before I vanished. I was drunk that night, made a fool of myself." He headed toward the door, then turned to say, "Hope they find your daughter."

The trouble was, no one was even looking.

The TV news and coffee and jitters kept me awake.

Around four-forty-five, there was noise at the kitchen door. Yazda had let herself in.

"Yazda! What are you doing here so early?" I asked.

She didn't answer immediately, just looked at me with sorrow in her eyes, and then she reached out for my hands.

"Ms. Aurora called me last night. Have you heard anything?"

"No."

She squeezed my hands hard, and held on. "I will make food," she said, "for waiting." And she went to work.

I sat down at the table with my coffee. It was a long time before we said anything else. Yazda poured the last of the coffee I'd made into a cup for herself and began making a fresh pot.

"Rihaan, my son, he ran with some bad boys. He said it was not a gang, but… it was a bad crowd. One night he didn't come home. Two nights and three days we waited, and then we got that call." She turned to face me now, haunting memories in her eyes.

"Oh, Yazda, that had to be so terrible," I said.

She raised her hands in the air and cried, "Why am I telling you these things! It's not the same with your daughter. She is a nice girl, Ms. Aurora says. She doesn't run with bad people!"

"It's all right," I said. "We're both mothers. I understand." Though I didn't believe I could ever understand the death of a child. A child of any age.

Yazda opened the refrigerator and began to take out ingredients, placing them on the granite counter. Another long silence before she spoke.

"I wanted to tell you that I know about waiting, too. Waiting for Rihaan to come home."

"What about the search for him? Did police make you wait twenty-four hours to begin?"

"He was seventeen, a high school student. Police searched, at first. But then… they said he was in a gang and was probably hiding because of gang activity. Something else had happened the night he didn't come home. They had arrested some gang members." She lowered her eyes in shame. "I don't think they searched hard after that. Someone found him, finally, with bullets in him."

"I can't imagine what you've been through," I whispered.

Yazda seemed to gather herself. "Food is necessary for those who wait. No one sleeps and the day begins early, after a night that does not end. Sometimes food is the only comfort in this life."

"Can I help?" I said. "Anything. Just keep me busy."

She smiled. "I will show you how to make *tahini.*"

First light began to streak the sky. Talking with Yazda about our families helped to pass the time. I realized my other children had no idea that Holly was missing. I would have to tell them soon, no matter what. I told Yazda about the day Michael went missing from our back yard. "I was a single mother. I felt overwhelmed. And I blamed my daughter for not watching him. She was only seven. I expected too much of her. I have never told her how sorry I am about that," I said.

Yazda was rolling out pie crusts for quiche. "You are a good person," she said. "A good mother, and you are good for Ms. Aurora. Some of her friends are not."

I remembered a conversation, earlier in the week, about her friends. Aurora had alluded to comments they made about race that made her want to scream, but she wouldn't let any of that get in the way of friendship.

"Aurora's a loyal friend," I said. "She may be too forgiving sometimes. Doesn't know where to draw a line."

"One of those women that you must know, Ms. Aurora calls a *sister.* I heard her say your name." Yazda turned to me, looked as if she was deciding whether to go on. What she saw in my eyes must have made her decision. "Yes, I heard her say, 'Jordan always judges me.' I don't know what that means. But the stories she told, how could Ms. Aurora believe her? They could not be true! I could hear the lies in her voice, myself. Ms. Aurora knew I didn't like that one.

She told me, 'Life has not been easy for her. Felicity tries to live up to her name, but she has never really known happiness.'"

I felt another storm. Lightning cutting through me.

"Felicity? Are you sure that's the name?" I managed to ask, though I didn't have to.

"Yes! I am sure," Yazda said. "It is not a name I would forget."

Chapter 34

I threw the door open. It hit the wall hard and bounced back, the noise matching my anger.

"How *could* you!" I shouted.

Aurora raised her head from her pillow, rousing from sleep. "Jordan?"

"Where is Felicity?" I said. I waited a beat, saw her reaction, and knew. Her face told me I was right. I marched to her bed. "No more lies, Aurora," I said. "Get up! I need to find Felicity."

Aurora pulled herself up in bed, reached for a big pillow. Taking too much time, precious time.

"I need to know *now!*" I said, before she was settled. "Where is Felicity?"

"Why on earth are you asking about Felicity?" she said.

"Because if I find her, I'll find Holly. And you know that." I felt impatience and fear and rage begin to gather. I wanted to shake the truth from her, but she raised her hands.

"Oh Jordan! Whatever are you talking about?"

"I know Felicity is in Nashville. She was at Tommy Kahn's office and she tried to get into Holly's house. She's been here. Yazda wouldn't lie about it." I stepped closer. "Please, Aurora, tell me, what did you say to Felicity? What did you tell her that led her to Holly?"

Aurora looked away. Not exactly an eye-roll, but disapproval. "It's hard to find help that will keep your confidences. Not that there was anything *wrong* with Felicity coming to visit me. She's an old sorority sister, or have you forgotten?"

I had not forgotten any of it. College, sorority life, the trust among sisters. And then Provence, where Felicity finally showed her true self.

"I haven't forgotten that she killed her husband and when I confronted her, she tried to kill me," I said.

Aurora shifted to give some room and patted the side of her bed. "Calm down. Sit here. Let's talk like reasonable women. Like sisters." Trying to be soothing. For a moment I wondered if she really had no idea about all that happened in Provence, that she was still seeing Felicity as she was thirty years ago. A fluttering butterfly. Aimless, and harmless. But no. If Aurora really believed in Felicity's innocence, why all the secrecy?

"Just tell me where she is," I said. "Please, Aurora. I need to find Holly. I *know* Felicity has done something to her."

Aurora kept patting the place on the bed. "You need to hear this, Jordan."

Reluctant as I was to waste any more time, I sat down. Aurora reached for a glass of water and took a drink. None of us look our best, waking up, but the kind of strain I saw in her eyes, around her mouth, added years to the face she showed the public every day.

"Felicity warned me. She told me that you'd twist the facts."

"She denied her part in killing Barry? She denied trying to kill me?"

"Yes. It wasn't like that. Barry was a scumbag," Aurora said.

"Even scumbags don't deserve to be murdered in cold blood," I said.

"It wasn't like that!"

"She confessed!" I shouted.

I heard noise in the hall. God, please don't let Notorious come in, I thought. I lowered my voice. "Felicity admitted it all to me. Barry had passed out, and she left the patio door unlocked to let a hired killer in. She said she didn't pull the trigger, but she's in no way innocent."

"The man was supposed to put a scare in Barry. Barry was cheating, you know, and also double-crossing someone, a collector who... Oh, I don't remember all the details. I just know the man who shot Barry had his own agenda—" Aurora was gesturing wildly.

"She held a gun on me, Aurora. I was there, in Provence, in the car! You have a second-hand account." I said, trying to keep my voice down, but the sound was fury, barely contained.

"Felicity told me what happened. I know she had a gun and she thought you were going to turn her in to the authorities. But think about what she did. She gave you a little bump on the head, so she could get away. She needed time to prove her innocence. Felicity *could've* killed you, but she would never, never hurt you—" Aurora paused. Maybe she hadn't heard herself. Felicity *had* hurt me. A concussion was no small thing.

"She would never hurt Holly," Aurora went on. "I don't know where you got that idea."

"I don't have time to explain," I said, getting to my feet. I pointed to her phone, lying on her night stand beside her water glass. "Give me Felicity's number. And any other information, like where she's staying. I know you have it."

Aurora crossed her arms like a petulant child.

I leaned toward her and grabbed her by the shoulders. "If anything happens to Holly, I promise, Aurora, you'll regret it!"

She shook herself free. For another moment our eyes met in sheer combat. Hostility. Determination. And then I could feel something relent in her. She reached for her phone and began to scroll through. "You're wrong about all of this, Jordan. Just talk to her. You'll realize that you're making a truly *bizarre* accusation. We were all sisters. Have you forgotten the loyalty we all felt for each other? Felicity would never do what you're saying."

I flinched, as my phone sounded. I snatched it from my pocket. A number I didn't recognize, not in my contacts, but I had to answer, just in case it was about Holly.

"Jordan," came the soft voice. "It's Willow. Can you talk?"

"Keep looking," I said to Aurora, and I hurried from her room, up the stairs.

"Have you heard something?" I asked Willow.

"No. But I was thinking... I haven't slept all night."

"Same here. What is it, Willow?" I was in my bedroom now. I closed the door.

"It's about Tommy Kahn."

I pulled back the draperies and looked out on a quiet morning. Limbs strewn all over the lawn, but now, absolute stillness.

"I'm listening," I said.

Willow's voice began to shake. "I don't really know where to start, but... I had a job at this place. A club. A kind of, well, they call it a gentlemen's club."

A stripper? Was Willow a stripper? But I wasn't going to interrupt. All that mattered was whether she knew something that could help us find Holly.

"I was a dancer," she said. An edge of shame in her voice. "I didn't do anything wrong. But it's the kind of place my aunt wouldn't approve of. I wouldn't want her to know."

"Go on," I said.

"Tommy Kahn used to come in."

I didn't ask if the place was Déjà Vu.

"I've made up my mind to concentrate on my music now. The money's not great at the club anyway, not unless you do more than dance," she said. "And I didn't do, you know, pole, lap, and all the rest. I didn't! I was more like a hostess. But I guess I know what you must be thinking of me."

"Willow, you called because you know something about Tommy

Kahn that might lead to Holly. That's what I'm thinking," I said. "That's what matters to me. All that matters."

"Well..." She let the word hang on the line for a minute. "So far my music doesn't pay the rent, so I've started helping out a woman in my neighborhood that cleans houses. Just so you know, I'm through with all that now. The dancing at that club."

Willow was right. Aurora, who would happily let her niece live with her in Belle Meade and pay her expenses, would not want to hear this. Not any of this.

"What about Tommy Kahn?" I sat on my rumpled bed, trying to control my impatience.

"I'm sorry. This is awkward."

"No, please, Willow. It's all right. Just tell me. The truth."

"Yeah, well, Tommy Kahn seemed nice enough, as far as those men go. Not like a lot of them, you know," she said. "He didn't try anything with me. Just bought drinks and looked lonely. Wanted to talk. He gave me his cell number and asked me to call him, but I never did."

How long will this take? I was wondering.

"If you need his number—"

"Yes! That'd be great, Willow. Let me get something to write on."

She gave me the number. Every little piece of information could help. Something else I could pass on to the detective.

I thanked Willow, thinking that was the end of it, but it wasn't.

"Before I quit," she said, "one night he was getting pretty wasted, and he got to talking about his business and how some of the girls at his office, he called them girls, were trying to take him down. That's what he said. Take him down. I said, 'Why don't you just fire them?' and he said, 'Better to keep an eye on them. When the time comes, they're gonna pay.'"

My blood suddenly ran cold at the thought that he was making Holly pay.

"I knew Holly worked for him and I thought about her when he talked about the 'girls,' but I figured, no, he couldn't mean Holly. Not Holly. She's so… professional. Such a straight arrow. But tonight when you said she knew too much, I kept thinking about it, and that's why I had to call."

"You did the right thing, Willow."

She kept talking.

"Something else happened," she said. "One night, I was leaving my house, waiting for an Uber to take me to work, and this woman was in my driveway. She came up on me, from out of the dark. She was just *there*." Willow sounded even more breathless. "She punched my shoulder with her finger and said, 'Get this: Tommy Kahn's taken.' I was so stunned. 'I haven't done anything,' I said, 'and you're not his wife.' Dee Dee Kahn's always in society news, so I would recognize her. Anyway, this woman said, 'Not your problem, bitch.' I don't know what she would've done if my Uber hadn't pulled up."

"Did she just walk away?" I said.

"Yes. Just disappeared into the shadows. That's really why I left Déjà Vu. Whoever that was, she was dangerous." Willow was crying softly now. "Please. You won't tell Aunt Aurora any of this, will you?"

"No," I said. I wasn't feeling any loyalty for Aurora, my sister, anymore.

Chapter 35

Aurora was still sitting up in her bed when I came back into her room and shut the door behind me. I made no effort to be quiet.

She remained silent and motionless. Reminding me of some Renaissance statue. The unyielding quality of her chin held high, lips pressed together. Her gaze fixed on the middle distance.

"Did you find it?" I asked.

For the first time, she acknowledged me. "That's the number," she said, with a little nod toward her night stand. She'd written on a note pad, large scrawly numbers, with a red pen.

I stepped up beside the bed, tore the page off the pad, and said, "Where is she?"

"I have no earthly idea."

"She didn't say where she was staying?"

"No." Aurora's cold voice matched the expression in her eyes.

I took the paper and started to go, but something wouldn't let me leave without asking. "Aurora, you're a smart woman. How could you be so naïve about Felicity?"

Her reply came quickly. "Why do *you* want to believe the worst about her? She always adored you. Always wanted your approval. You know that."

"Felicity was desperate for *everyone's* approval," I said. "Not mine any more than anyone else's."

"If you believed that, well, you were stupid," Aurora said. She finally shifted from her stone-like posture. "Felicity would've danced barefoot on hot coals for you, but you were too preoccupied."

"Preoccupied? Yes, I studied, had a job in the Dean's Office, spent a lot of nights working in the Architecture Building," I said, hearing the cold in my voice, too. "So maybe I was preoccupied. Weren't you? You sang in a band and kept up a 4.0. And Felicity was not the poor, pitiful soul you seem to think she was. She was beautiful, rich, stylish. Life of the party. The frat boys couldn't get enough of her."

"But *you* were her measuring stick," Aurora said, a new note in her words that told me she actually did believe it.

I shook my head, trying to clear my brain of everything except Holly. "I don't give a damn about all of that, Aurora!" I said, storming across the room. "This stroll down memory lane will have to wait. I need to find out what Felicity has done with my daughter!"

There was no sun. Just a shift of dark to early morning light.

I stood at the window of my bedroom, looking out on all the wreckage from the night before. A large oak near the street had split, one huge limb barely missing electrical wires. Notorious had said we were lucky. What I would give to be lucky now, to find Holly.

My hands trembled as I punched in the number Aurora had provided. She won't answer, I told myself. It can't be this easy. She won't answer.

But she did.

A fuzzy, sleepy hello. Unmistakable Felicity.

"It's me," I said. I would recognize her voice anywhere. She should recognize mine. She might even be expecting this call.

"Oh." A little laugh. I couldn't tell if she was surprised or not. "A blast from the past. Good morning, Jordan."

Something I hadn't realized, or had disregarded, was that quality about Felicity, always sounding as if she was playing a role. Or maybe I *had* known all along. Maybe that was why, even as sorority sisters, I didn't take her as seriously as Aurora thought I should have.

I wasted no time. "Where's Holly?"

"Holly?"

"I know you know. Just tell me, Felicity. I won't try to find you if I can find Holly, if she's all right."

Another little laugh but this time, an edge of contempt. "I figured Aurora would cave. She tries. She always tried, bless her heart. But she's weak, when it counts. Not like you. Oh no. Not strong like you, Jordan," she said, in that mocking voice that was so Felicity.

"Holly hasn't done anything to you."

"Oh! Well, maybe not to *me*. But she's not innocent."

"Tommy Kahn." I hadn't meant to say it. I hurried to dismiss any chance of an argument. Time was too precious to argue with her, to rehash sorority life or what she'd done in Provence that had changed everything between us. "Please, Felicity, I don't understand what all of this is about," I said. "Just tell me how to find my daughter."

"Maybe you'll understand after tomorrow," she said, the sweetness as false as everything else about her.

"What do you mean?"

"It will all be over after tomorrow," she said.

The call ended with a click.

"Felicity!" I shouted. "Felicity!" But the line was dead.

I punched in the numbers again, whispering, "Felicity, please answer!"

But she did not.

Everything that had kept me going seemed to fall apart, with that call. I had the feeling that whatever was solid in the center of me was collapsing, like the building downtown. Either outside forces were stronger that any person should be able to withstand, or I was never as strong as I pretended to be. Not as strong as I'd believed I was. Never as strong as Felicity had imagined. Why would I be a measuring stick for anyone?

So I had a good long cry. It was not like me to weep like that, something I hadn't done since the night police woke me with the news that my husband was dead. Dr. Stuart Mayfair, coming home on a rainy night after delivering twins. Our twins, just two years old. I always thought my tears had simply dried up after that, but it wasn't so. All the tears I might've shed in the years since that night had gathered somewhere behind my eyes, or was it somewhere in the recesses of my heart? And now what held back the dam of tears had burst, and there seemed to be no end to my weeping.

But after a while, it ended. Just like the storm.

Washing my face, I thought about knocking on Alex's door, but no. Whatever I had to find within myself, he couldn't do for me. Strength was part of it. Courage, I suppose, though it never occurred to me that there was anything courageous about trying to save my daughter. It was just what a mother would do. The part that always gave me an edge was putting my mind to work. Figuring things out. Working the problem.

I climbed onto the bed and leaned against the headboard, pillows behind me. Like I'd last seen Aurora. I took Holly's rosary from the nightstand and held it, prayer-like. A priest once told me that prayer helps if you know how to fight.

The call with Felicity had not given me what I wanted. Had she given me anything at all? Even if I'd had a recording of the conversation, she didn't admit that she knew what had happened to Holly.

I was the one who mentioned Tommy Kahn. Not Felicity. Still, I was certain now that Felicity had been the woman standing at the wall of glass in his office. I was sure Tommy was involved with her, and he was likely involved in Holly's disappearance. I remembered what

Willow had said about the woman who threatened her. *Tommy Kahn's taken,* she'd said, and now Holly was taken. And Felicity was at the center of both. Police knew where to find Tommy, if not Felicity.

On the back of the paper with Felicity's number, I wrote what Felicity had said so I wouldn't forget, in case any of it was useful. *I figured Aurora would cave… Not strong like you, Jordan.* I couldn't think that was helpful, but I copied it anyway. *Maybe not to me,* when I said Holly hadn't done anything to her. *She's not innocent.* Not an admission, but it was something. Felicity had some grudge not just against me, but against Holly, too. *It will all be over after tomorrow,* she said. What did that mean?

My nerves were frazzled. Coffee might not help the jitters but could still pump caffeine into me. Keep me awake. This was no time for sleep.

On the stairs, I heard Notorious's voice, coming from the media room. Monotonous three-chord tune and lyrics that would be, and should be, lost in the airwaves.

> *Today's heartache is gonna end,*
> *Tomorrow's just around the bend.*
> *Lay down all the worry and sorrow.*
> *It will all be over, come tomorrow.*

I sank onto the stairs and put my head in my hands. Didn't think I could stand another stupid song. But I didn't have it in me to do anything about it.

The song went on and on.

Tomorrow. Something about tomorrow. Felicity had said, '*It will all be over after tomorrow.*' What would be over? Did she mean Holly would be returned? Or dead?

What was happening tomorrow?

Only one thing I could think of.

The Eagles Nest was going down.

Chapter 36

The streets were still a mess. Detours all through Belle Meade and Green Hills, where trees blocked streets or water was too deep to cross, and many other streets narrowed to one lane. No traffic, except Nashville Electric Service and Metro Water trucks. Workers in orange vests were out, making repairs to power lines and the stormwater system.

My progress was taking much too long. That was the downside.

On the upside, the sky was getting light. No rain, thunder, or lightning. The storm had passed. Still, the storm inside me had not let up.

For the first time since waiting in Bobby's for Holly to arrive, I had a feeling that I knew where she was. That each heartbeat was bringing me closer to finding her.

Just a feeling, not certainty. That was why I hadn't told Alex or called Kyle.

But assuming I could get to her, what would I find? Was she hurt? Was she alive?

My mind started going to worst case scenarios.

I had to get hold of myself, or I'd be no good to Holly in any scenario.

As I turned around on another street blocked by orange and white barriers marking high water, I seemed to hear Alex's pronouncement about how I'd lost my senses. I'd left without telling anyone where I was going. But I was much too focused on making my way through all the obstacles to the Eagles Nest. And as quickly as possible.

Tomorrow, it would be over, Felicity had said. She could mean only one thing. Tommy Kahn was sending in bulldozers tomorrow to take down the Eagles Nest. That's where Holly was. In the addition, that echo chamber, Notorious called it. I knew it in my bones.

What had I ever done to Felicity? Aurora said I hadn't paid enough attention to her. And *that* was why she wanted to punish my daughter? I felt rage boiling in me. But there was something else. Something about Tommy Kahn and how Holly was not innocent.

Was Felicity's revenge toward me, or was she trying to protect Tommy? Or both? I couldn't quite put it all together yet. But I was close.

And I was getting closer to Holly. Belmont Boulevard. Past Belmont University, on to 16th Avenue. Down to Music Row. A turn onto Edgehill, and on to the Eagles Nest.

It seemed to take forever. Then, finally, the Eagles Nest came into view.

Yes, Notorious, it looked like the old girl had withstood the storm.

I parked on the side street, as I had done before. Was that two days before? Just two days? I had lost my sense of time. Holly had been missing not even twelve hours, but it felt like an eternity.

Grabbing my purse and phone, I left the car. Again, it crossed my mind that I should call Alex, but I was so close now. So close to finding Holly. I couldn't think of anything else. My shoes sank into the soggy ground as I plodded forward. I was trying to remember what had stood out to me when I was here. It was the haphazard way that the studio was attached to the house. That was as far as I went, that day. I was too terrified of darkness to go any further. But today, everything had changed. My daughter was in that dark place. I just knew it. And that meant I had to find a way in. I had to go into the darkness.

The abandoned studio had been a refuge for the homeless. It was habitable. Not attractive, not comfortable, but a place where Holly could survive, I told myself, trying to dredge up every bit of hope I could.

It was that early morning time when the light was coming fast. Enough light for me to examine the dead spaces between the house and addition. The pieced-together places. There had been attempts to cover the gaps with plywood. Some of it rotten, some of it in good shape, where the recent owners, the ones who sold the property to Tommy Kahn, must have tried to seal up any entrance from the vagrants who'd found a warm place to crash on cold nights.

But none of it looked secure. With the sale coming about, the owners apparently hadn't done anything to it recently. I tugged on one of the plywood sheets and felt it move. As I pulled harder, an opening to the addition appeared. An opening into the dark. I dragged the section of plywood onto the sodden ground, feeling my heart speed up. Took out my phone, for the flashlight. It wasn't a tight space. I was able to access the opening by bending over, but it felt like going into a crawl space, which had always given me the heebie-jeebies. And I had managed to avoid every crawl space since the claustrophobic experience in a priest hole. I'd never gotten past being trapped in that terrifying space in Ireland.

This was once a studio, I reminded myself. Just think of it as a studio.

One more silent prayer as I took my first step inside.

"Holly!" I called out.

I heard a small noise.

"Holly? Is that you?"

I pointed the flashlight, and a rat with an impossibly long tail darted across in front of me. Yelping, I jumped back. I grabbed at my throat, where my heart was thumping with such force, it felt like it was about to fly out of my chest. While I was still taking short, shallow breaths, I felt something else on my shoe and shined the light on another horrible creature, with wild, yellow eyes, turning its head, trying to reach my ankle. The noise I made was something between a scream and a cry as I shook my foot and the hungry rat scurried away. Into the darkness where no telling how many others waited.

"Nothing you can do to stop me!" I called into the blackness.

I shuddered and steeled myself. I swished the flashlight, hoping other rats wouldn't come out of their hiding places. Moved forward. Slowly. The space was littered with bottles and cans and food wrappers, rags, a blanket, a glove. A shoe? One shoe? Under any other circumstance, the stench would've made me turn back. And the rats. But after a minute, I took a step, and another. My breathing evened out. I had to do this.

I called out again. "Holly?" My voice a little shaken this time. The possibility struck me that someone else might be hiding back here. A different kind of rat.

And then I heard the muffled cry from farther back in the darkness, the sound that was music to my heart! I stumbled down into the echo chamber, calling, "Oh God! Holly! I'm here!"

"It was Felicity. She killed Caleb."

Holly's first hoarse words, when I freed her mouth from the nasty headscarf that must have been left by one of the homeless women. It wouldn't be anything Felicity would wear. Holly turned to wipe her mouth on her shoulder, looking like she would gag. Her lips were cracked. I tried to shut out what the past twelve hours would've been.

She was tied to one of the load-bearing posts, arms behind her, wrists and ankles bound with rope. It was hard for me to think of her as my grown-up daughter. In the eerie light from my phone, she seemed smaller, younger. Helpless. Pale. Dark-circled eyes. I had to get her out of here, but I indulged myself, drawing her face and shoulders against me, holding her for one brief moment.

"You're here." Her next squeezed-out words. And I saw something else in those eyes, the courage that had kept her going during this nightmare.

"Drink this," I said, reaching into my purse for a small bottle of water. A habit of mine I developed from being on job sites. I always carried one of those short water bottles in my purse. Holly drained the water in a few gulps. I should've had the presence of mind to bring more, and I should've thought to bring a knife. In all my imaginings, why hadn't I imagined that she'd be tied up? Felicity had a knowledge of knots that surprised me. A woman full of surprises.

I dug in my purse again for lip gloss and put it on Holly's dry, swollen lips. She licked it, and I applied more. Then I began to work on getting her hands untied.

"Caleb met Felicity at the river because he thought she had information about Tommy," she said. I could tell that her throat was dry, that it hurt to talk.

"You can tell me all of it later," I said.

But she kept on. "Felicity came into the church. Just like any other parishioner, at first. I shouldn't have gone with her. She had a gun, but I could've screamed. I just went like a lamb." Holly seemed to be in a kind of daze, remembering. "I was so foolish. And so was Caleb. Felicity laughed about shooting him. So easy. 'Like a lamb,' she said."

"You wouldn't expect her to have a gun. Neither would Caleb," I said.

"I let her walk right up to me, smiling. What was I thinking?"

Holly knew Felicity, from the time when Kyle worked for Barry Blake. She knew that Felicity had fled to somewhere in Europe, that she was at best an accomplice to Barry's murder. But I had not told her that Felicity had tried to kill me. Maybe if I had, Holly would've felt danger signals the moment she recognized Felicity in the church.

"People from our past, people we used to trust… it's hard to think of them with evil intentions," I said.

Squatting beside Holly, I was having trouble getting the rope untied from her wrists. It made me want to cry to see how hard she'd struggled to get free. Trying so hard that her wrists had bled, some of the bleeding scabbed over, some of the skin still raw. Maybe I could find broken glass and use it to cut the ropes. But first I had to call for help. I picked up my phone.

"Did you ever imagine we'd be here like this, Jordan?" came the voice, out of the darkness. "Put it down."

Chapter 37

"Felicity."

The air had gone out of me.

I shielded my eyes with my hand. Felicity was shining her flashlight into our faces. It made her barely visible, the outline of her and her outstretched arm. I could tell she held a gun.

She'd managed to get in without making a sound.

Now my foolishness came back to haunt me. If only I'd made a call when I had a chance. No one knew where I was. No one knew that I'd found Holly. No one would be coming to help.

My recklessness might cost both of us our lives.

I had pulled up Kyle's number and managed to hit "Send," but he'd have no idea where I was or what the call was all about.

"I said put it down! Toss it over here." Felicity took several quick steps toward us. "Or I'll shoot. I swear I will, Jordan."

I gave a gentle lob, and my phone hit the floor. Felicity picked it up, turned it off, and threw it over my head, far back into the echo chamber. Into more blackness.

She stepped closer. Held her phone so the flashlight pointed down, making everything around us shadowy. Creepy. Perfectly fitting for where we were, for the grim prospect that we were facing. In her other hand was the gun, aimed in our direction. Was it the gun I'd seen before, in Provence? She'd held it on me, making me drive her to her getaway plane, and then used it to knock me out. Aurora actually believed she deserved credit for giving me a concussion instead of killing me. I wondered if Felicity would have any qualms about killing me this time. My throat closed at the thought of what she'd do. Not to me, but to Holly.

"The minute I said what I did about tomorrow, I knew I shouldn't have. I knew you'd figure out where to go. So smart. Always so smart." Felicity gave a scornful laugh. "And I was so right. Here you are. Trying to rescue your daughter before tomorrow. I didn't intend for it to end this way, but you gave me no choice. It would've been so much better if the building had just... come down. So much, you know, *cleaner.*"

A chill ran up my spine at the thought of bulldozers demolishing the Eagles Nest, with Holly inside. And me, now. "So what are you going to do?" I asked.

"What do you think? I can't just let you go."

"Let Holly go. Please, Felicity." I put as much feeling into my words as I could possibly dredge up, when all I wanted to do was scream at her. Pull her hair out. Punch her in the face. I couldn't remember any time in my life that I'd felt violence would be so very easy for me.

"You know I can't do that." That put-on honey-sweet voice. "Besides, I already told you, she's not innocent. She tried to get Tommy in big trouble. She thought she was getting away with stealing from the company. Yes, it was *stealing*. But she's not as smart as you, Jordan. Tommy found out what her little game was. That reporter was stupid, too, trying to sling mud on Tommy, just so he could come up with a big story. Well, we know where *that* got him."

She spoke as if Holly was not even there. It seemed she only wanted a conversation with me. Wanted to tell her side, I suppose. All she had to do, really, was shoot both of us. Was Aurora right, that she couldn't find it in herself to do that? I could only hope.

Yet, she'd killed Caleb.

My mind kept working out how to handle her. Buy time. No

one was coming for us, but if I could keep her talking, maybe… was it possible I could take her gun away? I couldn't imagine how, but maybe… All I knew to do, until some opportunity presented itself, was to talk. And listen. Keep it going. I had the feeling she'd imagined this moment for a long time.

"How in the world did you convince Caleb to meet you at the river?" I asked.

"It was easier than you'd imagine," she said. "So easy, it seemed like… like it was meant to be. I just called his cell, told him I had information, and I gave him enough, so he knew I was the real deal."

"His cell? That's remarkable. How'd you get Caleb's number?"

She kept smiling a wicked smile. "He'd given Tommy a card, with a number in ink on the back. That was when he interviewed Tommy and pretended he'd be fair in the story he was writing. 'Call me if you think of anything else.' he'd said. But no, he trashed Tommy. And we knew that was not going to be the end of it!"

"I don't understand where you fit in, Felicity," I said. "Tommy, yes, he wouldn't want to go to prison or even pay huge fines, but what was it to you?"

"Oh, Jordan, everything I've done has been for Tommy. Surely you've figured that out. I love him, and he loves me."

"Don't you know about Dee Dee?" Holly chimed in. I couldn't help being proud of her, there with her hands and feet bound, bleeding wrists and cracked lips. Still having the courage to speak up.

An expression crossed Felicity's face that made me think she'd forgotten all about Holly. "That's what is known as a *transactional* relationship. An arrangement. Dee Dee has money. But then so do I." Looking at me again, "It may surprise you to know that I was busy, those years in Europe. You know, Jordan, if you hadn't been so smart, such an *infuriating* sleuth, working out what happened to Barry, it would've changed everything. I could've come home. And we wouldn't be here right now. Like this."

"I need to sit, Felicity," I said, and I shifted from my squatting position to sitting beside Holly. My purse wedged between us. Felicity aimed the gun more directly at me, a warning, but I kept my hands in her clear view so she'd know I wasn't trying anything. I kept wondering what her game plan was, but as long as she'd keep talking, and listening, I was buying time. Someone, maybe Detective Slater, might have the same idea I'd had about the Eagles Nest, and he'd see the car on the street. I could hope.

"But while I was running, hiding out, which you forced me to do, I learned a lot about finance from Antonio DeMarco," Felicity said.

"Antonio DeMarco is a crooked collector of art, antiquities, and all things Elvis," I said, glancing at Holly. "He managed to get Felicity away from Provence after she was an accomplice in Barry's murder, before she could be arrested."

Felicity gave a manic laugh. "You do have a twisted way of looking at things. Antonio is a businessman. I invested some of his money with Tommy."

"So you and Tommy have a business relationship," I said.

"Not *just*. Is it really so hard for you to believe that a man could be smitten with me, Jordan?" Her voice edged with irritation. A response would've required more words than I had in me. Possibly she was thinking, too, about her scorecard with men. So many smitten with her, yes, but not for long. She never could seem to keep them.

"Everything was always so easy for you," she said. "You didn't even have to try."

"If it makes you feel any better, everything *wasn't* easy for me," I said.

She let that glide by without a reaction. "It's not that you were *gorgeous*. Not in college when *my* boyfriend wanted to be *your* tennis partner."

"You didn't play tennis, Felicity. If you had—"

"Not when you were a poor, young widow with a litter of children," she went on, without a pause, "and men fell all over themselves trying to be helpful, to get close to you. Even that delicious patron of the arts." She gestured with her phone, and the light did an eerie dance. "Monsieur Broussard. Wasn't that his name? He wouldn't give me the time of day, but you made his clock stop. He took you to Paris in his private plane. So romantic!"

"Is that what this is all about?" I said, unable to keep from sounding annoyed. "Revenge for something petty that I wasn't even aware of? You think I had it easier than you, and this is payback?"

She seemed to consider it. And then she said, "Honestly, Jordan, it's survival now."

In the look she gave me, I saw something that had gone way beyond green-eyed envy. Felicity was truly unhinged. Any moment she might put an end to all of this rambling. She'd spoken the truth. It *was* about survival. She had to get rid of us, for her own sake, and Tommy's.

Our survival hung by a hair. I had to do something. Think of something quickly.

"Did Tommy know you were going to kill Caleb?" I asked. "Did he put you up to it?"

"Tommy? *No!*" she said, as if that was unthinkable. "He was even... *worried*, when I told him."

"But he gave you Caleb's number. He must've known you were up to something." Keep talking, keep talking, I told myself.

"He didn't *give* it to me. He threw the card in a trash basket when he saw that horrible article, and I dug it out, later." Her voice took on a ragged edge. "I knew what had to be done, and I did it. That's all there is to it. And I'm not sorry. I'm a stronger person than I used to be."

Meaning now, she could pull the trigger, I was sure. Something she hadn't been able to do in Provence.

"I never thought you were weak, Felicity," I said.

I shifted my leg and let it touch Holly's. Thinking it might give her hope, that together, we had a chance. I felt a surge of adrenaline coursing through my veins. It was all coming to an end, and I was going to do *something*. I didn't know what yet. But *something*.

Felicity noticed my movement and raised her gun. I lifted my palms slightly, waited a moment, and breathed relief when she didn't shoot. "I promise you, Felicity, I never knew how you felt about any of those things," I said, trying a conciliatory voice. "I guess I'm not as smart as you say I am. I should've caught on."

"Don't patronize me!" she said.

Time was running out. When she'd said all that she wanted me to hear, she'd be finished with us. Her sudden frown was even more worrisome than her bravado. As if she was thinking hard about what to do next. I was thinking hard, too.

And then her phone made a sound, a text coming in. She checked it, lowering her gun for a moment. And I knew that this was the advantage I needed. An answered prayer. My last chance to save us.

As Felicity glanced down at her text, I let my hand slide closer to my purse, jammed between Holly and me. I felt the brick I'd been carrying since the day Odelle was injured.

"Does Tommy know what you planned for Holly?" I tried to sound casual, unhurried.

"I'm sick of your questions, Jordan." Felicity tried to text something with her thumb. The light from her phone zigzagged here and there, giving an instant of darkness for me to reach into my purse and grab hold of the brick. Was Tommy trying to talk her out of her murderous scheme? At this point, her state of mind being what it was, I doubted he could. She looked up, but she seemed to be thinking, not staring directly at me. She lifted her hand again, with the gun.

Felicity might shoot me. Probably would. But if I could do enough damage to her, it might give Holly more time.

Felicity shined the light back into my face. I raised my left hand, as if to shield my eyes, but it let me squirm without calling attention to my right hand, and my weapon.

With all the power I could muster in one swift movement, I hurled the brick.

The blow landed on the side of Felicity's head. Just like Odelle's. It knocked her back. She stumbled and cried out. I was on my feet before she hit the ground, leaping on her like a jungle cat, taking her all the way down on her back. Ready to fight, so unlike me, but in that moment, it felt perfectly natural. All the fight I never knew I had in me.

Screaming something in her face. For the life of me, I couldn't say what.

But Holly's screams would be with me for a long time.

I scrambled for the gun, a couple of feet away, pulled myself off of Felicity, and stood.

Pointing her gun at her heart, I thought I could pull the trigger. It would be so easy. But I heard Holly shrieking, "Mom, no! No, no! Mom, please don't!"

Felicity lay motionless. A deep gash at her temple.

"Is she dead?" Holly cried.

I didn't know.

Chapter 38

She might be dead. I didn't care.

Blood poured from the wound. Just like Odelle's.

I didn't even feel for a pulse until I'd made a call on Felicity's phone.

The miracle was, I remembered his number. I held my breath until I heard Detective Slater's impatient voice. He wouldn't recognize Felicity's number. But he answered. I made it short, and the detective was not a chatty guy, either. In a couple of minutes, he had police and two ambulances on the way.

"Two?" he'd asked.

"One for Holly. One for the woman who kidnapped her and murdered Caleb Hunter. She might be dead."

"Damn," he whispered. Then back to his normal gruffness. "Got it."

Felicity wasn't dead. I touched her neck and felt a pulse. I didn't know whether to be relieved or disappointed.

And then I went to Holly and wrapped her in my arms, best I could, with her hands still tied behind her.

She was weeping and trembling. All that she'd endured coming out in spasms. I held her for a long moment, without taking my eyes off Felicity. Keeping her gun pointed at her.

At last, Holly got her bearings and said, "You need to call Kyle, and then, can you *please* get me out of these ropes?"

I remembered a manicure kit in my purse and dug for it. My hand closed around Holly's rosary, and I pulled it out, to show her. She gave a little cry. "I dropped it in the parking lot at the Cathedral!" she whispered. "I prayed someone would find it, and I'd live to get it back."

"That's where I found it. The first indication that you'd been… taken," I said, dropping the rosary back into my purse. And I started in with the manicure scissors, trying to cut the ropes.

A couple of minutes later the sirens started blaring. Help on the way. Police and EMTs.

I was making some headway with the small scissors when Felicity started to groan.

The police, four of them, came rushing to our rescue. They found me standing over Felicity, gun pointed at her heart, and God only knows what they saw on my face.

"We'll take it from here," one of them said. "Let me have the gun." I didn't know I was frozen in place until he said, sternly, "Ma'am, give me the gun."

A female officer finished cutting the ropes that bound Holly's wrists and ankles. She had her free before the EMTs arrived. And then Slater was there. He took off his jacket and draped it around me. I hadn't realized how violently I was shaking.

"My phone," I said, nodding toward the dark echo chamber. "It's somewhere back there."

"And mine, and my purse," Holly called to him. Her voice was still raspy, but as they helped her onto a gurney, I thought she seemed in far better shape than she had any right to be.

More policemen were piling in. It was a crime scene. Surely Felicity would be charged with attempted murder. And with Caleb's murder, if Felicity's admission counted for anything.

"I threw it and hit her in the head," I said, pointing to the brick, a few feet away. "The same brick that struck Odelle. It was in my purse."

Slater frowned. "You didn't tell me you were holding back evidence."

"Guess it's a good thing I still had it with me," I said.

The EMTs took Holly out first. "Are you coming, Mom?" she asked, reaching out as I followed the gurney to the ambulance.

"I'll be there," I said, taking her hand until the EMTs moved her on. I glanced at Alex's car, parked where I'd left it, but I was relieved when Slater said he'd give me a ride to the hospital. He thought I should be checked out, too. Probably a good idea. I was still shivering, even with Slater's jacket. Feeling the full force of all that had happened.

"Keys?" he asked. "I'll have somebody follow us in your car."

I dug in my purse. "Women get a lot of hassle about taking their purses everywhere," I said, "but mine came in handy."

"Yeah, most women's purses feel like they're full of bricks, but you're the first woman I ever saw that actually carried a brick around with her," he said. I think he wanted to smile, but wouldn't.

Felicity was moving, moaning. I took a few steps toward her, strapped to the gurney and handcuffed. I was wondering what she might say to me now, but she hadn't completely come around. It was just as well that I didn't have to hear any more of her ravings. As they loaded her up, I took a long, hard look at her face, one side of it drenched in blood. It didn't look like the face of a killer. But that's what she was. Not what she used to be. Police had done the right thing, putting her in cuffs.

I tried to feel something for her, but I couldn't.

"I could've shot her," I said to Slater. "I really could have."

The havoc wreaked by the storm seemed like a distant memory.

Hard to believe, it was still early morning. Early Sunday morning. Not even time for church. The sun was bright, the sky a deep blue, spring in the air.

Kyle was already at the E.R. He had called Alex, and after a while, Alex arrived in an Uber. The E.R. was an erratic place, still spilling over from the usual Saturday night emergencies. Gunshots and broken jaws that happen, one of the nurses remarked, even during a storm. And on this Saturday night, victims of the storm had come in, as well.

Only two visitors at a time were allowed in the cubicle with Holly, one of them Kyle, who refused to leave her side. Slater spoke with her, and then a homicide detective came to get her story. All of this, Alex told me, as I was confined to another cubicle.

Slater spent a little time with me that was not necessary, but I didn't mind his company.

"You'd make a good detective," he said, adding, "Jordan."

I smiled at the thought, but he said, earnestly, "You figure things out. You put yourself out there. Bringing that woman down like that, with the brick, that took some steel."

"Only because it was my daughter," I said. "I don't think much about the law when it comes to my children."

"Mama Bear and her cubs." His scowl told me he was still annoyed that I hadn't given up the brick earlier.

"Do you think Odelle can have the brick back?" I asked. "I know she wants it."

"Why?" he said.

"I'm not sure."

He shrugged. "It's evidence now, but we'll see."

It took too long for me to get checked out, considering that there was really nothing wrong with me. The shakes had subsided, and I had no injuries. Detective Horowitz, a short, stocky, no-nonsense homicide detective spent a while questioning me. Too long. My memory was starting to go fuzzy.

Finally he said, "We'll let you know if we need you to come downtown." Fine with me.

I couldn't remember my last real meal. I was suddenly starving. Alex and I made our way to the cafeteria, where breakfast was still being served. From my tray with all that I chose from the line, you would've thought I was a refugee.

"Do you want to talk about it?" Alex said.

"Not yet," I said, through a mouthful of French toast. I washed it down with half a large glass of orange juice.

Back in the waiting room, we texted Kyle, who was still with Holly. She was getting an I.V. No surprise that she was severely dehydrated, suffering from shock. Or that she was sleeping, after the previous nightmarish night. Kyle said she hadn't seen a doctor yet. Someone had told them it would be a while. No one had attended to her wrists, and she might need another unit of saline before they let her go, but she probably wouldn't need to say overnight.

"I'd like to get out of here for a little while," I told Alex.

Alex raised his eyebrows when I said I wanted to go to the Cathedral. But he was agreeable. Two lapsed Catholics, struggling with our own disbelief. The early mass was over, the sanctuary empty except for a priest who was putting a prayer book into the back of a pew.

"Father, do you have a minute? I need to talk to you," I said, approaching him.

"We have another mass at eleven, but I have time. What can I do for you?" he said.

"I'm Jordan Mayfair. The mother of the young woman who was taken from the church last night," I said. "We found her. She's safe. She'll be all right."

He made the sign of the cross and said, "Someone came by last night to ask about her. He said she was missing. I've been praying."

"The thing is," I said, "I was the one who found her. She was kidnapped by someone I'd known for a long time. A woman I used to think was my friend, but… I could've killed her, Father."

He waited, patiently.

"I wanted to kill her. I've never felt murder in my heart before." Silence for a long moment, and then I asked, "Would you hear my confession?"

I suppose he was used to hearing all kinds of stories. His expression didn't change. Not much. Just a flinch when I mentioned Confession, as if he was thinking about it. "What did you do to her?"

"I hit her with a brick and knocked her out. And then the police came."

"And you did that to save your daughter?"

"Yes. She would've killed Holly." I swallowed. "Should I go to Confession, Father?"

He smiled at me. "You've already confessed." Tenderly, he said, "I don't see that you committed a sin, my child. I think you were being a mother. Protecting your daughter."

I thanked him, and he said, "Go in peace."

Alex was walking through the sanctuary, his hands behind his back, studying the ornate ceiling. I caught up with him. "I need a few more minutes," I said.

I went to the altar and knelt. And prayed. A moment later, Alex knelt beside me.

Chapter 39

One more stop.

From the Cathedral, we drove farther toward downtown and pulled off on a side street. It was not possible to get any closer to the Gulch, where the high-rise fell in the storm. But we could see cranes in the distance, working to pull up steel girders, trying to raise order from the rubble. Lights and emergency vehicles all around the chaotic site.

We sat in the car for a few minutes, taking it all in. Quietly.

"The New Nashville," Alex remarked, finally, with a woeful look. "You would not find me in one of those towers when the next storm rolls through."

It did seem that all the tall, thin skyscrapers rising above the city, the Twenty-first Century giants of downtown Nashville, looked frail, suddenly. Like trees in a forest, realizing the storm had taken down one of their own that should've been as sturdy as any of them. As if they had overnight lost confidence in themselves. In their own strength. In their own roots. In their ability to stand against time and storms.

"You know, Jordan, you're like Old Nashville," Alex said.

"Oh, really? Is that supposed to be a compliment?"

"It is, indeed," he said, turning to me with a smile. He pulled away from the curb. "You withstood the storm."

"Are you ready to talk about what happened?" he said, as we made our way to the hospital.

He'd asked before, but now I said, "It might help me to make sense of everything if I talked about it."

So I did. I told him everything. But when I'd finished recalling what Felicity had said and done, there at the Eagles Nest, it still didn't make sense that she should hate me so much.

"So Felicity killed Caleb?" Alex said. "She admitted it?"

"Yes. She did it for Tommy. He had nothing to do with it. That's what she said."

A long pause, and Alex raised his voice. "Jordan, you should have *never* left the house without letting me know where you were going! I know how independent you are, but, mother of God, Jordan, there's a *limit!*" All that he'd held back, coming out like this. My uncle had scolded me before, quite a few times, in fact. But this time his display of emotion shocked me.

There were no words to express how much I regretted going off on my own, but there was no apologizing for what mothers sometimes do for their children.

The tension between us hung in the air while Alex maneuvered onto West End, lined with traffic, even on a Sunday morning.

I was relieved to hear a calmer note when he spoke, after a few minutes. And I knew he had forgiven me. Forgiveness coming more quickly than I deserved.

"Aurora thought you'd gone to find Felicity, but if she knew where Felicity was, I could never get her to admit it. Probably she didn't know," he said. "We had a huge row when she said she'd simply befriended Felicity."

That made me smile. The part about the huge row.

"That's what she called it. Befriending Felicity. How appallingly naïve! Like trying to make a pet of a rattlesnake. Not realizing what Felicity's motive really was."

"That she wanted to kill me." The thought still made me shudder.

Alex looked straight ahead. His hands tightened on the steering wheel, knuckles white. "When Kyle called me and told me about you and Holly—the worst was over then and you were on your way to the hospital, but I was *furious* with Aurora!"

"As well you should've been."

"It didn't start out just about Holly, you know," he said. "And Caleb just got in the way. Mostly, it was about you. Months ago, Felicity came to Nashville to wind up her dead husband's business. She must've believed enough time had passed while she was hiding out in Europe. It was safe to come back to the States," Alex said. "She heard about my book, and the Parnassus date. That's when she first called Aurora, knowing you'd contact her when you were in town."

"She knew I wouldn't miss your event at Parnassus."

"She knew you always support me."

"Of course," I said.

"And she began filling Aurora's head with... with lies. Playing the victim."

"Laying the groundwork," I said. "Considering how she felt about me, it must've been a double-whammy to find out that my daughter was about to get her lover in trouble."

"I always thought of Felicity as flitty. Capricious. But..." He shook his head. I could see something agonizing in his face, as he remembered. "She was poisonous, a soul in ruin."

"It's hard to believe what she was capable of doing," I said.

"Even the people you know best," he said. "I suppose everyone, at the core, is a stranger."

I still didn't know if Felicity would've killed us in cold blood. Could she have pulled the trigger? One thing was certain. She had no qualms about stowing Holly in that awful place, to let the bulldozers do the job for her on Monday. And she knew what that would do to me. I shivered, thinking about what Holly had gone through, and me, too, all because of a rancid friend, a so-called friend.

We were silent as Alex turned into the parking garage across from Vanderbilt Hospital.

"I don't think Holly and Kyle will mind if I stay with them," I said. "I will not go back to Aurora's."

"Nor will I," he said. "I've already made a reservation at the Hermitage Hotel for tonight. None of the new hotels for me. The Hermitage is Old Nashville."

I smiled. Grateful to be assured once again of what I'd always known, that my uncle was on my side and would be, no matter what.

We spent most of that Sunday in the waiting room. Holly was released, finally, after getting the I.V.'s and having her wrists bandaged. A strong young woman. Old Nashville.

Alex went back to Aurora's for our belongings. Late that afternoon, he brought my things to Holly's house. He held Holly in a tight embrace, telling her how brave she was, and had a drink with Kyle.

I walked to the porch with him as he was leaving for the Hermitage Hotel. He said, "I've decided to go home tomorrow, Jordan. I suddenly feel like a stranger in this city. You'll want to stay here a few days, I expect."

"If Holly will have me," I said.

"I have no doubt she will."

That evening, Detective Slater came to the house with my phone and Holly's phone and purse. Our phones looked as hygienic as new ones. Perfect working order.

"That brick," I reminded Slater.

"I know, I know," he said. "I told you I'd see about it. It's evidence."

"You'll let me know?"

"Yes," he said. "I have your number."

"And I have yours," I said. "Memorized."

"Thank God," he said.

There were messages from two of my children. Julie, in Chicago, and Catherine, in Atlanta, had become increasingly concerned, unable to reach me or Holly. I was afraid they'd hear something on the news—To me, it was a huge story that might make the national news!—so I called both of them and had long conversations, explaining in broad strokes what had happened, assuring them that we were all right.

"You always seem to get into trouble," Julie said, "but you find your way out of it."

She didn't know the half of it.

I had a message from Paul Broussard. *"We found Bella at a terrible place on the lower East Side of Manhattan. She'd been in New York since she left Geneva. Her sisters arranged for her to enter a psychiatric hospital. I look forward to talking to you, Jordan. Much to tell."*

I dashed off a quick text.

> Much to tell you, too. Will call soon. So happy Bella is safe. I understand how terribly frightened you must have been. Truly, Paul, I understand, more than you know.

Nine-fifteen marked the end of a day, the end of a weekend, that had left all of us sleep deprived and emotionally drained.

Holly was already in bed. A lamp in the living room shined on Kyle when I finished in the bathroom, ready for bed, myself. He was slouched in the big chair, his feet propped on the coffee table. Television on, muted. He looked up from whatever he was checking on his phone.

"I hope Holly can get some rest," I said, standing in the doorway.

"Yeah. She's exhausted. More than exhausted, seems like she's… I don't know." He frowned, shook his head, as if trying to figure it out, and clicked off the TV. "Helluva week."

Traumatized was probably the word he was looking for.

"You get some sleep, too," I said.

Kyle sat up straighter, putting his feet on the floor. "Do you think she'll be all right?" he asked, his eyes pleading for a prediction I didn't think I could make. I tried to reassure, best I could.

"Holly's strong," I said. "And resilient. But she'll need time. And she'll need you, Kyle."

He seemed to think about it for a minute. Then he managed a smile. "Well, goodnight, Jordan. Hope you sleep well, too."

"Oh, I will," I said.

You would've thought.

Chapter 40

Kyle left for work Monday morning, reluctantly. He lingered at the door, touching Holly's arms gently, as if he thought she might break. I didn't think she would break, but I heard him say, "You should've slept in. Take a nap," and I figured she'd had a sleepless night. Like me.

He hadn't wanted Holly or me to turn our hands to do anything considered work. Sunday evening he'd started to launder the clothes we'd been wearing at the Eagles Nest, until both of us protested. We wanted it all destroyed. Even our shoes. So he put everything in paper bags and took it outside, not for the garbage can. He dropped it in the fire pit and burned it all. I went out later and looked at the ashes and wished the memories could burn away like that.

Kyle had handled dinner Sunday night, meaning he'd ordered from Door Dash, and Monday morning he'd made a handsome pancake breakfast. Cleaning up the kitchen both times, scrubbing and bleaching until it was implausibly spotless. Holly barely touched her food, but she teased him, calling him June. As in Beaver Cleaver's mother, of the shirtwaist, heels, and pearls.

As the morning dragged by, she said, "We need to *do* something. Not just sit here."

"Take a walk?" I said.

"*Something.*"

Both of us were accustomed to being purposeful. With the day stretching before us, we had too much time to think. We needed something to liberate us from the inertia of our memories of the dark place, with the rats and stench and fear of death that still held us hostage.

It was a welcome diversion when my phone rang.

"I wondered how Holly's doing," Skye said.

"She's all right," I said.

"I'm sorry I was kind of a, well, a bitch, when you said she worked for Tommy Kahn."

"You didn't know the whole story."

"I still don't!" Skye said. "I don't know how you found Holly at the Eagles Nest, or who the woman was that they arrested, or why she wanted to hurt Holly. All I know is what I've heard on the news. Maybe you can fill me in."

"I will, but not now. I'll tell you everything when I can," I promised.

"Well, I know Holly is one of the good guys."

"Yes, she is." I changed the subject, asking about Odelle.

"Odelle's better," Skye said. "She's like this city of ours. Strong, but might not ever be right again. Her memory comes and goes. She's in better spirits now that the Eagles Nest is getting a reprieve."

"What do you mean, a reprieve?"

"Well, it's a crime scene, for one thing."

"I should know that." I laughed. When Slater came by, he hadn't mentioned whether investigators were still at the Eagles Nest, but I could imagine yellow tape still up, all around, even if the CSI people were finished.

"Yeah, you should know." I could hear the smile in her voice. "And the hotel chain that Kahn was counting on, well, they pulled out of the deal. Part of it, I suppose, is all the publicity about what happened to you and Holly. I'm sure Tommy Kahn is involved in that."

"Maybe not," I said. "Not directly."

"Aw, you think? I was hoping he'd go down for kidnapping."

"People are like water. They find their own level," I said. "Tommy Kahn still has plenty to answer for."

"You're right about that. His biggest worry now is the building that collapsed in the storm. Tommy's up to his neck dealing with those problems."

"You mean that was *his* building?"

"He's one of the principal investors." Skye sounded absolutely delighted as she said, "Maybe this will topple the whole Tommy Kahn empire. I heard on the news that there's an investigation into what happened, why the building fell, whether the materials were inferior or the construction was shoddy. That kind of thing. He might lose everything. Wouldn't that be poetic justice? You're an architect, Jordan. You know what they're looking for."

I had a good idea what an investigation like that would involve, and that it would take time. "I know until it's all cleared up, Tommy Kahn's not a good risk for a business partner. One look at his credentials, and anyone could see that he was a man who never had a strong foundation."

"That's a good one!" Skye said.

I told her that I'd asked Detective Slater to get the brick back to Odelle. "It might not matter, if the Eagles Nest isn't demolished, but I know it meant something to her."

"It's not just a sentimental thing," Skye said. "Odelle told me it was a very old brick. There was a word imprinted on it, she said, but she couldn't remember what it was. She's been racking her brain trying to come up with it. She said they used to do that, stamp the company's name on their bricks, back in the day."

"Wolford," I said.

Skye was silent for a moment. "That's the name? Are you kidding? You remember?"

"Can't believe I carried that brick around for days and never thought there was any significance to the word. I could barely make it out, but I'm sure it was Wolford." I spelled it.

"If it's old enough, if it's really a historic brick, we might have something to go on. Something that would get the Eagles Nest designated a historic landmark. Now we have a place to start. Wolford. Thanks, Jordan. That's gonna make Odelle *so* happy!" Skye laughed out loud. A musical laugh, from deep within her. I hadn't heard anything like that from Skye before.

Maybe something good could come out of a nightmare.

Holly set a fast pace on the long walk in her neighborhood. We didn't say much. Chatted idly about how Tennessee springs went from the teens one day into the high seventies the next, and from storms that could topple towers to tranquil days like this. Warm sunshiny morning, not a cloud in the sky, and a soft wind out of the south.

The Eagles Nest could've come down today.

It was a crime scene, protected from Tommy Kahn's bulldozers for the time being. But I couldn't help thinking about what might've been. What could've been happening at that very moment. It was too painful to contemplate. Certainly too painful to talk about.

"Oh, there's Miss Miranda!" Holly said, trying for a cheery note as we approached her driveway. The old woman was at her mailbox, dressed exactly as I'd seen her before, in an old housecoat and orthopedic shoes, laces untied. Waving us over.

"Come on," Holly said. "I need to let her know I'm all right."

"You were on the television, honey!" she said. "I *knew* that bitch was up to no good."

With women like Miss Miranda, it's not necessary to say much.

They don't even ask a lot of questions. Miss Miranda elaborated on her worry for Holly and repeated what she'd heard on the news, as if we hadn't been there, ourselves.

And then, she reached out an arthritic hand and touched Holly's arm. "I am so sorry about all that happened to you, honey. I can see the weight of it in your eyes."

"I'm all right," Holly said.

"Well, you will be. And so will you," she said, looking at me. "Take it from an old woman who could tell you stories to make your hair stand on end. Time heals just about everything."

Holly picked up her phone from the kitchen counter. "It's Willow," she said. "She texted 'Call me, please.' Sounds like it might be important, not just asking me to come to another gig." She gave me a knowing look and punched in the numbers.

I grabbed a bottle of water and left the kitchen. I expected it would be a private conversation, but a minute later Holly followed me to the living room. "Willow wants to come over. She said she's in the neighborhood. Whatever she's doing, she'll be finished in about an hour. I don't know what it's all about, but I said sure. You'll enjoy seeing her, won't you?"

Holly must've read something in my face. She groaned. "How could I forget? You saw her Saturday night, didn't you? Kyle told me how terrible it was, there at Bobby's, everybody waiting for me, not knowing, worrying…" Her voice trailed off.

"Not as terrible as it was for you, Holly."

Neither of us said any more about that.

"Did Willow sing?" Holly asked.

"Yes. Three songs. None of them anything like the one we heard at The Bluebird."

"That's too bad. Songs she wrote?"

"She said yes. But she said she wrote the one she sang at The Bluebird, too." I frowned, puzzling over how it could be. "Hard to believe that someone who wrote a song that could shake your soul would write the kind of middling tunes we heard Saturday night."

"Well, look at Notorious," Holly said. "Kyle talks about the ridiculous songs he plays, out in front of the Hall of Fame. But remember the tape player that we found in his old room? And the song he'd recorded that probably could've been a hit if he'd done something with it?"

I had heard plenty of Notorious's ridiculous lyrics, but now and then there was one that rose above all the others. One that sounded like it was coming from an ancient place, the kind hidden inside every person's heart. "You're probably right," I said. With Notorious, though, it seemed to depend on his level of sobriety at the time. Drunk, he thought his inane lyrics were brilliant. Sober, he knew better than anyone else when a song was a flop. And when it was right.

As we waited for Willow, it occurred to me that I'd never mentioned Willow to Detective Slater. The phone call, early Sunday morning, when she told me how Felicity had threatened her. Something else I should probably do, tell Slater about it, but I'd want to talk to Willow first. She had peeled away some of her own layers, out of worry for Holly, when she called to tell me about Felicity.

That was what real friends did.

Unlike Willow's aunt.

Chapter 41

Willow and Holly embraced, both teary, unable to speak.

Holly pulled back first. "Sorry I missed your show Saturday night," she said, finally.

"Yeah, shame on you," Willow said, wagging her finger.

And they both laughed, the initial awkwardness dwindling, but not entirely gone.

I offered to make lunch. My default, food, when I don't know what else to do, but Willow said no, she had to get back to work soon.

"Maybe a water, if that's all right?" she said, the sweet, innocent voice of the Willow I remembered.

"I'll see what I can do," I said.

I heard them laugh, giggle, really, while I went to the refrigerator. Like old roommates, again. I couldn't help thinking about Aurora, a snapshot of us as sorority sisters, but I quickly put the memory in a far corner of my mind.

"I was just over on Lischey," Willow was saying, as I handed her a bottle of water and sat down on the sofa beside Holly. "Right down the street from Winfrey's Barber Shop. Vernon Winfrey, Oprah's daddy, he died sometime back, but the barber shop's still going strong."

"What were you doing on Lischey?" Holly asked.

"Cleaning a house." Willow met Holly's gaze, then looked down at the water bottle. "That's what I'm doing now. Working for a neighbor of mine, cleaning houses."

"Oh." Holly was stunned and not able to hide it. "I didn't know. I thought you were probably still waiting tables."

"You wouldn't have any reason to know. I haven't waited tables in a while." Willow sighed. "And I haven't been a very good friend."

Holly gave a gesture of dismissal. "Don't, Willow. Yeah, we've been out of touch, but it's my fault as much as yours."

"No, you tried. You kept contacting me, trying to. I pushed you away. I was embarrassed."

"Why? Because you were cleaning houses? You shouldn't be."

Willow took a drink from her water and ran her tongue around her lips. "That's recent," she said. "Before, I was working at Déjà Vu. Dancing. Always trying to believe that the money was worth feeling like crap about myself."

I could tell how hard Holly was trying to take in these revelations, how hard she was trying not to show discomfort. Clearly, Willow could see it, too. She gave a little laugh. "I know. It's not exactly singing on the Grand Ole Opry."

"Well... no. Doesn't mean you won't sing on the Opry someday," Holly said.

"See?" Willow directed her gaze at me. "That's how Holly's different from me. Better than me. Always tries to be supportive." She turned back to Holly. "Me, I just stopped returning your calls. But the truth is, I didn't believe you needed anything from me."

"Willow," I put in. "Why don't you tell Holly what you told me—was it yesterday morning? About Tommy Kahn and Felicity."

Holly inhaled, and exhaled slowly. Realizing, I suppose, how in the dark she was about so much, but ready to listen.

Willow told everything as a matter of fact. Just as she'd done on the phone with me. But when she'd finished, she choked up a little. "I was so worried about you, Holly," she whispered.

"You did what you could, Willow," I said. "I know that wasn't easy for you. But after what you told me, I had no doubt that Felicity was the person we were looking for."

"But how did you know it was the Eagles Nest? I didn't tell you that," Willow said.

There was a moment, a flash. I was struck by how I could hurt Aurora, and I wanted to hurt her, with everything in me. She loved Willow like a daughter, the daughter she'd never had, with a future Aurora might've had. Willow loved her aunt, too, but what if she knew how devious Aurora had been? Just when Willow had started to consider what it meant to be a friend, how would she react to knowing that her aunt had betrayed me, and that her deception had led excruciatingly close to Holly's death?

I swallowed back every harsh word I could've spoken about Aurora. "That's for another time," I told her.

Willow let out a long breath, as if it was all too hard to think about. She stood up then and said, "I have to get back to work."

At the door, she stopped and seemed to consider whether to say something else. Turning back to Holly then, she said, "I'm thinking about going home. Closer to home anyway. To Atlanta."

"Oh no!" Holly said. "Why? Just when we, you know, we've *found* each other again!"

"Yeah." A sweet smile. "That means a lot, Holly. It does. But my music isn't working out like I thought it would. I don't feel that connection with the audience."

"You have an amazing voice," I said. "That night at The Bluebird, the song—"

She interrupted, and I could tell I'd hit a nerve. "That was not... that was, what do they call it, an anomaly?"

And then she seemed so sad, all at once. I touched her arm. "I know you're not a big fan of Notorious, but I agree with what he said after you sang at Bobby's Saturday night. Something like, 'Voice of an angel, needs a good hymn.'"

"You have the voice, Willow," Holly added. "There are millions of songs waiting to be sung. Maybe you could just sing. Every singer isn't a songwriter."

"I always planned to sing *my own* songs," she said, a little like a peevish child, but she took a breath and seemed to get her bearings. "I need to start over. Maybe I can, in Georgia."

"You can start over, here in Nashville," Holly said.

"You've already made a new start," I said. "Just now. Coming here, making things right with Holly. Starting over doesn't have to mean relocating."

Willow made no promises, except that she'd call Holly soon. She left, wiping her eyes.

Holly closed the door. "I would miss her. I wouldn't have thought so, but now, I would."

"She'd miss you, too," I said. "I don't think going to Georgia will make her happy."

I was certain of one thing. Willow wouldn't be happy until she made her wrongs right. And I had a feeling I knew what that meant.

Kyle had news that evening.

"Guess who was back in front of the Hall of Fame, playing his music today?" he said, taking a beer from the refrigerator.

"Notorious?" Holly and I said at the same time.

"Yep."

"Did you talk to him?" I asked. Wanting to ask if Notorious said anything about Aurora, wondering if he'd heard the skirmishes that Alex and I had with her. But I didn't.

"Yeah, we had a long chat. He's moved back to his old room," Kyle said. "He promised the landlady, no more binges. Not sure he can keep his promise but he seems to think so. I never met her. She must be a kind of softie."

"We met her. Remember that errand you sent us on?" Holly said, smiling a gentle rebuke.

"I wouldn't call Theodora a softie," I said. "But I think she has a good heart. She has a feeling for poets and lost souls. If Notorious can stay sober, they might make quite a pair."

"Didn't he and Aurora have something going?" Holly said, getting a beer for herself. "Want one, Mom?" I shook my head, and she picked up a half-empty bottle of chardonnay from the refrigerator door. "Or some wine?"

"*That* sounds lovely," I said, and took a wine glass from the cabinet.

"Notorious mentioned Aurora," Kyle said. He took a long pull on his drink. "I don't know what he meant, because Aurora *did* take him in when he had no place to go, but he said he figured it all out and couldn't stay with her. I asked what he meant and he said, 'She's not the woman I thought she was. A river with just ten percent arsenic is still poisonous.'"

"I would have to agree," I said. I knew exactly what he meant.

"Was it Aurora who told you I was at the Eagles Nest?" Holly asked me. "I never got it all straight. Did she know Felicity wanted to kill me?"

"She didn't know, but… she should have known. Without Aurora, well…" I pulled up one of the stools. As we sat around the kitchen bar, I filled in the gaps for them.

Holly and Kyle let me tell the story, without interruptions. Only when I'd finished did Holly ask, "How much of this does Willow know?"

"Not much," I said.

"I don't mind telling her!" Holly said.

I raised the wine to my lips and thought more about it. No, I didn't want to do that to Willow. Aurora would never betray her niece. She might even come clean about all of it, eventually.

"I'll leave it to Aurora to find her own way to redemption," I said.

Chapter 42

Sometimes the stars align. And our best intentions don't *always* pave the way to perdition.

Kyle called mid-morning the next day, from work. Holly put her phone on speaker when he asked if I had ever toured the Country Music Hall of Fame.

"The original one, on Music Row," I answered. "Not the new one."

"It's not that new, Jordan," Kyle said. "It's been downtown since 2001. You missed the first *new* one, when it moved to downtown, but this one—it was a $100 million expansion in 2014 that doubled its size. It's amazing. You'll love it."

"Did you call to do a commercial for the Hall of Fame?" Holly asked.

"No, I called to ask if y'all wanted to come down this afternoon. I can make some time and give you a personal tour. Interested?"

"Sounds like fun," Holly said. Flashing me a questioning look. "What about it?"

"Definitely interested," I said, glad to hear Holly say *fun*.

"Should we plan for right after lunch?" she asked.

"How about 3:00?"

Giving them some space, I left the kitchen, where Holly and I spent most of our time together. Tea or coffee and talking about everything except what happened over the weekend.

A few minutes later, she joined me in the living room. "I'm afraid

Kyle had an ulterior motive," she said, but her smile was brighter than I'd seen in a while.

Notorious, playing out in front of the Hall of Fame again, had been asking Kyle about his belongings, now that he was back at Theodora's. The duffel, bag of clothes, and the cassette player that Holly and Kyle were storing for him, here at their house.

"Kyle had the bright idea that we should take all of it to the Hall of Fame, and he'd give Notorious a ride home at the end of the day." Holly gave a little laugh, a sound that relieved me. "Kyle really does have a big heart," she said.

"Maybe we should ask Willow to go with us this afternoon," I said.

"Sure."

I could see Holly was surprised, and wondering why.

"Just something I was thinking about," I said. I scrolled for Willow's number from our very early Sunday morning call.

Not optimistic that she'd want to go, or that she'd even answer her phone. Not optimistic that she'd get the point of it when I said, "I think Notorious wants a new start, too."

But she did.

Another call to Holly from Detective Horowitz. He wanted to interview both Holly and me and asked if we could go down to the station. She told him we had some time in early afternoon, as long as we could be finished by 3:00.

I had not anticipated what it would be like to relive the nightmare. Bad enough for me. For Holly, it had to be so much more terrifying. The dark, the restraints, the fear that no one would find her. Did Felicity tell her the bulldozers would be taking down the building on Monday? Holly never said, but she had to know. It had been in the news.

When she came out of the interview room, she said to me, "I don't want to talk about any of it." Neither did I.

While Holly parked the car, Willow and I dashed across Demonbreum at the Country Music Hall of Fame in front of a Hop-on, Hop-off bus. Notorious was at the top of the steps, singing for a handful of smiling tourists who might've believed they were listening to a country music legend.

"How did you know?" Willow said.

"I didn't *know*," I said.

"It was when I sang at Bobby's, wasn't it? I had to sing my own songs that night because Notorious was there. I sure didn't want another scene like the night at The Bluebird."

"That was what you meant when you said it *messed you up*, that Aurora brought him."

She nodded.

I said, "I heard one of the songs Notorious wrote a long time ago"—when he was almost somebody, I thought—"and there was something about it. Something at the heart of it like the one you sang at The Bluebird. But I didn't *know* anything. It was just a feeling. I saw a chance for you to make things right, Willow. For *you*. If what I was thinking was true."

"Well, it's true." She held up a red tote bag.

Notorious finished a tune with a solid lick on his guitar, as we stepped up to meet him, and when we started talking, the tourists moved on. Kyle had come out from the building, and Holly was coming across the street. And there, with all of us around her, in front of the Country Music Hall of Fame, Willow put on a brave face and said to Notorious, "I stole your songs. Not just the one from The Bluebird. All of these."

I wouldn't say it was shock on his face. More like he'd been struck by a wave of sadness. But Kyle and Holly were definitely shocked.

Staying at Aurora's when she had COVID, Willow had found the songs. It felt like she'd discovered a pot of gold, she said. Not just lyrics. He'd written the scores, too.

"I didn't know who they belonged to," Willow said. "I asked Aunt Aurora whose foot locker was under the bed, and she said… 'I don't know, but I got the feeling it was somebody that wouldn't ever need those songs again.'"

Notorious listened, his head bowed, as if all of it was too heavy to bear. Whatever had passed between him and Aurora when he left her house, I was sure he knew she had betrayed him. The woman he'd loved, the inspiration for that song, "When I Don't Have to Love You Anymore."

Willow held the red bag out to him. "Everything I took is in here. And I've been through every one of them. Notorious, these songs ought to be cut. The world needs to hear. Please do something with them. Don't let 'em just die."

"You have more notebooks in our car," Kyle put in. "The ones Holly and Jordan found in your room. My God, man, you have more than a pot of gold. You have a gold mine."

Notorious was quiet for another moment. He looked up, his eyes glistening, stared at the bag, and reached for it. "I thought they were lost forever. Lost like me."

Finally he met Willow's gaze. "Thank you," he said.

And she said, "Forgive me."

I knew I would have to face Aurora once more. I put it off for another day, until the day before I was scheduled to fly home to Savannah.

The UGA fight song on the doorbell didn't make me smile anymore.

Aurora was good at playing nice. Wasn't she always? Better than I was, though I'd promised myself I would not be rude. We exchanged pleasantries, passing through her spacious house. "It would be a shame not to take advantage of a day like this," she said, leading the way to her sunny patio, the table covered with the cloth I'd brought her from my trip to Provence.

"Yazda quit, but I managed to make sweet tea," she said. "I'm not totally useless."

It was harder to confront her than I'd expected.

"How is Holly?" was her first question.

"She'll be all right." I didn't feel like sharing intimate details with Aurora. Like Holly's fatigue, the restless nights, with nightmares, symptoms Kyle and I privately called PTSD.

My nightmares now weren't about my own fear of the dark so much. They were about Holly. Imagining rats crawling on her, all the pitch black hours that she waited for help. She had never mentioned rats, but Kyle said they'd treated her for rat bites in the E.R. and she had worn long sleeves every day since we were at her house.

"And how are you, after that ordeal?" Aurora asked.

"Thankful," I said. "Thankful beyond words."

She poured ice tea in two glasses from a crystal pitcher. "I had no idea what Felicity wanted, when she kept coming around and calling, asking about you and your plans. I just thought it was more of the same. At first I thought she was jealous of you, when we lived in the sorority house, but somewhere along the way I realized she was *obsessed* with you."

"You told me," I said.

A wrinkle found its way into the bridge of her nose, her Botoxed forehead, too. "Well, it's true." With a little wave of dismissal, she said, "Felicity's problems reach way back. You remember, don't you? She told us that her mother put her in dozens of beauty pageants, where the little girls are made up to look eighteen. She never won, and her mother would always tell her she was too fat, which she certainly wasn't, or that she didn't smile enough at the judges."

I remembered those late nights in the sorority house when Felicity talked about those horrible pageants. Maybe I wasn't sympathetic enough. Maybe I thought all of that should be locked up in the past, since she had grown into a stunning young woman. Maybe I didn't realize how those things could scar a little girl.

"None of that is an excuse to murder," I said.

"No." Aurora sounded annoyed. "What *I'm saying* is that I had no idea how *damaged* she was when I was just trying to be her friend."

"Look," I said. "I didn't come here to ask you for an apology. We are way past that."

Her eyes widened. "Why, Jordan, I'm not apologizing! I didn't do anything wrong!"

The breeze kicked up, carrying the scent of Aurora's flowers from her perfect garden to this perfect patio behind her perfect house. I was tempted to keep up the debate, but mostly I wanted to say what I came to say and get out of there, leave this place that now held only unhappy memories.

"I thought you should know, I didn't tell Willow about any of it," I said.

Aurora couldn't have wanted her relief to show in her eyes, but it did.

"Any of it?" she said.

"I didn't tell her how you, what did you say, *befriended* Felicity. And I didn't tell her that you knew the songs she took from the foot locker belonged to Notorious, someone who had meant something to you, but you betrayed him. I don't know exactly what you told her when she asked you about those songs, but you let her believe stealing them was fine."

Aurora looked away. That "looking into the middle distance." I couldn't tell if it was genuine or an affectation. "You know, Jordan, I didn't approve of what Felicity did, but she was right about one thing.

Your piety can be terribly tedious sometimes."

"Piety?" I had to smile at that one. "You mean when I try to get at the truth."

"Just like that reporter. The *truth!* Truth at any cost. And see what it cost him. You are so meddlesome." She hiked her chin. "What's between my niece and me is not your business."

"But I *am* right about it. You tried to move the foot locker from under the bed, in the room where Willow had slept," I said. "You must've been getting the room ready for me, but you changed your mind. When you hurt your back and couldn't move the foot locker, you couldn't risk that I'd find it and ask questions. Being that I'm so meddlesome."

I could almost hear Notorious accusing Aurora of doing something with his songs. Later, he'd said his mind was muddled, but he'd been so *sure* his songs were in the foot locker. And I could almost hear him telling Kyle, "Rora's not the woman I thought she was." He knew she was trying to buy her niece's future with his past.

"Willow gave Notorious all his songs back. Did you know?" I asked.

At that, Aurora flared. Her face no longer a mask of civility. "No! She didn't!"

"Yes, she did."

The silence was heavy around us, a feeling of finality.

I pushed my chair back. "I can find my way," I said, standing. Turning to leave, I had one more question. "What *did* you tell Willow when she asked you whose foot locker was under the bed?"

Aurora looked like one of those marble statues, framed by her lush garden. "I told her the truth. That it belonged to someone who wasted his gift." She gave a soft, cynical laugh, reminiscent of Felicity. "That foolish child. With those songs, Willow could've been somebody."

Chapter 43

The *Nashville Voice* came out on Thursday, rocking Nashville with the first in a series of investigative reporting on "Dirty Dealing in Nashville."

Tommy Kahn was the star of the article, but not the only crooked developer who had received PPP funds and had suddenly made a substantial purchase. A beach house, a plane, or, in Kahn's case, a building. One that he'd intended to demolish so he could partner with a syndicate to build a luxury hotel. A deal that had fallen through when the Eagles Nest became a crime scene.

I had to believe Caleb, the truth teller, would've been proud of what Walt had done with his investigation. And Walt was just turning over the first rock. He promised much more to come.

I was scheduled to fly out to Savannah that afternoon. That morning, Holly and I went to see Odelle Wright.

Odelle lived in Hillsboro Village, a neighborhood nestled between the ever-expanding Belmont University and Vanderbilt, the university and medical center complex. An eclectic mix of private homes, apartments, condos, shops, offices, and churches. While attempts had been made to interweave Old and New Nashville, it seemed the new was winning, especially along Twenty-first Avenue with its unbearable traffic. But there were side streets where you could believe there was still some sense of community. A real neighborhood.

Odelle's street was one of those streets, lined with pre-World War II houses. She lived near a dead end in a 1920s elegantly renovated bungalow befitting an architect, where Time seemed to be suspended.

"Welcome, Jordan! Come in! Come in! And I am *so* happy you brought your daughter!" Odelle sang out from her door while we were still coming up the steps to the wide front porch. The already slender woman had lost weight, but in spite of her spindly arms and tiny waist that you could put your hands around, Odelle did not seem frail. She used a walking stick but her good posture made me stand a little straighter, myself. An upright woman, Odelle Wright, in ways that had nothing to do with her stature.

The gash on her temple was still bandaged.

She led the way into her comfortable living room. Furniture with classic lines, in excellent condition. She'd made tea, serving from an ornate teapot that I expected was authentic, from England, as were the cups and saucers, crème pitcher and sugar bowl.

"You look great, Odelle," I said. "And that's a beautiful blouse." It was cobalt blue. A complement to her white hair, it brought out the blue of her eyes.

She looked down and touched the silky material, as if reminding herself. "I got it at Harvey's. Their after-Christmas sale. I hadn't taken it out of my closet until today. But what's the sense in waiting for an occasion? I could die tomorrow! Besides, *this* is an occasion."

Harvey's was one of the big downtown stores, once famous for its carousel horses and live monkeys. The department store was also known for the sit-ins at its lunch counters during the Civil Rights demonstrations of the 1960s. I knew this because Alex had written about Harvey's in his book.

The store had been closed for decades. Holly and I looked at each other. Neither of us seemed to know quite what to say.

But Odelle quickly corrected herself. "I don't mean Harvey's.

What is that store in Green Hills? Macy's! That's it! That's where I bought the blouse."

More idle chatter and drinking tea. Odelle had a grandmotherly way about her when chatting with Holly. "Are you an architect, like your mother?" she asked.

"Oh no," Holly laughed. "I had an administrative job, but now I'm, well… I guess they call it *between* jobs." She seemed quite at ease saying it.

Odelle frowned, as if searching for a memory. "Now I remember. Skye said you worked for Tommy Kahn, but you quit because of the Eagles Nest. Did you realize he was as crooked as an old man's back?" And she pulled herself up, even straighter.

"Something like that."

I wasn't sure how much Odelle knew about what happened over the weekend, but I didn't think Holly wanted to go into all of that. It was a good time to reach into my purse.

"Detective Slater, you met him, returned this yesterday," I said. Odelle held out her thin, blue-veined hands with their long fingers, and I put the brick in them.

"Wolford," she said, running her finger over the word, her face glowing. "Oh, Jordan. You won't believe what we've discovered. It's really quite extraordinary!"

Odelle settled back in her chair, set the brick on her lap, and told her story. It didn't sound like much was wrong with her memory.

"Back in the 1850s, a man named Isaac Wolford started a brick-making company up in Robertson County," Odelle began. "He raised tobacco. Had as many as a hundred slaves. But he'd married a woman from Massachusetts from an abolitionist family. Don't ask me how they got together in the first place." She trilled a little laugh. "Eliza Wolford was appalled that the slaves were illiterate, with no opportunity for education. So she took it upon herself to teach the slave children to read. She thought if she could begin to educate even a few, some small percentage of the county might finally begin to see them as human beings, not property, to be exploited. As a compromise, I guess it was, Isaac Wolford built her a little schoolhouse on their land. You know the saying, 'Happy wife, happy life.'"

Odelle took a minute to gather her thoughts, or to ponder over what she'd told us.

I knew I was getting ahead, but I said, "This brick came from that schoolhouse?"

"Yes, it did."

"This *particular* brick?" My mind was already flying to other possibilities, that it could have come from any structure that used Wolford bricks. "How can you be sure?"

"Skye and the staff at the Coalition worked their butts off this week, to answer that question."

Her confidence dispelled any doubts I'd had.

"The brick-making company was successful through several generations, up until the Depression," she continued, in her storytelling voice. "The property up in Robertson County was divided up time and time again, passed down to descendants, until the land with the dilapidated schoolhouse came into possession of one, oh, what was his name? The Wolford that built the studio at the Eagles Nest? I can't recall. My poor memory. But the Coalition has a record of all of it now."

"I don't think there's much wrong with your memory, Odelle."

She smiled. "Comes and goes." She took another moment, sipped her tea, and started again. "Around 1980, he bought the Eagles Nest. The publishing company was struggling. Hadn't kept up with the times. Andrew. That was his name. Andrew Wolford. He had other enterprises—" she raised an eyebrow, the kind of look that covers a whole conversation—"and eventually the Eagles Nest housed some of those businesses. But Andrew Wolford wasn't ready to give up on the music business yet. So he added a recording studio to back of the house, the way they were building studios on Music Row, with the echo chamber. To get the reverb."

She raised her teacup to her lips again, her hand shaking a little. I didn't want to interrupt her train of thought. After a minute, she said, "Maybe the costs were more than he'd budgeted. I don't know what he had in mind when he did such a slapdash job of tacking on that addition. Anyway, he'd inherited that land up in Robertson County." Her thin face broke into a big smile. "You can probably take it from there, Jordan."

"I suppose he tore down the schoolhouse, what hadn't fallen down already, and brought those bricks to Nashville," I said.

We let a minute pass, the words hanging in the air.

Odelle said, "Isn't that extraordinary?"

Holly and I both agreed that it was.

"We think it was the first slave school in Tennessee. Maybe in the entire South. Based on those bricks, we believe the Eagles Nest property can qualify as a historic landmark," Odelle said. "The studio for sure. The big house, we don't know, but our people are hard at work."

"You're much closer to it than you were when I met you, just a little over a week ago," I said.

"Is that all? Just a week?"

"It seems longer, doesn't it?" I said.

"It seems like we've been friends forever," Odelle said.

Chapter 44

There is no place in the world like Savannah in April. Nothing like the way the breeze carries that first smell of spring jasmine, as Time seems to regain its stride after a sluggish winter and walk in full bloom toward summer.

What Felicity had done had stained Nashville for me, but I hoped that someday all that Nashville was, the small city with its southern sophistication, would rise above the tarnish. Old and also New Nashville. Reinventing itself like a country song. Forever changing, yet always, underneath, somehow the same.

But Savannah was home. My roots were as deep as a sweet gum tree. And coming home had an effect I hadn't expected. A profound sense of renewal.

Spring was once again at its peak, fragrant azaleas and camillas, temperatures hitting high-seventies. Running in Forsyth Park with Winston, my wordless companion, or walking, if that's what the-best-mutt-in-the world preferred at the end of the day, I was filled once more with a whisper of joy. I was more grateful than I'd ever been for my home. My routine. My quiet, unremarkable life.

Unremarkable except for nights that Paul Broussard and I met on Zoom, telling each other everything that we'd held back for so many months. Each of us expressing the depth of our distress when our daughters were missing, and each understanding the other's anguish. Confessing our hopes and doubts and trusting the speed of light to reach across the ocean into each other's hearts. That was enough, for now. It would have to be. It was Zoom, but it felt intimate in a way I'd thought I had lost forever.

Holly and I talked every day, and I could hear the calm, the expectation of happiness, gradually returning to her voice. One day she sounded absolutely giddy. "I have a new job! You'll never guess."

At Odelle Wright's request, Holly was going to work for the Nashville Coalition for Historic Preservation. Skye was one of two paid employees, and the other one, eight months pregnant with her third child, had an offer that would allow her to work from home.

"Imagine!" Holly said. "Now I'll be *saving* history, not tearing it down."

Joshua had asked Kyle and Holly to take charge of planning Caleb's memorial, so she was waiting until after the service to start her new job.

"Kyle and I are both still shaken up by it all. This is the last thing we can do for Caleb," she said.

Holly made sure I kept up with the *Nashville Voice* weeklies, the "Dirty Dealings in Nashville" series. Tommy Kahn was sharing the spotlight with other flash-in-the-pan, three-thousand-dollar suit developers and bankers. Like Dillion Lowe, who had funneled his PPP funds to an offshore account, and now *he* was missing. Rumor was, he'd fled to Cuba, from which he could not be extradited.

The investigation into the building that fell in the Gulch continued. A sub-contractor had pulled out of the project some weeks before the building's collapse, citing concerns about safety practices and substandard materials.

Tommy Kahn was being questioned by the U.S. Attorney's Office in Middle Tennessee. I could see Joshua's hand in that.

Felicity Blake was behind bars, charged with murder. No bail.

"Tommy knew Felicity was Caleb's killer. Remember, she said he was worried when she told him," Holly said. "According to Walt,

Tommy will probably testify against her, if it comes to that."

"Not exactly honor among thieves," I remarked.

"Do you think you and I will have to testify?" she said. "She confessed to us, too."

"We can do it if it means putting Felicity away for a long, long time," I told her.

"She's nuts. A real mental case. I could almost feel sorry for her if she'd shown even a shred of kindness or remorse," Holly said.

I told her she was a better person than her mother. "And isn't it poetic justice that her lover has betrayed her?" I said. "Just as she betrayed her friend."

Time roared by, and it was May.

Alex and I returned to Nashville for Caleb's memorial.

"Kyle said he was sure Caleb would've chosen Benton Chapel, himself," Alex told Joshua and me, as he maneuvered us through downtown, to West End Avenue. Driving west to the Vanderbilt campus from the Hermitage Hotel, where the three of us had rooms.

"Kyle took me by the chapel yesterday, on our way from the airport," Joshua said, from the back seat. "It's perfect… for what we need," and his voice trailed off.

A silence settled around us, and Alex tried to fill it with words. He had plenty to say about the chapel, how it was a place for ecumenical worship and ministries, not aligned with any single church. The Vanderbilt Divinity School was known for its commitment to social justice.

Joshua didn't seem to be paying attention, but Alex's history lesson was as a good as any way to pass the time as we traveled to the place where we would say that final goodbye to Caleb.

We were early, so Joshua could meet with the woman who would be conducting the funeral. "She's a priest, but much more than a priest," Alex said.

We arrived before he could elaborate.

Alone, I entered the chapel.

Benton Chapel was as impressive as Alex had promised. A serene space, lofty ceiling, with gentle light flooding in from dozens, maybe hundreds, of small windows, exquisite stained glass. Under other circumstances, I could've spent much longer in the sanctuary. I promised myself I would return someday, not as a mourner, but as an architect, to examine the architectural features, the symbolic details. To appreciate the design of a space where man meets God and grief meets mercy.

Walking down the center aisle, I approached the gold cross that hung above the altar. Looking down, then, at the photograph of Caleb Hunter set against a backdrop of peace lilies, I felt the sadness begin to splinter at the pointlessness of it all. Was Caleb's truth telling worth his life? A life cut short, ending all the good that he might've done? What wrongs could he have righted, that we couldn't even imagine, if he'd lived for three more decades, or four or five?

Suddenly, I wanted to cry out about how unfair it felt. How hope seems to break beneath the grief and the loss. Loss from so many years ago came rushing back with the force of a storm, the injustice of my children having to grow up without their father. My husband, not much older than Caleb, a doctor who did no harm.

I gazed up at the cross, asking once more for answers.

I would not have made a good divinity student, I thought, turning away.

Alex had parked the car, and now he was part of a small gathering on the lawn, exquisitely landscaped with shrubs and colorful flowers. Kyle and Holly had arrived, as had Skye and Odelle. Odelle using her walking stick, upright as always. Skye wearing a red dress and red flats, her hair in attractive, complicated braids.

"It's a time of celebration," she said. Her voice broke as she whispered, "Caleb's moved on up to a better neighborhood."

Walt joined the group.

"Skye has been telling us about what's happening with the Eagles Nest," Holly said.

"Seems every day there's something new," Skye said, getting her bearings. "We located Andrew Wolford's granddaughter in Hollywood, of all places."

"Hollywood?" Walt said.

"Yep. Andrew Wolford, the guy that used the bricks from that old slave schoolhouse to build the studio behind the Eagles Nest. His granddaughter's name is Eliza. She's like, thirty. My age," Skye said. "She had no idea that Eliza was her great-great-great grandmother's name."

"More greats than that," Odelle said. Her lipstick was red as flame, her rouge a little too rosy, but the cobalt blue blouse that she'd bought for an "occasion" made her eyes sparkle. "The first Eliza lived before the Civil War. Been a whole lot of begetting between then and now."

"Eliza Wolford—she goes by her maiden name—she was over the moon when she heard the about the bricks from the schoolhouse," Skye said. "I told her everything. About Tommy Kahn and his PPP fraud. About why the Eagles Nest was a crime scene." She darted a quick glance at Holly. "We must've been on a dozen calls this past week. That girl can talk some! But from the first time I spoke with her, I just knew something great was gonna come of it."

"She's married to a producer that makes documentaries," Odelle put in.

"Educational films," Skye said. "Like Ken Burns."

It seemed all of us in the little circle held our breaths, suspecting where this was going. A big smile flashed across Skye's face as she made us wait a moment.

"Eliza Wolford says her husband wants to make a film about the Eagles Nest," she said. "They're flying into Nashville Monday."

"My first day of work at the Coalition!" Holly said.

"Yeah, looks like we're gonna be busy, girl."

"How come I'm just now hearing about bricks from an old slave schoolhouse?" Walt said. "Sounds like something for the *Voice*. Something besides dirty deals."

"Tommy Kahn owns the building, and didn't he purchase it with PPP funds?" I said. "What about that? And wouldn't the filmmakers have to work with Kahn?"

"*Dee Dee* Kahn," Skye said. "They're working with Dee Dee."

"Word on the street is, Tommy and Dee Dee have gone their separate ways," Walt said. "Headed for divorce court. She's the one with the money."

I couldn't help remembering what Willow said about Double D.

"And that gives her the upper hand, when it comes to the Eagles Nest," Alex noted.

Tommy Kahn's troubles seemed to have no end. But I couldn't feel anything but gratitude that justice, slow as it is, was finally finding its way.

"That building should be a historic landmark," Odelle said, her old voice rising. "We are not giving up on that!"

"We're gonna keep trying." Skye touched Odelle's fragile arm. "What I'm hearing from Eliza, Dee Dee's making sure nothing happens to the Eagles Nest. It's still a win for us. For all of Nashville."

People were arriving already, entering the chapel.

It was time.

"We ought to go in." I said.

As we started toward the stone steps, Willow hurried to meet us. She locked arms with Holly. In her other hand, she carried her guitar case.

"I don't think I told you," Holly said to me. "Willow's gonna be singing today."

Willow's face glowed with the look of youth and health and promise. She whispered, "Notorious wrote something. For Caleb. And for me."

Chapter 45

All the three-hundred-plus seats on the main floor were filled and it looked like the balcony was full, too. The Reverend Becca Stevens prayed and read from the Scriptures before those who knew Caleb best, and loved him best, came to the pulpit.

Joshua spoke with a tenderness he hadn't shown before when talking about his brother. He said, "Caleb was my twin. More than a brother." His voice began to quiver. "My heart has been cut in half."

Walt said, "Caleb believed in the power of words. He believed words can change what we feel and believe." All who listened seemed to hold their breaths for a moment, carried along by his eloquent voice. "Words can change hearts and remind us of who we are, remind us of all we might yet be if we just speak the truth."

Kyle was a more confident public speaker than I'd expected. At the end of his eulogy, he said, "The truth in my heart today is this. That I miss my friend. That I know I always will."

And then he looked at the choir, twenty or so teens that could've been an artist's portrayal of diversity. And perhaps of New Nashville, I thought. The generation that was rising up to someday lead this city. "These young people are here because they knew Caleb and wanted to do this for him," Kyle said. "They asked if they could sing, and I knew Caleb would want it."

I remembered what Kyle had told us about the singing group

from the community center. Here they were, doing the last thing they could do for Caleb.

An ancient choirmaster, dwarfed even by the youth surrounding him, turned to his choir and raised his arms. The young people lifted their voices in a stirring rendition of "It Is Well With My Soul," an old hymn that took me back to summers with my grandparents in Georgia, when I sometimes went with Aurora and her family to a small country church. The sound circled from grief to hope, filling the chapel, hanging in the air, until the last note fell away.

A girl of no more than fifteen stood then and began to sing "The Prayer." She sang in English, and the old choirmaster answered each stanza in perfect Italian. What a tribute to Caleb, Old and New Nashville finally joining in harmony.

Clearly, the Reverend Becca Stevens knew Caleb personally. Like every true spiritual guide, she found a way to transform mourning into celebration.

Skye, I thought, had the right idea all along with her red dress and shoes.

And when Willow sang, I knew she had finally found the right hymn. A Notorious hymn.

Some of us lingered in the chapel long after the service ended. Joshua, Holly and Kyle, Willow, Alex and me. All of us, reluctant to let go of the moment, kept recalling one thing and another, this moment and that. The girl with the Celine Dion voice. The tough-looking boy with dreadlocks who was crying when he stood to sing, and only the music quelled his tears. Willow. We could not say enough about Willow's voice, Notorious's song. The eulogies, each so different and so true. And the priest, Becca Stevens—it was Becca to all who knew her.

"Caleb profiled Becca and her work with Thistle Farms," Holly told us, explaining that Thistle Farms was an organization founded by Becca to help prostitutes, addicts, women who were survivors of life on the streets. And now the ministries had spread to other countries.

"Becca started it all with Magdalene House," Holly said. "It's a program for women in recovery. Provides housing and counseling, helps the women learn marketable skills. Some of them work in Thistle Farms Café and gift shop." All the Nashvillians seemed to know these things. Alex, too. Maybe it was for my benefit, and Joshua's. Or maybe it just needed to be said.

"In her spare time, Becca writes books," Holly added, with a smile.

Much more than a Sunday morning priest.

Joshua spoke up. "Spend a few minutes with her, and you think she might be a saint."

Kyle laughed. "Funny you should say that. Caleb once told me he said, 'You must be a saint, Becca.' She shot back, 'I'm every bit the sinner you are, Caleb Hunter.' And then she reminded him of the quote. Oscar Wilde, I think. 'Every saint has a past and every sinner has a future.'"

Amen to that.

The light that had colored the chapel was starting to fade. I was starting to fade, too.

I looked up once more at the magnificent cross. Looking heavenward, which, I suppose, is the whole point.

As we turned to leave the chapel, Willow said, "A man from a record label handed me this and asked me to call him." She showed us a business card. "He's in A and R."

She said it matter-of-factly, but a smile broke on her pretty face when Holly gasped, "Willow! You're gonna do it, aren't you?"

"Yeah," she said. "I don't know if anything will come of it, but he must have liked the song today."

"You *think?*" I said. "Willow, you aren't really giving up on Nashville, are you?"

She took a long breath. "It was just something I thought, when nothing seemed to be working out for me. But no. I'm not running away."

Joshua opened the heavy doors. Familiar chords reached toward us on the breeze.

"Notorious," Kyle said, and there he was, leaning on one of the fences. My first thought, was, Is he drunk again? But he stood up, propped his guitar against the fence, and seemed as sober as I'd ever seen him.

He said, "I didn't make any noise while the funeral was going on."

"Why didn't you come inside?" Holly said.

"I wondered where you were. You said you'd be here," Willow said.

Notorious gave a sideways grin, "I used to say I didn't want to go to any church that would lower their standards enough to let me in."

He looked a little scruffy, his hair tangled and sweaty. But he was wearing the clothes he'd bought for that night at Bobby's, obviously his best.

"You walked?" I asked. "From East Nashville?"

"From the Hall of Fame. Not that far. I just didn't know exactly where the chapel was." Looking at Willow, he said, "You told me, but I forgot. I asked around, and when I got here, well, I didn't want to drag in late to a funeral. That'd be just plain uncivilized."

Willow stepped up beside him, and said, gently, "I think everybody liked your song."

We all agreed. We had *loved* the song.

"I hope that boy up there liked it." Notorious glanced at the sky.

"Notorious and I are writing together," Willow said. "We're working on something new."

Astonishing. But the words came back: *Voice of an angel. Needs a good hymn.*

Notorious had told Kyle he'd written a song for Caleb, and he wanted Willow to sing it. Kyle clasped Notorious's shoulder. "I had a feeling that was the start of something big."

"Why don't you and Willow play it for us," I said.

Willow started to open her guitar case.

Notorious shook his head. "It ain't ready. It's nowhere *like* ready, Willow. You can't hurry a song like that. Not the kind of song this one's gonna be."

Willow frowned, but then she said, "You're right."

Joshua said, "Would you sing the one you did at the service, Willow? I'd like to hear it another time, myself."

Notorious pointed his finger at her and smiled.

Something had changed in Joshua. The outpouring of affection for Caleb, perhaps, gave him a glimpse into his brother's life that he hadn't imagined. Though the sorrow was still there, and I supposed it would be until sweet memories took its place, the weight, the burden no longer seemed to fill his eyes.

Willow brought out her guitar.

I thought about the man from A and R and wondered if Willow would tell Notorious. And if the man asked for more songs like that, would she tell him about the ones Notorious wrote? Would Notorious let her cut his songs, the ones from his notebooks?

Time would tell, I supposed, but I believed Willow would try to do what was right from now on. I hoped Notorious would try, too. Try was all any of us could do.

A breeze blew Willow's hair and she pushed it back from her face, her skin almost luminous in the light. Like that night at The Bluebird, her voice, *that voice,* seemed to capture something larger than any of us, and carry us along like a warm wind. Where? God only knew.

*One day we'll feel the wind and rise
As some part in us all takes flight
To shed this flesh and blood disguise
For all we are is dust and light.*

Acknowledgments

I am deeply grateful to the writer-friends and readers who persuaded me to write about Nashville. With three books of the series set in Provence, Ireland, and Italy, I had assumed I'd need to travel to some other exotic location to write the fourth. The more I thought about it, the more I knew I had something to say about the city that has been my home for many years, the city I love, and I had overwhelming encouragement to write this mystery in the context of the clash between Old and New Nashville, which is real.

The scenes are set in locations that actually exist, in most cases. I tried to authentically portray restaurants, bars, tourist attractions, churches, colleges, neighborhoods, and the like. However, this is a work of fiction, so I admit to taking a few liberties, as with the Eagles Nest. All characters, with one exception, are imagined and are not intended to resemble real individuals. The exception is Becca Stevens, who is well-known and respected in the Nashville community. Thank you, Becca, for letting me write about who you are and the important work that you do.

My writers group, serious writers who meet every week, have for many years provided a creative space for me to write and grow. Nashvillians all, they offered valuable suggestions as I shaped the story. Thanks to Rita Bourke, Doug Jones, Mary Buckner, Mary Bess Dunn, Ed Comer, Jack Wallace, Randy O'Brien, and especially to Shannon Thurman, who gave an extra effort to the manuscript before I submitted it.

I couldn't have written about the Eagles Nest without the technical assistance of studio recording engineer Billy Sherrill. Drawing from his long career on Music Row, he was gracious enough to lead me through how the recording studios were built to get that special Nashville sound at the time I referenced in my story. I hope I got it right, Billy, but if there are any inaccuracies about the Eagles Nest studio, they're on me.

Much appreciation to architect Ron Gobbell, for insight into Nashville's historic architecture, commercial development, and the processes that go into the designation of historic buildings and overlays.

I owe a special thanks to songwriter Will Maguire, who told me more about country music than any New Yorker has a right to know and for giving me permission to use his songs: "Fade Away," "When I Don't Have to Love You Anymore," "Listen to the Rain," and "Dust and Light."

And I would be remiss without thanking Eddie Vincent and Deirdre Wait at Encircle Publications for believing in the Jordan Mayfair series and making it possible for me to continue the story.

As always, gratitude that cannot be measured goes to my daughters and their families, who keep me grounded as I write about murder and mayhem.

About the Author

Phyllis Gobbell is the author of the Jordan Mayfair Mysteries, *Pursuit in Provence, Secrets and Shamrocks, Treachery in Tuscany*—which won the 2019 Silver Falchion Award for Best Cozy Mystery—and the newest, *Notorious in Nashville*, published by Encircle Publications in October 2023.

She is also the co-author of two true-crime books based on high-profile murders in Nashville, Tennessee: *An Unfinished Canvas* with Michael Glasgow (Berkley, 2007, reprinted by Diversion, 2022), and *Season of Darkness* with Douglas Jones (Berkley, 2010). Gobbell was interviewed on Discovery ID's "Deadly Sins," discussing the murder case in *An Unfinished Canvas*. Her narrative, "Lost Innocence," was published in the anthology, *Masters of True Crime* (Prometheus, 2012). She has published and won awards for short stories and creative nonfiction, and has received Tennessee's Individual Artist Literary Award.

Faculty Emeritus at Nashville State Community College, she taught composition, literature, and creative writing. Recently she has taught creative writing in Lipscomb University's Lifelong Learning Program and has worked as a writing coach. Find Phyllis on Facebook and Instagram, and visit PhyllisGobbell.com for the latest news.

If you enjoyed this book,
please consider writing a review
and sharing it with other readers.

Many of our authors are happy to participate in
Book Club and Reader Group discussions.
For more information, contact us at info@encirclepub.com.

Thank you,
Encircle Publications

For news about more exciting new fiction, join us at:

Facebook: www.facebook.com/encirclepub

Instagram: www.instagram.com/encirclepublications

Sign up for the Encircle Publications newsletter:
eepurl.com/cs8taP